This is Susie Polzin's first novel. It has always been a dream since she was a little girl to write one. She grew up in the Blue Mountains and moved to Queensland at the age of seventeen as a single mother with a one-year-old boy in tow. Then got trapped for three years in a violent relationship. After hiding out for many years, she married and had another boy at the age of twenty-nine. Susie spent many years working in factories and waitressing most nights. She has also become a palmist since the age of sixteen and did this as a hobby ever since and has recently published a book called *Modern Day Palmistry*. She has remarried after twenty years and has lived and traveled extensively around Australia's top end in a bus coach motorhome from 2014 till 2020. Then settled down just west of Brisbane in Queensland, Australia, with her husband, Shane.

I dedicate this book to my nanna, Kathleen Halliday; and mom, Paula Goddard. Both of whom I got my love of books.

Susie Polzin

Secrets of the Past Revealed

AUSTIN MACAULEY PUBLISHERS™

LONDON · CAMBRIDGE · NEW YORK · SHARJAH

Ordering Information
Quantity sales: Special discounts are available on quantity purchases by corporations, associations and others. For details, contact the publisher at the address below.

Publisher's Cataloging-in-Publication data
Polzin, Susie
Secrets of the Past Revealed

ISBN 9798886932966 (Paperback)
ISBN 9798886932973 (ePub e-book)

Library of Congress Control Number: 2023918095

www.austinmacauley.com/us

USA
First Published 2024
Austin Macauley Publishers LLC
40 Wall Street, 33rd Floor, Suite 3302
New York, NY 10005
USA

mail-usa@austinmacauley.com
+1 (646) 5125767

I would like to thank my husband, Shane, for putting up with me while writing the book, and family and friends for their ongoing support.

Chapter 1

As I opened my eyes, the sun was starting to appear through the blinds in the bedroom. A memory of the night before started to flood my mind and with that came the anger, embarrassment, and shame that I had felt.

I had decided to get some take-away on my way home, after a long day of meetings. As I waited for the chicken chow Mein and fried rice I had ordered from the local Chinese shop, I heard a familiar voice coming from the restaurant inside.

It sounded like Andrew, the guy I had been dating for the last six years. (Which I still didn't have a ring on my finger from.)

I always went along with the excuses he made about it and just thought I was probably not ready to settle down myself.

I couldn't help my curiosity, so I walked over to the door that stood between the restaurant and the take-away area. He had told me he was going to his mother's for dinner and, to save driving back to the city tonight, he would stay the night and catch up over the weekend.

I didn't think anything of it as he did that quite often. When I stepped into the doorway, I heard another familiar voice. When I looked toward the sound, I nearly lost my balance. I grabbed onto the door frame to stop myself from collapsing on the spot.

Andrew was there with Fiona, a friend of Andrew's little sister, Erin. At first, I was just confused. Then I saw him holding her hand and laughing and talking like he didn't have a care in the world.

I should have yelled and screamed and really made a scene. But the shock and confusion just made me turn and run out of the shop and out onto the street. All the way to my small apartment three blocks down.

My thoughts were racing. Thinking about every excuse Andrew had been making and the worst part about it was it made sense. All the late nights spent working on different assignments and all the weekends off, looking after his mother and younger sister. Because his father had left them when he was very young. Took off with the town bike, his mom used to say.

His mother hadn't been well for a while. But not that bad that they couldn't get by without him. Never did like his mom. She was always drinking and had the mouth of a sailor. Didn't really like people as such. Always complaining about who in town was doing what and with whom.

Andrew was always giving her money and excuses for the way she was. His sister Erin was living in a granny flat out the back of his mother's house. People would come and go at odd hours. I must admit, I may have been dating this guy for the last six years.

But I still never felt close to his family. I remember seeing this woman with his sister a few times over the years. Turned out Andrew was going to take after his father.

I was ashamed because I ran. I was angry with myself for not knowing sooner and embarrassed that I'd been stupid enough to picture a life and a future with Andrew for this long. I had met him fresh out of law school. While I was out celebrating a friend's birthday at a club in the city, I had been attracted to him by the confidence he had in himself.

He was wearing a suit and celebrating some deal he had just made at work. Which meant he would be promoted and become a partner in the advertising company he worked for.

He was somebody I admired. As the years went by, that admiration had definitely began to wear thin. Although in the back of my mind, I often dreamed that we would get better and get married and buy a house in the suburbs and have children.

As I stood up to go to the bathroom, I realized my head was pounding. Must be hung over from the night before. I remembered emptying two and a half bottles of wine I managed to find in the apartment last night when I came home.

Bawling my eyes out for hours before finally falling asleep. Standing in front of the mirror, I took a couple of Panadol for the pain. I looked at myself and my eyes looked swollen from the night of crying.

I looked a lot older than my 31 years. I couldn't believe my whole world had fallen apart overnight. I looked at my hair, it was a mess. Still tied up from the day before. I had a long hot shower and washed my hair. Wrapping it up in a towel, I put on a pair of track suit pants and a black T-shirt. I wasn't planning on going anywhere today. So I didn't bother with putting a bra on either.

I went out into the kitchen and found some bread. Made myself a coffee and some toast and sat at the dining room table trying to think about how I was going to deal with Andrew. I wondered how long this had been going on and if Fiona was the only one.

The phone interrupted my thoughts. I was afraid to answer in case it was him. I wasn't ready to see or hear from him at the moment. So, I let the machine pick it up.

The sound of my sister's voice surprised me. I hadn't heard from my sister since our mother passed away a year and a half earlier after a long battle with breast cancer. We had drifted apart since then. Maree was three years younger and the one who had taken the time off to nurse our mother toward the end.

Of the both of us, we had just known that she was in a better position to be able to as my career seemed more important at the time. I came out of my reflection and grabbed the receiver.

"Hi Maree, what's up?" Her voice was running a mile a minute. I said, "Calm down and tell me what's happened."

She said, "I'm not really sure but I got an email from a solicitor named Harry Goldman. I don't know if you know of him but he wants us to meet him at an address not far from your apartment, at three o'clock this afternoon. I rang him but he wouldn't say what it was about. I'll drive down and meet you at your place at 2 o'clock and we can walk there together, if you want."

I agreed and replaced the receiver.

If anything, it was a welcome distraction. I went and blow dried my hair. It was definitely getting longer, dark brown in color. The same color of my eyes. People were always commenting on my looks and saying how pretty I was. I was short in stature but really fit too. I went to the gym every morning before work and sometimes I would go for a run.

It was only 10 am, I still had four hours to kill before Maree turned up. I decided to go into the bedroom with a few garbage bags in hand and bagged everything that belonged to Andrew. By the time I had finished, there were two boxes and three garbage bags. I took them and put them near the front door ready for him to pick up.

The day went by quite quickly. I not only cleared out Andrew's stuff but went through and cleaned the entire apartment. It was one o'clock, Maree would be here in an hour. So I had another shower and dressed in jeans and a pink cashmere top.

Maree showed up on time and we walked and talked. I told her about last night. She couldn't believe it. But secretly she was glad that Andrew would be out of the picture. She always thought I was too good for him and she was sure I could do a hell of a lot better.

We arrived at Harry Goldman's. It was just a frosted glass door with his name and credentials on it, which led upstairs to his office. We climbed the stairs and I knocked on the door. We heard a lady's voice telling us to come in. It was his secretary.

She knew who we were. "Hello," she said, "Harry will be out in a moment, just take a seat," and gestured toward the waiting area. My sister and I had tried to imagine what this meeting was about but still had no idea. We took a seat in the waiting area.

His secretary with her curly brown hair and glasses hanging on her nose continued to tap away at her keyboard. She was about 60 years old and looked like she had worked here for years. In the waiting room, there was a beige colored lounge and glass coffee table with a few outdated magazines on it. We sat there for about ten minutes, still wondering what this was all about.

The door finally opened and Harry came with his hand out and shook both our hands as he introduced himself and thanked us for coming. He had gray hair with a bit of a bald patch and a kind and caring way about him. "Come into my office and I'll explain why you girls are here." We followed him into his office and took a seat across from him.

He opened a file he had in front of him and said, "This is the last will and testament of your Aunt Mary. Your late mother's sister, I believe. It turns out that you are both the only living relatives."

He began to read, "I, Mary Sullivan, leave my house in Limpinwood and the sum of all monies and possessions I may have, to my nieces Amber and Maree Stokes." He looked up to see the girls looking quite perplexed.

"I have worked for your Aunt Mary for about 35 years. She was a very lonely woman. It is a huge house. She was never the same after her daughter went missing. Alice Sullivan was only 12 at the time. But you probably already know about that."

We both nodded, feeling a bit guilty that we hadn't reached out to her since our mother died. "We just knew that for some reason they didn't get along, for as long as we can remember. So Maree and I never really knew her, only the odd mention of her, every now and again. She never came to Mom's funeral either."

Harry went on to say that the money that she had left them was close to 6.2 million dollars. I looked at Maree in shock and amazement, bewildered. She had the same look on her face. Then we broke into laughter and hugged each other saying, "Oh my god, I can't believe it."

"I know," said Maree. They both looked back at Harry who was also smiling from ear to ear.

He said, "You girls are the only living relatives, so it's all yours. It will be good to get some life back into that place."

After exchanging bank details and keys being given to us, we left the office and wandered back to the apartment, laughing and giggling in disbelief. We bought a couple of bottles of wine and the ingredients to make spaghetti Bolognese on the way home. So we could celebrate our new found fortune and talk about the house and what we were going to do with it.

As I kicked my shoes off, I looked at the boxes and garbage bags and said, "This is something I need to deal with first." Maree was in the kitchen putting the groceries away and pouring us both a wine. I grabbed the phone and rang Andrew.

He answered on the third ring, "Hello darling, how are you?"

"I'll tell you how I am. I saw you with Erin's friend, Fiona at the Chinese restaurant last night. How long has it been going on, Andrew? I am so angry right now." He had gone quiet. "Andrew, I need to know, how long?"

"Eight months," was his reply. Sounding sullen.

"I have packed your stuff. I'll put it outside, you can come and pick it up. I never want to see you again as long as I live." With that, I slammed the phone down. I felt better now and went to put his stuff out the front. An hour later, it was gone.

Chapter 2

Maree and I were getting along really well. Nursing Mom had really matured her. We drank wine and cooked dinner and talked about what we were going to do. Maree was working as a teacher's aide while doing her degree. She was always good with kids; so patient and kind.

The summer holidays had just started so apart from her studies, she was free to do what she liked for the next six weeks. We talked long into the night and decided it would be a great time for me to get away for a while and reevaluate my life. We were also really curious about this house Aunt Mary had left us.

Over the next week, I wound up all the cases I had and handed them onto the other lawyers at the firm where I worked. By Friday, I was free. I was going in a new direction. I would keep renting my apartment and have a bit of a holiday, I thought as I packed my bags. Maree arrived Saturday morning.

I had a little black BMW and we packed all our bags into it and left the city and my old life behind. It was about a three-and-a-half-hour drive. We sang and laughed and talked about the old days. It was nice to reconnect with my baby sister again.

I apologized for not being there more. I knew it would have been hard for her. She went above and beyond and I was grateful. Mom and I used to press each other's buttons just about every time we came together.

She was proud of me with my career and all but she hadn't liked Andrew or his family either and had always made it known. Love is blind; she had probably seen what I couldn't.

We left the city and crossed the Brisbane River via the Gateway, down the Pacific Highway, over the Queensland border and into New South Wales. We turned off at Murwoolinbah and drove another 40 minutes. Then onto a smaller road. It was a beautiful day; the sun was shining and it was so green, everywhere I looked rolling green hills on one side and nothing but trees on the other.

This was just what I needed, to get away in the country. The Navman said there was a small lane coming up on the left and we would have to turn there. The sign said 'Sullivan's Lane'.

"Wow! We have our own street," we laughed. As we turned onto the lane, it was bitumen but one lane only. There were trees on both sides all the way; along two kilometers later, the black wrought iron gates came into view.

Maree pressed the button on the keys Harry had given us. The gates swung open and we drove through. It was strange to think that this was all ours. The house was massive like Harry had said. It was three stories high and the 1st and 2nd floors had a wooden veranda surrounding them and a five-car garage on the right. The house itself was painted white with French doors and there were wooden shutters on all the windows.

We couldn't believe our eyes. It was beautifully kept. The gardens and the lawns were immaculate. I thought I would just park out the front till we unloaded the car. It was a circular driveway covered in white gravel and a beautiful rose garden in the middle with every color you could imagine.

We could smell their perfume as soon as we got out of the car. A huge expanse of lawn was to the left, had to be at least two full acres and surrounded by trees.

We both grabbed our bags and headed up the three steps that led to the front door. I put the key into the large double wooden doors that both opened as I turned the key. We dumped our bags on the floor and went to explore.

The foyer had a huge chandelier hanging and the staircase was so wide with a dusty pink carpet with gold edging and went separate ways at the top. There was also a lift under the staircase. It went to the basement as well as the second floor.

We decided to stick together and check the place out. We went to the door to the left first which opened up to a huge lounge room, a hundred-inch television hanging on the wall and a fire place just to the right of that. A massive lounge suite which could easily fit a dozen or so people. Maree and I ran to test it out.

"Oh! So comfy," I said. The room itself was massive and included half a dozen French doors leading to the veranda. There was another fire place at the far end, there was also a library and a couple of computers set up on old mahogany desks.

There was another comfy lounge just a little smaller than the main one and so many books. All in order of fact and fiction as well as alphabetically. We both loved reading. I looked over at Maree and she smiled back at me. We had not felt this happy in a long time.

The right-hand side corner had a massive DVD movie library separated into different sections, everything from thrillers to children's movies. Then there was a door that led to a bathroom which included a makeup room with two sinks and a really big mirror; it had a nice big artificial flower arrangement on the marble top, another door led to three toilet cubicles.

We left that room and went to the right which opened up to a chef worthy kitchen, dining room and another lounge room with a seventy-inch television and another fire place. French doors that led out to the veranda which had a big barbeque and another big twelve-seater table and a huge outdoor lounge.

There was a gate in the veranda which led to a beautiful heated swimming pool surrounded by lounges and deck chairs with little tables in between. It had trees all around it, so it felt really private. It was like a scene in a movie; there was a bit of a rock, plant and waterfall feature down the far end.

It was about 30 meters in length and about 20 meters wide. It went up to two meters at the deep end and had a decent size spa on the left-hand side halfway down. It would have fitted a dozen people quite easily.

There was a digital sign on the side of the pool house saying the temperature of the pool was at thirty degrees Celsius. I bent down to feel it saying, "I know where I'll be most of the time."

Maree bent down to feel it too and said, "Me too." Down the other side of the pool was a building where the filter and chlorine and other things that kept the pool operating all year round were.

It was also connected to another room that had three toilets, three showers and a fair-sized changing room with a full-size mirror that covered half the wall. Also a cupboard full of bath and beach towels. There were also a few blowup toys for the pool in the far corner.

We went back to the veranda and went through the next set of French doors. There were half a dozen doors. Three belonged to the living area where we had come from. So we went to the next set and used the same key that opened the others. It took my breath away when I entered.

Even my sister had to whistle and say, "Oo, la, la." It was a complete gym with every bit of exercise equipment I had ever seen. The front of the room was a mirror wall.

"Oh my god, I can't believe how lucky we are." It even contained three toilets and three showers with a fair-sized changing room. It also had half a dozen lockers with keys for people to lock up their valuables while they did their workouts. Maree was just as in awe as I was.

The next door led to a room with a fully stocked bar, a pool table and lounge area with a television as big as the one in the front room and another fire place. In one corner, there was a section of computer games with another television to play them on and a box of toys and a chalk board on the wall.

So people could enjoy a few drinks and relax, knowing their children were being entertained. There was also another bathroom with a makeup room and half a dozen toilets. The last set of French doors led to a guest's bedroom with enough beds to sleep a family of five and included an ensuite bathroom and kitchenette.

Chapter 3

There were some pictures of people around the house but mostly of people we didn't know. We had heard that Aunt Mary had made a lot of money on the stock market and they had built this house together and planned to fill it with children.

They were said to have tried for years and finally at the age of 47, IVF had given them a beautiful baby girl. Her husband had died in a car accident when her daughter Alice was only three years old and had never been known to be with anybody since.

He was the love of her life and by the look of the photos around the house, they had known a lot of people and the house had a lot of good memories too.

There was a beautiful full-scale picture in the front room of Aunt Mary and Uncle Tom looking adoringly at each other, obviously very much in love. With their daughter Alice in his arms smiling cheekily at whoever was taking the photo, she would have been about two and a half. Not long before he died.

Other than that picture, there was only one more I had seen of Alice that was the one the police had used. Taken outside on the lawn, all dressed up in a pretty yellow sundress and smiling happily. It was taken a few days before she went missing.

Alice had gone missing when she was 12 years old while out playing on the lawn. Aunt Mary had gone inside to get her a jacket and when she came back out, Alice was gone and was never to be seen again. She obviously blamed herself and ended up having a mental and emotional breakdown.

The maid had found her in the ensuite bathtub in a pool of her own blood with barely a pulse. The ambulance was called and Aunt Mary went to the local mental hospital for the next couple of years. The locals and police had searched everywhere and followed every lead but had absolutely nothing to go on. That's what Mom had told us anyway.

Harry Goldman said that Aunt Mary had a maid and a guy who did the maintenance, lawns and gardens but she herself never left the house. Nor would she allow visitors to the house either. She never got over the loss of that little girl he'd said.

It made us feel really sorry for the poor lady. Especially after seeing this house and imagining how happy this family once was and the incredible sadness that there must had been as well.

We went back into the kitchen and put the kettle on while we reflected on the house and the people who had once lived here. After our coffee, we decided to check out the second floor. We ended up counting twelve bedrooms, all with ensuite bathrooms attached and two separate toilets.

Also two fully stocked linen closets and two fully stocked cleaning cupboards. Not counting the ones we found downstairs and the laundry that was near the mud room at the back of the house behind the kitchen. Maree and I chose a bedroom each.

They were both huge with an ensuite and walk in robes. Both of us chose the left side of the building and I had French doors opening out onto the veranda overlooking the lawn. Maree chose the one near the stairs because she liked the layout for its office study area.

I was checking out the view I had, after the lawn there was nothing but trees. Then I noticed a guy coming out of the woods at the edge of where the lawn finished and the woods began. I knew the woods were owned by us as well.

He had sandy brown hair with well-built arms and chest. He was quite tall, maybe six foot three or a little more. He was dressed in a white polo shirt and a pair of black cargo shorts. As he strode across the lawn toward the back of the house, he looked up to where I was staring at him.

He stopped for a second and he stared back. My heart skipped a beat then he broke into a beautiful smile, white teeth and blue eyes. I smiled back and waved.

"Oh my god!" I turned away and thought, I better go and find Maree and tell her. We will have to go and find out who he is and what he's doing here.

Down the hall, I found Maree setting up her desk with her laptop. Her bedroom was almost as big as my apartment, I thought as I looked around. Maree had Spotify going from her mobile phone and was happily singing a song I'd never heard before. I caught her attention by yelling above the music. She stopped and gave me her full attention.

"I have just seen a guy out the window, coming out of the woods, walking toward the back of the house. Would you come with me and we'll find out who he is?"

"Oh, OK, what did he look like?" I went bright red and couldn't help the smile that spread across my face and the dreamy look in my eyes as I went on to describe him. I finally got her to settle down and follow me downstairs to go find him and see what his story was.

They headed down the side of the house. The lawn felt so good under foot. As we rounded the corner that led to the back of the house, I could hear him chopping wood. *What the hell*, I thought and then I spotted him. He had the polo shirt off and his chest and muscular arms were glistening with sweat.

For a minute, I didn't think he had heard me shouting, "Oi."

He stopped chopping and waved. "Hi, I'm Jimmy Slater," he said, "you two must be Mary's nieces." Maree and I introduced ourselves. I noticed he held onto my hand a little longer than Maree's hand shake.

"I know I should have left when Mary died but I just love my job and I was hoping I can continue to work for you guys now instead." He pointed to a building I hadn't noticed over behind the garage. "I was living here for free but I do all the maintenance, lawns and gardens. I've been doing this since I finished school. It's all I really know."

I looked at Maree to see what she was thinking. She just shrugged and said, "Why not Amber, we would only have to pay somebody to help us anyway with the up keep. It's not like it's costing us at all this way."

I shrugged too and said, "OK, you can stay but it's just a month's trial to see how things go." He thanked them profusely. Then gave her another one of his heart-melting smiles before he went back to chopping wood.

Maree and I returned to the house to continue unpacking and getting settled in. We had brought the food I had left in my fridge at the apartment. We did need to get more supplies but we could do that tomorrow. I knew I had enough to put a couple of corned meat and tomato sandwiches together for a late lunch.

We sat at the kitchen bench and talked about the gorgeous guy out the back chopping wood for the fire places in this house. "We still have a bit to explore, plus that one room upstairs that we couldn't get into. We haven't even checked out the attic yet either," I said.

So after we had lunch and put the dishes in the dish washer, we went to check out the attic. There was a door leading off the mud room at the back of the house. I went ahead, it was a steep narrow staircase that had three levels; each one had a door to each floor.

We went down first and I turned the lights on as we went. I opened the door and entered a massive concreted space under the house; it had a generator that would back up the power if it ever went off and another door to the right and the lift was to the left.

I looked at Maree and she gave me a nod to get me to keep going to the right and open the door. I did and turned the light on as I went.

"Wow!" Maree followed me in, gasping at the sight. It was a wine collection like we'd never seen before. Obviously, they liked to party way back when. There was a huge fridge on the back wall that housed all the different bottles of white wine and all the red were in rows in the middle of the room.

Also stacked on shelves on the right-side wall was every type of spirit you could ever imagine. And on the floor to our right were boxes full to the ceiling of coke, lemonade and any other drink you could imagine to mix with the spirits.

Then I looked to the left and it was stacked with premixed drinks, cans and bottles. I found a carton of southern comfort and coke cans and put them in the fridge. It was ridiculously amazing. I turned toward Maree who already had a bottle of Jonnie Walker Red Label in her hand and two bottles of diet coke she had found in the fridge, under her arm.

With a big grin on her face she said, "I think all this calls for a celebration." I totally agreed and turned to go. I turned the lights off and closed the door. We put the alcohol into the cool room off the kitchen on the way through and continued our way up to the attic.

When we got to the last door, it opened into a huge space. It was here where you realized just how big this house really was under the roof. We wandered around for a good hour or so.

It was mainly outdated broken furniture, old luggage bags and trunks full of old clothes and a lot of old linen and sewing machines that had seen better days, some old toys (something we hadn't seen much of) but they were everywhere up here. Even Alice's old cot and cradle was up here. We were starting to feel a bit sad again seeing all this.

We left and went back down to the kitchen where we poured ourselves a scotch and diet coke and took a seat in front of the fire place that was now crackling away. It shocked us to begin with, that somebody had been in here and we weren't even aware. But then we decided to make the most of it and enjoy celebrating.

There was a stack of wood beside it so we wouldn't have to worry about going outside to get more. The sun had gone down and the fire was a welcome bit of warmth. We both just sat staring at the fire, sipping on our scotch reflecting on the day.

After a while, I got up to make something for dinner, we had some left-over spaghetti from the night before. I had brought the container with me and I had a half of a bread stick there, so I made some garlic bread to go with it. After dinner, I finished loading the dish washer and turned it on.

Then we both went around to all the windows and doors and made sure they were locked. Then we both went upstairs to settle in for the night. I went straight for the shower. It had been a long day. I was looking forward to going to bed. My room was massive, it had a lounge area kitchenette and a four-poster bed.

A television hung on the wall in the lounge area that I could even see from the bed if I wanted to. The walk-in robe was huge with a dressing room and full-length mirror that led through to the bathroom which had a spa bath and separate shower that had enough room to fit two people in easily and the shower itself had such good pressure. So much better than I was used to.

A big mirror hung on the wall above the two sinks and had lights all around. I could see every pore in my skin it was so bright and a door separated the toilet and the bathroom, which I liked. I got into a nightie and turned the lights off and climbed into bed.

It was 10:33 pm on the alarm clock on the bed side table. I had put my phone on charge beside me. I picked it up and texted Maree. "Are you in bed?" I asked.

"Yes," she answered.

"Goodnight, I love you."

She texted me back. "Goodnight Sis, I love you too." I smiled to myself and put the phone down and snuggled down under the covers.

I must have fallen asleep quite quickly because the next time I opened my eyes, it was morning. I got out of bed and went straight in to clean my teeth and wash my face. I put my hair up and dressed in jeans and a T-shirt.

Looking around, I still felt like I was living a dream. I grabbed my phone and went downstairs to put the kettle on. I met Maree on the way. "That was good timing, how did you sleep?"

"Like a baby," she said.

"Me too, as soon as my head hit the pillow, I was out."

I put the kettle on and Maree made us some toast. While we were eating and enjoying our morning coffee, we were both busy in our own heads. I was remembering a dream I had had last night; it was really vague but I was dreaming about Alice and her parents.

They had looked just like they had in the photo in the front room. The little girl was running around on the lawn laughing and dodging Uncle Tom, who was chasing her and making out he was a tickle monster. Aunt Mary was watching them and laughing.

She came to join in when he finally caught the little girl and they both tickled her, then they all fell to the ground and hugged. They were so happy, I thought as I came out of my dream. Maree was asking if I wanted another cup of coffee.

I said, "Yes please," handing her my cup. We were sitting at the kitchen bench. It was a white marble top. I told her about the dream I had and we made a shopping list. We thought we would probably have to go into Murwoolinbah where there was a Woolworths supermarket to really stock up. We also made a plan to check out the small town of Limpinwood before we went.

Chapter 4

The car was still parked out the front. We got in and drove around the drive to exit. On the way past the garage, we agreed we would have to check that out when we got home. We imagined no cars at all would be in there, especially because Aunt Mary hadn't left the house in 20 years.

Maree pressed the button and the gates swung open. As I drove through, I noticed a mail box built in the brick wall beside the gate and took a mental note to stop on our way back and have a look. As I slowly drove down the lane, I looked over at Maree. She had dark brown hair like me but she had hers cut short; just a few little curls framed her face.

She had green eyes though, the same shape as mine. You could tell she was my sister. We both had the nice brown Mediterranean skin that we got from my father's side of the family.

Our parents had met when my mother was on an overseas holiday, she had taken a tour to some waterfall and he just happened to be her guide. She said it was love at first sight and I believed her. He was a great father, always there for us all.

He had passed away when I was only fourteen, he had got mugged on his way home from work one day and died from his injuries in the hospital three days later. The police never found out who it was. After a couple of months, we stopped hearing from them and in a strange way I guess that's why I got into law.

I turned left at the end of the lane and we headed toward the little town of Limpinwood, it was only a four-kilometer drive. The first building we came across was a little cottage with gnomes all through the gardens in the front yard. Next door to that was a newsagent which doubled as a post office.

Then a bakery and a general store that doubled as a liquor shop on the corner. Next door to it around the corner was a petrol station. Across the road on the same side was a police station with two police cars in the parking area.

And on the right-hand side was a small primary school and a quaint little church to the right of that. It was a beautiful little town. We passed another couple of houses before there was nothing but trees.

We turned around and had another look at the town as we drove through. One of the police officers was coming out of the police station adjusting his hat as he walked toward one of the cars in the parking area. There was a couple of teenagers standing on the corner, outside the general store. A teenage boy was sitting on his bike and a teenage girl was playing with her hair and laughing at whatever he was saying.

There was an old lady out walking her dog with a cane in one hand and the lead in the other. There was a guy at the garage filling up a red pickup truck or Ute as we say in Australia, meaning utility vehicle. The school was deserted but there were cars parked everywhere around the little Anglian church. It looked like a typical Sunday morning in a small country town.

So we headed into Murwoolinbah and filled the trolley with a good four weeks' worth of food and loaded it all into the car. Murwoolinbah was not a huge town but they did have all the shops you would ever need from Bunnings Hardware, to Woolworth's, Coles, Target and quite a few specialties shops also all the fast-food shops you would find anywhere like KFC, MacDonnell's or Macca's as we say, Hungry Jacks and Red Rooster.

We stopped in the drive through at KFC on the way home. To be honest, we were glad to get home. Neither of us liked food shopping.

We put everything away in the cool room and the walk-in pantry. Then sat down to have a coffee. We were discussing what we may find in the garage, when we heard a knock on the French door near the fire place. It only had a lace curtain, so we could see it was Jimmy, the guy that we met yesterday.

I got up from the kitchen bench where Maree and I were sitting, unlocked the door and told him to come on in and went back to sit.

"Hi," he said as he came in. I pointed to one of the empty chairs and told him to have a seat. He flicked his sun-bleached hair as he took a seat.

"I just came in to see how you guys were settling in and ask if there is anything you need me to do. I hope you didn't mind me getting the fire started last night. I always did it for Mary," he said.

"I must admit it did surprise us but it was a welcome surprise though," I said giving him a big smile. You could see the tension leave his body, as he started to relax.

That's when Maree decided to start the interrogation. "I know you said you have worked here since school but you are not that old. I was imagining somebody a bit older the way the solicitor was talking," she looked at him expectantly.

He said, "I'm 30 years old, I left school after grade ten so it's been about 14 years. Before that my father did the job. My mother was your auntie's maid for 30 odd years. My parents split up while I was in grade 10. I only had a month to go and I had just finished all of the exams I needed to do."

"So, my parents let me apply for the job and leave school early and besides, I basically grew up here with my parents being here all the time, so I already knew the job my dad did. Hell, I used to come and play when Alice was here. She and I were the same age."

He turned inward as he said this last bit. Like it still affected him to think about her. "What is your mom doing now?" Maree asked.

He looked up and said, "Oh, she's just at home; since Mary died, she doesn't really know what to do with herself. It's a bit sad really. We have a house outside of town. Mom still lives there. My Dad moved downstairs and brought himself a truck and now he does cross country loads, so he's hardly ever home."

I began thinking about his mom and kind of felt sorry for her at home with nothing to do after sticking by their aunt for so long. Then my mind came back to the house and how massive it was knowing the dust was starting to be seen already on the furniture. I turned to Maree and it was like she was thinking the same thing.

She said to me, "We should see if she wants to come back and help us with this place, maybe."

I said, "I was just thinking the exact same thing."

I looked at Jimmy and he was nodding and said, "She would be over the moon if you did that. I can give you the address if you wanted to go and talk to her." I got a pad and pen from near the phone on the kitchen bench and he wrote it down for us.

We chatted for a little while longer then I asked him about the garage and what we could expect to find. His eyes lit up and he said, "come with me, I'll show you."

I looked at Maree and she shrugged and said, "OK, let's go," we jumped up and followed Jimmy out onto the veranda and went to the right and through a gate which led to the garage door. He unlocked the door with a bundle of keys he'd pulled from his shorts pocket. As the door opened, he reached in and switched on the lights.

We entered a hallway with six doors, one leading to each garage space. The first room was a lot bigger than the rest and was full of tools and a hole in the middle of the room so they could work under the cars. Every tool you could ever need was hanging on the walls and mobile tool boxes full to the brim.

A mechanic would have been in heaven. The next space had a silver Mercedes Benz. "This was Mary's," he said, "I look after them, even though nothing has been driven since Mary went to that hospital. My Dad taught me a lot about cars and how to fix things and keep them running well." I couldn't help but think this guy really was the full package.

I stopped when I realized he was talking to me. "Sorry, what were you saying?" I said.

"I was just saying, I'll move that car out and put yours in there if you like."

"Oh, yes please that would be great. My keys are hanging on the hook in the kitchen, thank you," I said with surprise. I wasn't used to a man doing things for me.

We moved on and just before he opened the next door, he turned toward us and with a sparkle in his eyes, he said, "You may just prefer to drive this one though," he opened the door and we followed him in.

"Wow!" Maree exclaimed, "It's a mussy." It was a Mustang, Metallic Blue. Maree's favorite color. She was already sitting in the driver's seat, playing with the gears and adjusting the mirrors.

"I know who will be driving this one," I said, happy to see Maree's reaction to the car. *She deserves this after all she did for our mother*, I thought.

"Come on Maree, we haven't finished looking at the other ones yet," she jumped out and closed the car door and followed us through. Jimmy was having as much fun as we were.

He turned to me and said, "It's so good to have some life back around this place." I smiled up at him and he winked back. Making my heart melt just a little bit more.

I couldn't help but ask, "Do you have a girlfriend, Jimmy?"

"Nah," he said, "too much to do around here. Not that much to choose from around town either, I guess," he said.

Maree asked, "Have you ever had a girlfriend, Jimmy?"

I shot her a look but he answered anyway, "I've had a couple but nothing too serious," he said. Well, I guess it was a good question. *Saves me having to wonder*, I thought.

The next door revealed a model T ford, looking like it had come straight from the factory floor, shiny and new. The last door we entered was as big as the first room but looking around, I could see three road/trail motor bikes. Three kayaks, two double seated jet skis and even some archery equipment in the corner.

Fishing and camping gear. Jimmy could tell we had seen enough and followed us back out, turning off the lights and locking the doors. We headed back to the house.

He took my keys from the hook in the kitchen and went to park my car. He said he would park Mary's car in the last garage with all the bikes and sporting gear. It would easily fit in there, he said. Maree couldn't stop talking about the Mustang. She said she was taking it for a drive this afternoon.

It was quite a warm and sunny day; they decided to go for a swim before they left. Jimmy dropped the keys back to the hook in the kitchen and he also put the keys to the Mustang there for Maree as well. While we were in the pool, we talked about going to see Jimmy's Mom this afternoon and offering her a job.

Maree would get to drive the Mustang. She was so excited. She had an old Ford Focus 2007 model hatch back still parked at the apartment in the city.

After having a shower and getting dressed we headed out the front door where Jimmy had parked the Mustang. He stayed out there so he could see their faces. It looked even more amazing in the sun.

Maree and I were grinning from ear to ear when we waved good-bye to Jimmy. I pressed the button and the gates swung inward. The motor sounded as good as it looked as she drove slowly through the gate and put the gas down a little as they went down the lane toward the main road.

The Navman told them to turn right and head away from town back toward Murwoolinbah. After about five kilometers, we had another right turn. Then five minutes later, we were turning right into her driveway. The letter box had Slater in block lettering so we knew we were at the right place. We parked behind the red Tesla in the driveway.

The house itself was set back off the road, it was a two-story building, white in color and brickwork downstairs. The downstairs had newspaper up covering all the windows. We thought that was a bit weird. We went up the stairs to the front door. Just as I went to knock, it opened.

It startled us a bit. The lady who answered the door, we knew must have been Jimmy's Mom. He had obviously got his looks from her; even at her age, she was gorgeous. She had long blonde hair put up in a loose bun. May have been dyed but it would have been that color naturally in her younger years.

Steel blue eyes which matched the summer dress she was wearing. We introduced ourselves and asked if we could have a chat. She invited us in for a coffee.

We followed her through the front room which had a little table and lounge chair where she was obviously reading the newspaper when we arrived. It gave way to the living area and dining room and into the kitchen. It was a lot nicer inside then it looked outside. Lace curtains hung in the kitchen windows showing a veranda out the back.

I could see some hanging plants out there and not much else from the position I stood. We helped her carry the cups over to the dining room table. She got some biscuits out of the pantry and put some on a plate. She still had a great figure, I noticed.

She came over and sat down across from us and poured herself a tea from the teapot she had filled. Maree and I opted for a coffee. She had introduced herself as Silvia Slater. She finished pouring her tea then looked up at us both and said, "So, what brings you girls here? Is Jimmy giving you trouble?"

"No, no, not at all, in fact we've kept him on," I said.

She smiled and said, "He'll be so happy. He was really worried about leaving and what he was going to do. He does do the job well though. He's a good boy," she said as her thoughts trailed off with the thought of her son.

I took the opportunity to bring up her job. "We," I gestured toward Maree and I, "we were wondering if you would come back and work for us as well?"

She was about to take a sip of her tea. She nearly spilled it and had to put it down before she did. "Really!" she exclaimed; she looked down for a second as if to gather herself. When she looked back at us, she had tears in her eyes. Maree and I both leapt out of our chairs and came around to hug her. She was shocked but hugged us back and we all laughed.

Then she threw her hands in the air and said, "When would you like me to start?"

"Whenever it suits you," I said. "Bring me an old pay slip and we will get that sorted too." The truth was we had no idea what our aunt was paying her but I'm sure we could work something out. This was an idea Maree had and it made sense to me too.

It worked because she agreed and couldn't stop talking about all the work she would have to catch up on. We all agreed she could start tomorrow. We hugged her again before we left.

"So glad we did that," I said to Maree as we hopped back into the car.

"Me too," she said as she hit the button that started the engine with a big grin on her face. As she backed out of the driveway, I looked up and waved back at Silvia and caught another look at the downstairs windows that had newspaper around them and wondered if the dad did live there still. Why was it like that anyway? It made me feel uneasy. Maybe it's just all his stuff in storage there, I told myself.

Maree had turned the stereo on and was singing away to 'The Love Shack' song. I joined in. I had a thought. Mom would love to see us now. I could almost picture her in the back seat, singing away with us too. I could feel her energy. I yelled above the music and told Maree what I was feeling.

Surprisingly, she winked and said, "I feel her too," and went back to her singing as did I, both smiling while we did. All the way home we sang; even as the gates opened, we were still singing out loud with the windows down. It was Queens 'we will, we will, rock you,' all the way into the garage in the third bay down. Jimmy had given her the button with the key ring.

We entered the house though the garage door and gate onto the veranda and through the French doors near the fire place into the lounge and dining area through to the kitchen. We poured ourselves a wine and sat at the dining room table to relax and chat about everything.

There was a stereo in the lounge beside the sofa. I cranked up the music and we were up singing and dancing away to Katie Perry's Firework song when Jimmy came in to get the fire going. We talked him into having a wine with us and got him up dancing too.

He got the fire started and we ended up sitting around on the lounge, chatting away with the music in the background. At 6pm, I got up to put something together for dinner and Jimmy helped while Maree stayed on the lounge gazing at the fire.

It was the first chance I got to spend with Jimmy by myself. He was chopping the tomatoes for the salsa. We were making tacos. I had given him directions and he was happy to do whatever. I was stirring the mince on the eight-burner stove.

I noticed his muscles moving under the thin pale pink polo shirt he was wearing. He was wearing the same kind of black cargo shorts I'd seen him in yesterday when he came out of the woods. It jolted my memory and I had to ask.

"Jimmy, what were you doing yesterday in the woods?"

He looked up from his chopping and said, "It's a path that leads to the river, I often go there to think."

I said, "Oh, I'll have to check it out," he looked back to the tomatoes, then back at me, being careful not to slice his fingers.

He said, "Yes, I'll take you there tomorrow if you like. It's a beautiful spot. We could take a picnic down there for lunch if you want to, it's just a short hike. It's a great place to go kayaking and fishing. There is also a small boat ramp on the opposite side, which you can get to via the main road if you ever want to go jet skiing too. It's a tributary of the Tweed River."

"It's a date," I said.

"I've got a few chores to do in the morning but we can leave about 10 o'clock if you like," he said.

"Sounds great," I said as I put the spice mix satchel into the mince and continued to stir. When the mince was ready, I turned the stove off and started shredding the lettuce. Jimmy had finished doing the salsa and was now grating the cheese.

After I finished the lettuce, I made up some guacamole. We put all the ingredients on the dining room table including the wraps, sour cream and some chili sauce.

Maree turned the music down a little. Got up off the lounge and joined us at the table. When we finished eating, Maree got up. Stacked the dish washer and cleaned the kitchen. She then said she was going upstairs to finish unpacking and left us to it.

"I guess I better get going," Jimmy said as he got up to go.

I put my hand on his arm and said, "I'd rather you stay a while."

He said with a shrug, "Well, I guess I have nothing else planned." We moved over to the lounge; Jimmy restocked the fire and came to sit by my side.

The more time I spent with Jimmy, the more I liked him. I told him about Andrew and what had happened the night before I left. I talked about my mother's illness and our childhood and how I had lost my dad and got into law. He was just so easy to talk to.

He was telling me about his childhood and how he basically grew up around this house. He even confided in me that Alice had been his first girlfriend. This I didn't expect but the more he told me about their lives and the people and the parties, the more I wanted to hear.

He described my Aunt Mary and Uncle Tom as real socialites back in the day. He said Uncle Tom ran an import, export business from home and was quite well off himself.

"I have to ask, if you live in the house up the back for free and work around the place for your board. What the hell do you do for food and clothes, etcetera?" I asked.

"I chop wood for people around town. I don't mind it; keeps me fit. I do quite well with it really, most people buy a ton at a time. I always replace the trees I cut down, so it keeps it sustainable. Dad used to do it too, so I already had his old clients plus I've added to the list. I hope you don't mind that I do that?" he said.

"No, not at all. It saves me worrying about how you were able to eat," I said with a chuckle. He was surprised that I cared. After a while, I laid my head on his shoulder and in silence we just watched the fire crackling away mesmerized by the flames. I couldn't help thinking how quickly my life had changed and how lucky I was that it did.

About 10 pm, he got up to leave and I got up to lock the door behind him. He turned and put his hand on my cheek and said, "I'm happy to be here for you, if that's what you want."

I nodded and said, "Yes, I would like that," turning a little pink as I leaned into the hand. That was when he leaned in and kissed me. I responded; it wasn't just a kiss. We could feel our energies coming together and had a really good pash. As we parted, we agreed to meet back here at 10 tomorrow morning.

I turned everything off and checked that the doors were locked. Then went upstairs to take a shower and hopped into bed. I laid awake for quite some time trying to digest everything that had happened that day. I'm sure I went to sleep with a smile on my face.

Something woke me up; in my groggy state, I was wondering what it was. Then I heard it again. It sounded like a little girl whispering, "help me," again and again. I was fully awake now, I looked at the clock, and it was 2:45 am. I listened for a while; it had gone silent again.

I thought about going to Maree's room and telling her but when I didn't hear it again, I decided not to bother waking her. It was probably just my imagination anyway; I thought as I snuggled back under the covers and tried to get back to sleep.

Just as I was about to drift off, I had a feeling that somebody was in the room. I wasn't game to move but I opened my eyes and there was Alice standing near the bed staring right at me. I couldn't believe my eyes, so I closed my eyes then had another look and she was gone. Well, that was weird. I tried to get back to sleep but couldn't, so I decided to go downstairs and have a hot chocolate and see if that helped.

Maree and I always had an uncanny connection. Like we always knew if something was wrong with the other. So as I put a dressing gown on, on my way out the bedroom door, the clock said it was 3:30 in the morning. As I was passing Maree's door, it opened.

She wasn't really surprised when she saw me, she asked, "What's up?"

I said, "I really don't know," I noticed my voice was shaking, "I have just seen Alice. She's gone now, she just disappeared. I woke up and she was standing there watching me. It was creepy. I couldn't get back to sleep. I was just going to make a hot chocolate and hope that helps. Do you want to come?"

She nodded and ducked back in to grab her dressing gown and side by side we went down the stairs. I couldn't help but look around as I went in case I would see Alice again. I didn't see her again that night. The hot chocolate did help though and Maree's company, of course.

We sat at the kitchen bench and I told her about the whispering that had woken me up and the apparition of Alice looking like the picture the police had used for the media. She had long curly red hair, pale blue eyes and beautiful olive skin. She was dressed in a blue and white checked tunic type dress. White lacy socks and black leather shoes.

"I wonder what she wants," Maree was saying. I was stirring the milk on the stove. "I woke up and could not stop thinking about you for some reason, I felt like I needed to check to see if you were alright. So that's why I couldn't sleep," Maree was saying. We finished our hot chocolate and went back to bed. When I finally fell asleep, I slept well.

I slept in till 8am. I'm glad I did though and I was feeling refreshed after my shower. I blow dried my hair while I reflected on last night and what it all meant. I was none the wiser. I didn't know how I was supposed to help her.

I put a pair of leopard skin bikinis on under black shorts and a yellow blouse with three buttons down the front and tied at the waist. I put my runners on and my hair up. Then headed downstairs grabbing a beach towel out of the linen cupboard in the hallway, then I grabbed another one for Maree.

As I ran down the stairs, I could hear Maree talking to somebody in the kitchen. As I rounded the corner, I remembered Silvia was starting today. "Good morning," I said as I sat at the kitchen bench. Silvia already had the kettle on.

She said "good morning" and asked what I would like for breakfast. She said she had made bacon and eggs, so I said I would love some. Maree said good morning when I walked in and was busily eating bacon and eggs herself.

"It smells divine," I said. Silvia smiled as she handed me my coffee made just right. I said, "Wow, I could get used to this," and took another sip.

"So could I," Maree and Silvia both said at the same time, we all laughed.

Silvia asked, "Would you like some tomato with that?"

"Yes please," I said. She handed me my plate. And two pieces of toast. "Oh, thank you," I said and got stuck into it. I didn't realize I was so hungry. "Hmm, yum," I said and rolled my eyes back a little to emphasize how much I was enjoying it.

Silvia said, "Maree tells me Jimmy is taking you girls down the river for a picnic lunch. I've made a basket up with enough food to feed an army. Don't worry if you can't eat it all though," as she was loading up the dish washer and cleaning the stove and wiping down the bench and counter tops.

I wondered if Maree had mentioned what had happened during the night. For some reason, I didn't really want to tell Silvia at this stage anyway. She made me another coffee then asked if we were OK with her tidying up our rooms while we were gone.

I was happy to oblige and so was Maree. Neither of us had anything to hide. She handed me the sunscreen which I used then handed it to Maree to use.

I was just putting my plate into the dish washer when I heard Jimmy on the veranda and ran to open the door. "Hello ladies, good to see you back Mom," he said.

"It's good to be back, I made you guys up a basket, but you'll have to carry it though. I may have gone a little overboard," she said smiling up at him.

He gave her a hug and said, "Thanks Mom, you're the best." He turned to me and said, "Are we ready to get going?" I turned to Maree, then we both thanked Silvia for everything and headed out the front door.

We were excited to be out exploring again. Jimmy led the way carrying the basket like it weighed nothing at all. Across the beautiful spongey green lawn. "I have to ask Jimmy. What's the secret to this amazing lawn?" He went on to explain about a machine that put little holes in the lawn and it makes it retain the water better.

It also had a huge sprinkler system that came on at a certain time of the day. I asked if that meant we would have a huge water bill. He laughed and said, "Don't worry your pretty little head about that. It runs off the bore water which comes up out of the ground."

He then went on to tell us about being able to tap into an underground river system that supplied it freely. It was interesting the way he explained everything. We definitely were city girls.

The track was through thick forest but the track was well used, so it was easy enough to keep up. There was a bit of a decline coming up. We had been walking for about an hour.

"It's not too much farther." Another fifteen minutes went past and the path started to open up to a beautiful view of the river. It even had a little beach about a hundred meters long made up of little pebbles. The water looked so clear and inviting. Maree and I looked at each other then started stripping down to our togs. Maree's bikini was an aqua color with hibiscus flowers on which really accentuated her beautiful Mediterranean skin.

We were pretty sweaty after our hike through the woods so we both dove straight under. The water temperature was a little cool and felt really refreshing. I looked back to see if Jimmy was coming. He had put the picnic basket on a table and chairs I hadn't even noticed till now and was taking off his shirt as he headed toward us.

He ran down to join us, splashing us as he did. Then ducked his head under the water to cool off. I couldn't help but admire his gorgeous, well-built body and the way he flicked his hair as he came up out of the water. He splashed me and I dove out of his way and splashed back. Then had a bit of a swim.

Maree was asking Jimmy about the table and chairs and he was explaining how he had built them himself and was pointing to a bend in the river where we lost sight of it. "There is a little bridge up that way. I made that too," he said with a smile. "It leads to the woods on the other side. Which also leads to a place I can drive down to and that's how I got the materials down here."

He was so clever, I thought. "We can go have a look after lunch if you like. It's only a short hike," we both agreed. Jimmy had come up behind me and put his arm around my waist and pulled me onto his lap. I wrapped my arms around him.

I looked over at Maree, she was busy floating. I turned back to Jimmy and he kissed me again. I felt like I hadn't felt in a very long time, loved and appreciated.

After a while, I heard Maree saying she was starving. I looked at my hands and my fingers were looking all wrinkly where my finger prints were. I'd had enough too. We all got out and grabbed our towels and dried ourselves off. Wrapped in our towels, we went and sat down at the table and admired how well it was made.

Jimmy opened the basket and took out a table cloth. He handed it to me and I spread it out on the table. It had some really pretty rosellas on it. He put the basket back down and started to unload the contents. We arranged all the food on the table and put the basket down on the bench seat beside Maree. Jimmy and I sat opposite.

There were four different kinds of sandwich meat and all the salads you could imagine. Silvia had even made a fresh fruit salad with cream for dessert. We definitely couldn't eat it all but we all had a red hot go at it. We were starving after our long walk and swim.

We packed everything back up and left the basket on the table with our towels and went off to have a look at the bridge Jimmy had made.

The path followed the river. It was just around the bend; the water narrowed down a little. It was about twenty-five meters wide where the bridge crossed over. It swung a little when I tried walking on it but it had netting on the sides, so it felt quite safe. You could hang onto the sides as you went. Maree was right behind me when I reached the other side, so it was strong too.

I decided to give it a test on the way back and rocked from side to side a little. Maree was screaming and laughing at the same time, which made me do it more. Jimmy was just watching us with a big grin on his face.

"You did a good job with it Jimmy, I love it." He went a little red, he was hoping I would like it and relieved when I did.

We headed back through the woods, stopping to pick up the basket and our towels on the way home. It felt weird to be thinking of this place as home and I said what I was thinking to Maree. Just to see how she was feeling about that prospect.

"I was just thinking about that," she said. "It's absolutely magic out here and I love the house."

"And the people," I added.

"Yes definitely," she said. We arrived home around five. We thanked Jimmy for taking us and he left to do some chores.

Silvia had left us a note on the kitchen bench. It said, 'Dear Amber and Maree, I am over the moon to be back. I have made you a lasagna and some cheesy garlic bread, it's in the oven. You just need to heat it up. I have also made a salad to go with it in the fridge.'

'You just need to put the salad dressing on it. Thank you again. See you tomorrow. I've also made an apple pie. It will go well with ice-cream if you want dessert. Love Silvia'

"Wow, aren't we lucky?" I said to Maree. "Let's go have a shower and meet back here for dinner about seven." Maree agreed and we both took off to do what we needed to do. I took our towels to the laundry. Something caught my attention out the back yard.

I could hear two men in a heated discussion. I peered out the laundry window, careful not to make my presence known. The window was closed so I couldn't hear what they were saying. One of the men was Jimmy, he had the axe in his hand and was obviously in the middle of doing his chores.

There was also another guy I'd never seen before. He had dark, oily looking, shoulder length hair that looked really messy, like he'd just woken up. He was a little shorter than Jimmy and had quite a big belly. He was dressed in a dark blue bonds singlet and a pair of brown stubby type shorts, which looked like they belonged in a rag bag and black rubber thongs.

He was angrily yelling at Jimmy. The guy looked back at the house. I stepped back from the window so as not to be seen. He looked a bit scary with his wild hair, crazy eyes and his angry attitude.

I left the laundry and took off through the kitchen and ran upstairs. I had figured the guy must be Jimmy's Dad, the truck driver. By the time I'd finished having a shower and washing and drying my hair, it was time to meet Maree for dinner.

I went downstairs and the fire was already lit. We didn't see Jimmy at all that night. The lasagna was amazing and so was the cheesy garlic bread and salad. We chose a red wine to go with dinner and had a quiet night. Then we sat near the fire talking about what we wanted to do the next day.

The plan was to have a workout in the gym first to work off the apple pie and ice-cream we had eaten for dessert. Then check out the right-hand side of the house upstairs on the second floor. We had only had a brief look while we were choosing a bedroom the day we arrived.

Aunt Mary's room was at the far end and the locked door was next door to that. The rest were guest's bedrooms, a toilet and another linen closet. Also another closet for the cleaner. Stocked up with all the cleaning products. Also a vacuum cleaner, mop and bucket and whatever else a cleaner would need. We both wanted to check out Aunt Mary's room. Just to get to know her a little better, if that was possible.

We were also intrigued to check out the locked room. We both had a feeling it would belong to Alice. We would have to ask Silvia about it tomorrow and where the key to it was kept. We had an early night and promised to set our alarms for 6:30 am so we could go to the gym together and start the day in a positive way.

Chapter 5

I dreamt about Alice again, it felt so real. I was wearing my pajamas and she had woken me up. I followed her out of my room and down the hallway past Maree's room. I banged on her door and screamed out to her, getting no response as I followed Alice past the stairs and down the other end of the hall. Then she disappeared into the locked bedroom door. As I reached for the handle, the alarm clock sounded. It was 6:30 in the morning.

I brushed my teeth and splashed my face and got dressed into my Lorna Jane workout gear. Silvia didn't start till 7:30 am so the house was still quiet. I grabbed a towel out of the linen closet and went downstairs. I turned the light on in the kitchen and grabbed a water bottle out of the fridge and went straight to the gym.

10 minutes into my workout, Maree turned up. I had the stereo on random play and music videos were on a television that hung from the ceiling at the front of the room. We spent a good hours' worth of sweating it out on the different machines, it was better than any gym I had ever been to.

We both felt very spoilt. After our workout, we both went back upstairs to shower and get ready for the day.

We said hello to Silvia on the way through. She was in the kitchen preparing a pancake mix for our breakfast. An hour later, we had been upstairs had a shower and dried our hair and got dressed and were sitting back at the kitchen bench stacking them onto our plates with butter and maple syrup.

I was washing it down with a second cup of coffee when I remembered the dream I had this morning. I was telling Maree and Silvia just how real it felt. "That reminds me," I said, "have you got the key to the locked room upstairs? Maree and I want to have a look."

"You'll find it in a secret drawer in a desk, in your Aunt Mary's room. It's Alice's room. Nobody has been in there since she's been gone. After the police were finished with it, Mary locked it up and told me where to find the key so I could do the dusting once a month and that was it. I was instructed to not move a thing and never to mention it again. I always cleaned it when Mary was downstairs so she didn't have to look in there."

"After her breakdown, it just seemed easier not to have the reminder but this house belongs to you girls now, so I guess it's up to you both now. If you need me just give me a hoy. I've got some laundry to do. So if I'm not in here, I'll be out at the clothes line." We thanked her and headed upstairs to explore.

We went straight to Aunt Mary's room first. I opened the door, there was a beautiful arrangement of artificial flowers in a huge Chinese vase in the middle of the first room. An antique gold trimmed red velvet settee to the left and a side table with a lamp beside that.

There was an old telephone on the table which obviously still worked and an intercom system attached to the wall. One button was labeled the kitchen, another Jimmy's house. There was also one for emergency 000 which would automatically put you in contact with police/fire or ambulance.

I opened the drawer on the side table and found a pen and paper. Also Aunt Mary's phone book that had everybody's contact details in. I closed the drawer and went through the doorway that led to her bedroom. I was surprised to see she had a king-sized bed and the room itself looked very modern, compared to the front room.

It had a walk-in robe big enough for a couple but Aunt Mary had managed to fill it with her own stuff anyway. We must have spent a good two hours just going through her wardrobe. It was like going back in time, it was quite sad really.

It had so many pretty dresses with sequins, skirts, tops, shoes, bags, scarves, hats and jackets and heaps of costume jewelry to match them all. The sad part about it was you could tell that none of it had been used since she had come home from hospital 20 years ago.

In the bedroom itself, was a large set of wooden drawers and the clothes in there were the ones she had obviously worn. All blacks, grays and dark in color.

We went over to the desk that Silvia had told us about. It was really old maple wood and had a front like an old bread bin. I sat on the pink padded wooden stool in front of it and opened the front. It had three little drawers on the left-hand side and the rest was desk area. There was a writing pad on the desk and pens and pencils in the drawers.

There was another drawer under the desk and I pulled that out. There were places inside for paper clips, rubber bands, liquid paper and anything else you would need in a desk. I crouched down to have a look up underneath inside the drawer on the right-hand side. There I found the little button that opened the secret drawer. I pressed the button and the little drawer opened.

I found the key to the room but I also found an envelope with our names written on, in what must have been Aunt Mary's hand writing. "Oh my god," I said as I looked up at Maree who was looking over my shoulder. "I wonder what this is."

It was quite heavy and it was sealed with one of those old-time red wax stamps. I opened it with the letter opener that I found in the drawer and emptied the contents onto the desk. There was a letter and another key. I opened the letter and read it out loud.

Dear Amber and Maree,

I know it must have been hard for you girls to understand why your mother and I weren't talking to each other for so long. But she was my sister and for a long time we used to be close. Life just gets in the way sometimes. I'm sure she will be there to meet me when I cross over and all will be forgiven. I truly believe in the afterlife. Which brings me to the reason I am writing you girls this letter.

It's about Alice, I know her spirit is stuck in this house and I haven't been able to help her cross over properly. Your mother and I, we had an uncanny connection and I know you girls have it too. It's our gifts we have inherited through my mother's side of the family.

I have dreams and I see spirits at times. I see Alice a lot, from a few months after she disappeared. That's how I know she is dead. I thought I was going nuts at first but you learn to live with it. I was afraid to leave her here by herself. If you're reading this letter, you may have already met her.

She is very clever at being seen. Although it is only me who sees her. I hope you can help her somehow and I will try from my end too. Don't say anything to anybody. They will just think you're nuts and for some reason, Alice doesn't like other people knowing she's there. Thank you in advance.

The other key belongs to a safe deposit box at the Heritage Bank in Murwoolinbah. Lots of love, Aunt Mary.

Maree said, "It makes sense now, your dreams and your visions."

"Yes, I wonder why she's hanging around. I guess we will soon be finding out," I said. "I wonder why her safe deposit box wasn't mentioned in the reading of the will. We will have to keep that to ourselves as well. There's a reason it was hidden in that letter."

"Yes," Maree agreed.

We left Aunt Mary's room and went to the bedroom next door. We both looked at each other not knowing what to expect when I put the key into the lock and turned. The door swung open and we entered the room. It was everything you could imagine a twelve-year-old girl would wish for.

The walls were painted as if you were in a magical land with flying carpets, castles and stars. She had a beautiful pink bed spread on a queen size four poster bed and pink and purple curtains hanging around the top. It was a room fit for a princess with a teepee cubby house in one corner and a massive doll house in the other.

I walked over to get a better look at the doll's house. It was an exact replica of this house. "Wow, Maree check this out." The more we looked, the more curious we were. Every piece of furniture had been hand made. "I wonder who spent all that time making this."

I made a mental note to ask Silvia. There were even little matchbox cars parked in the garage that matched the ones that were in there. I noticed there were little handmade dolls in there as well. One that looked like Silvia was in the kitchen with pot holders on her hands, putting a cake into the miniature oven.

There was also one that looked like Jimmy's Dad but he was dressed in overalls and working on one of the cars in the first bay of the garage. There was one that looked like Alice in her room. She was laying on the bed and one that looked like Aunt Mary sitting at her dressing table in her room.

She had a little hair brush in her hand. We must have been in there for another hour or so just looking at all the bits and pieces. You could even turn the lights on in the different rooms.

We continued to explore the real house. Alice had her own little library of children's books to one side of the bed. On the other side of the bed was a table with an alarm clock, a pretty colored light with stars cut out and when you turned it on, it went in circles making stars shine onto the walls and ceiling.

There was a toy room off the main room filled with all sorts of dolls and teddy bears. Also everything the dolls would need as in little prams, cots, clothes, Barbie campervan and sports car. Also a dress up corner with dresses and tiaras and all sorts of costumes a little girl would want.

Another room that was her wardrobe filled with a twelve-year-old girl's clothes, a full-length mirror and dressing table with a makeup mirror surrounded by lights. Then it led through to an ensuite bathroom also themed toward Disney's princesses from the electric toothbrush to the shampoo and bubble bath. It was sad to think these people were so happy, once upon a time.

We purposely left the door unlocked when we left Alice's bedroom. If we were going to get to know her better and more importantly, help her to cross over if we could; although if Aunt Mary couldn't do it, I didn't hold out much hope.

I will try my best, I thought. As I closed the door and turned the lights off, I said out loud. "If I can help you Alice, I will, I promise. But you may have to help me do that."

We went back down to the kitchen to have something for lunch. It was already 1:30 in the afternoon and we were starving. Silvia must have heard us coming, she was getting out the sandwich meat and tomatoes. I grabbed the bread and started buttering. Maree was on her phone at the kitchen bench.

"Silvia, who made the doll's house upstairs?" I asked.

"I don't know if you knew Uncle Tom's younger brother or not, Kenny was his name." I vaguely remembered something about our Uncle Kenny.

"I just remember him being in a wheel chair. I think he had MS. or something, didn't he?"

"Yes well, he used to live here back in the day. He built that; he was a very clever man. Good with his hands. He's the reason Uncle Tom put the lift in. He died while your Aunt Mary was away in hospital. They didn't think he would live past twenty-five but he was well into his forties. Alice and he got along really well. He spent every bit of his spare time on making that house."

We finished eating and Maree said she was going upstairs to do some study. I decided to go for a swim, so I went upstairs to change. I put my togs on thinking I would have to go shopping and get more. I only had the one set of togs, the leopard print ones.

Now that we had our own pool and money was no option. I didn't even need them in the city. I had brought them in case I went away but we never did go anywhere. I ran back downstairs, grabbing a beach towel out of the linen closet on the way through. I decided to take the lift down to the basement and find something to sip on while I was in the pool.

I pressed the basement button and the lift door opened. This was the first time I had used it. It had pretty green painted walls and a built-in intercom system. It moved smoothly and quietly. I arrived at the basement. The door opened up onto the room where the generator was.

I turned right and turned the lights on as I went. I got a six pack of Southern comfort and coke premixed cans out of the carton that I had put in the fridge the last time I was there. I turned the lights off and went back the way I had come.

Silvia was in the kitchen cooking a lamb roast for dinner. I stopped for a quick chat and to have a look. "It smells amazing," I said looking in the oven "I'm going for a swim. Is Jimmy here today?"

"Yeah, he should be around here somewhere. Check the intercom first, if he's at home he will answer or in the garage but if he's chopping wood, you'll hear him outside anyway. I don't think he was going anywhere today. He would have said," Silvia said as she peeled the potatoes.

"All good, I'll go find him and Silvia, can you make enough vegetables for Jimmy too, please," I said as I got up to leave. Silvia could not hide the way she felt. She was beaming. *She obviously approves of me*, I thought and it felt good to know that too.

I was thinking that I wouldn't mind having a look around out the back. So I was going to find him and see if he wanted to go for a swim too. I also thought it would be a good excuse to check out where he lived. I went through the French doors and I hung my towel on the railing near the gate that led to the pool.

I went through the last gate at the end of the veranda and closed it behind me. There was a path that went to the left and another that went straight ahead which I gathered would lead to Jimmy's place. I went left first; it had a beautiful garden along the back of the house and the path was made of the same white gravel that was out the front.

I was glad I wore my thongs. It stopped near the back door and opened up to a grassy area and that's where three clothes lines were. Just beyond that was the place we had seen Jimmy chopping wood on that first day. I went to the shed to get a better look.

The walls were made from timber and the roof was made with corrugated iron. There wasn't really a door as such, so I just walked in to have a look around. There was tractors and machinery, zero turn mowers, whipper snippers and every tool a landscaper would ever need. There was also a boat under a tarp and a huge pile of firewood and a white ten-ton, dual cab truck parked in there.

I yelled out Jimmy's name but got no reply. I retraced my steps back to the veranda and took the other path that went straight ahead. It had big trees either side of the path; after about fifty meters, it opened up onto another expanse of lawn.

Then the building came into view. It looked like a huge log cabin, not what I was expecting. The chimney had smoke coming out so I knew Jimmy would be home. I took the eight steps up onto the veranda and knocked on the front door.

Jimmy opened the door and said, "Hey it's you, what's up?"

"Nothing, just thought I would go for a swim and then I got side tracked." I held up the six pack of cans and said, "Would you like one?"

"OK, why not, would you like to come in?" He stepped to one side and gestured for me to come in. I was still in my togs, feeling a little shy all of a sudden. I asked if he had a T-shirt I could borrow.

"Of course," he said as he closed the door and pointed to the lounge. "You sit there and I'll get you one." I watched him walk off down the hallway then looked around the room. It was an open plan living area and everything was made from timber. Except the fire place it was made of stone. After a few minutes, Jimmy came back and handed me a light blue polo shirt. I gratefully accepted it and put it on. I felt so much more relaxed.

He came and sat beside me; I took a sip from my can then put it down on the table beside the lounge. I leaned over to kiss him and he kissed me back. His voice was husky when he spoke.

"Would you like me to put those in the fridge for you?" Pointing to the rest of the cans.

"Yes please," I followed him over to the kitchen. "Have you finished with your chores for the day?" I asked.

"I've only got to light the fire shortly but that's about it," he said. "Why's that?" he asked as he wrapped me up in his arms from behind. I felt the heat radiating off his body.

"I just wanted to know if you would be free for dinner. Your Mom has cooked a beautiful lamb roast."

"I could never say no to that," he said as he spun me around and kissed me again. Then he picked me up and carried me down the hallway to his bedroom. He lowered me onto his bed as his kisses went from my lips down. I pulled the polo shirt off and continued to remove his as well.

His head went further down as he removed my bikini bottoms. My body went into orgasmic explosions. I had never felt this way. His tongue and mouth just totally explored my whole body and just when I thought I couldn't take any more, he put himself inside me.

My body arced and responded to his thrusting body movements then we finally climaxed together and collapsed in a sweaty heap on his bed. We just laid there in each other's arms and talked for a while. I forgot what it was like to have somebody that's interested in me instead of themselves.

You could tell Jimmy really did care and loved to listen to anything I had to say. It was getting late and it was starting to get dark. Jimmy said, "Come on, let's go. I'll walk you back to the house and you can go have a shower while I get the fire going."

I got up and put his polo shirt back on then watched him get dressed, every little muscle showed as he put his shirt back on. "I'll come back here for a shower and meet you after that for dinner. What time do you think?" I looked at my watch. It was six o'clock already so we agreed on 7:15.

Jimmy grabbed the drinks on the way and we walked hand in hand back down the path to the main house. "Maree must be still upstairs," I said as we walked into a dark house. We turned the lights on. "I'll let her know what time we'll be eating on my way through," I said as I kissed Jimmy and left him to get the fire going. I ran up the stairs. As I reached the top, Maree was on her way downstairs. I told her what the plan was and kept going to my bedroom.

I got into the shower and thought about the afternoon as the water cascaded over my body. I washed my hair and used the hair dryer afterwards. Then dressed in a pair of jeans and a black top that accentuated my cleavage. I put just a little bit of makeup on. I made it look natural and not too cheap. I was glad to see Maree was still dressed and not in her pajamas when I saw her earlier on the stairs.

She noticed I was humming as I entered the kitchen. She was sitting at the kitchen bench talking to Jimmy. "Have I missed something?" she said laughing as she watched us kiss.

"Never you mind," I said as I picked up the note that Silvia had left on the bench. It said 'Dear Amber and Maree, the meat and vegetables are in the oven on a low heat. Just get Jimmy to slice the meat, the peas and corn are on the stove and just need heating up. I have made some gravy, it's in the microwave and there is some mint jelly in the fridge door. Enjoy, love Silvia.'

I got the lamb out of the oven and put it on a chopping board. I soaked the pan and got a big knife out of the block on the counter top. I gave it to Jimmy to cut the meat. He went to work while I got the plates out of the cupboard and turned on the peas and corn.

I used a pot holder and removed the vegetables out of the oven and turned it off. I got a pair of tongs out of the drawer and shared out the potatoes, pumpkin, carrot and purple sweet potato. Then put some meat onto everybody's plate. I also got the mint jelly out of the fridge and put it on the table.

Maree had already set up the dining room table with cutlery and the salt and pepper; while the gravy was heating up, I served out the peas and the corn. Maree took the plates over to the table and Jimmy wrapped up the left-over lamb in some foil.

I took the jug of gravy to the table and we all sat and ate. Maree had got a bottle of red from the cellar and I stayed with the southern comfort. I didn't want to mix my drinks. I had slowed right down anyway. Jimmy opted for a beer.

So we were just enjoying the meal when I remembered to ask Jimmy about his father. I told him I was in the laundry and seen them out the window. "It looked a little heated," I said watching for the way he reacted.

"No, it's OK. Dad he just has a bit of trouble with his mental health, that's all."

"Is that why he has newspaper up on all his windows?" I asked. I couldn't help myself. I had to say something.

"Yeah, he gets a little paranoid sometimes," he said.

"Well that makes sense than. We were wondering about that, weren't we Maree?" She nodded in response and went onto another subject when we noticed the mood change at the mention of his dad.

After dinner, Maree stacked the dishes into the dish washer while I wiped down all the surfaces and Jimmy restocked the fire. We had decided to watch a movie, so Maree and I went into the front room to have a look and choose. We settled on a good action movie starring Bruce Willis 'Die hard IV'.

Jimmy put the television on and put the CD into the machine. We all laid down on the lounge and got comfy. Jimmy used the remote and got the movie started. When it finished, Jimmy stretched and got up to leave. Saying he had to go to town early in the morning to pick up some part that had come in for one of the cars he was fixing. We said our goodbyes and he left.

Maree turned to me and said "Did you see how he reacted to you mentioning his father?"

"Yeah, and the windows at the house," I said. We both went up to go to bed ourselves, it was already 10:30. 11 o'clock by the time I hopped into bed. It took a while for me to drift off. I couldn't stop thinking about Jimmy and the incredible sex we had had.

When I finally fell asleep, I dreamed I was following Alice down the hallway again and again she went through her bedroom door. When I grabbed the handle to open the door, again I woke up. I looked at the clock on the bedside table and it said 3:10 am.

I was just lying there and I couldn't get back to sleep, so I got up and put my dressing gown on and went down the hallway to Alice's room. I put my hand on the door handle and turned. It opened and I walked in and sat down on the side of the bed.

I turned on the pretty lamp beside the bed and looked around the room. That's when I noticed Alice, she was over sitting in front of the doll's house. She had her back to me but I knew she knew I was there.

"Hi Alice, I'm Amber. I'm your cousin," I said. The little girl got up and floated toward me. She stopped at the end of the bed and just stared. "I'm here to help you. You need to cross over to where your mother is now."

She came around to where I was sitting and stood right in front of me. Then she started to cry and said, "Help me, please," I reached out to comfort her but my hand went straight through her.

"I want to help you Alice but I don't know how, can you help me?" She turned and floated back out through the door. I turned the lamp off and followed her out the door and down the hallway. When we got to the stairway, I heard a noise and looked up to see Maree coming out of her room.

I looked back down the stairs but Alice was gone. I told Maree not to worry and go back to bed. I went back to bed myself and laid there till day break. I finally went to sleep then and didn't wake up till 11.

"Good morning, Silvia," I said as I entered the kitchen and sat down leaning my arms on the bench with my chin down on my hands. I was still in my dressing gown. Silvia put the kettle on.

"You look terrible, did you have a rough night?"

"Yeah, woke up at three and couldn't get back to sleep till the sun came up. Still feel tired though, I'll have a coffee and see if that helps." Silvia was asking if I ended up finding Jimmy yesterday. I told her I did and how much we loved her lamb roast. Plus we all watched a movie afterwards.
"What would you like to eat?" asked Silvia.

"Just some vegemite on toast will do, thanks." I didn't want to say anything about Alice. Especially if she was just starting to trust me. I remembered the letter saying Alice didn't want people to know that she was there. So I kept it to myself. After eating I went back upstairs to lay down and read a book for a while then drifted off to sleep.

The next couple of days I just spent relaxing around the house and enjoying the pool. I slept in till nine on Saturday morning because my sleeping pattern was still a bit out of whack. I rolled out of bed and had a shower and got dressed. Then went downstairs.

"Hi Silvia, where's Maree?" I asked as I entered the kitchen.

"She went to town; they have a market down there on Saturday mornings. There is always live music and heaps of stalls, food and jewelry and clothes, etcetera. It's the best place to get fresh fruit and vegetables. That reminds me, how would you like me to do the shopping? I noticed we were starting to run low on things like that."

She handed me my coffee and toast. "What did Aunt Mary used to do?" I asked while enjoying the welcome aroma of the coffee.

"She just had an account that I used for housekeeping. I only ever replace what gets used, unless something special comes up."

"We will have one made up for you on Monday. I do have some money on me if you need anything in the meantime," it reminded me about the safety deposit box. *It will give us a chance to look at that*, I thought.

"Maree gave me some to go to the markets this morning, thanks anyway. So we have the best fresh produce now, so if you're wanting fruit," she pointed to the cool room and the fridge. "They have all the stone fruit in season at the moment," she grabbed a bowl out of the fridge. It had apricots, plums, peaches and cherries. I picked a plum and starting eating. It was so juicy and sweet.

I thanked Silvia for the breakfast and took my second coffee upstairs with me. I turned my television on and the 11:30 news was just finishing up with the weather and a midday movie was about to start. I hopped back into bed and enjoyed a lazy Saturday morning. I fell asleep half way through the movie and didn't wake up till five in the afternoon.

I couldn't believe how much I had slept. I was wide awake now and keen to get in a nice hot shower. I put some track suit pants and a T-shirt on and went looking for Maree. I found her in her room at her laptop bopping away to one of her favorite bands off Spotify.

I knocked on the door but she didn't hear me. I didn't want to scare her but she jumped anyway when I called her name. "Sorry, I was miles away. You've slept a lot, are you OK?" she asked.

"Yeah, I'm fine, just out of whack with my sleeping pattern, I'm wide awake now. I'll probably be up half the night." I told her about the housekeeping account that we needed to set up for Silvia and talked about going to the bank on Monday.

Out of curiosity, we decided to check our bank balances while she was on her laptop and I checked mine out on my mobile phone I had in my pocket.

"Oh my god," I said and Maree squealed. It said $3,185,289.37 had been credited to both their accounts. Harry had said it could take a week or so to go in. We both took a minute to let it sink in. Maree was the first to break the silence.

"Let's go shopping," she said as she got up and threw herself backward onto the bed.

I joined her laughing saying, "I'm getting some new togs and shoes and clothes and jewelry."

"Me too," said Maree, "and a new laptop." We both went quiet for a minute, both lost in our own thoughts.

Then Maree surprised me by saying, "Amber, I have a date coming up on Friday night."

"What, when did you get time to get a date?" I asked.

"As you know, I went to the markets this morning. I'll have to show you what I brought," she said as she got up and went over to the dressing table. She showed me a nice dainty looking set of gold earrings, there was a pearl in the middle of a heart and the necklace to go with it.

"They're beautiful," I said. She also showed me a little leather shoulder bag she had brought. I said, "Hang on, what's this date you were talking about? You can't just say that, then not tell me about it."

"OK, OK, I'll spill." She paused for effect. "I had just finished looking at the markets and decided to try the car out a little. I went out the other side of Limpinwood, about thirty kilometers, it was a beautiful drive and there was a couple of nice little towns, you'd love it and everything being so green."

"Anyway, I got caught speeding, didn't I? I pulled over when I heard his siren and saw his lights in the rearview mirror. Oh my god, Sis, you should have seen him, so cute. He let me off with a warning if I promised to have dinner with him. He said I wasn't going that fast but he just wanted to check out the chick that was driving the Mustang. I love a man in uniform," she said.

"So when and where do I get to meet him?" I asked.

"He'll be here to pick me up Friday night at 6:30. I'll have to find something to wear. What do you think?" As I followed her over to the walk-in robe, "a dress, a skirt or jeans?" she seemed wistful as I watched her search through the clothes hanging in her wardrobe.

I hope he treats her well, was what I was thinking but I was glad to see her happy at the same time. "We can always find something pretty in town on Monday if you want," I told her. "Do you know where he's taking you? It won't matter what you wear, you'll be gorgeous anyway," I said.

She blushed and said, "I might have to get a trim too. His name is Eli," as she made her way back into the main bedroom playing with her hair. She was so excited; it had been a long time since she had been with a man. Before Mom got sick, she'd said.

"I'm going downstairs to eat now, are you coming Sis, I'm starving?" I looked back as I started moving toward the door.

"Me too," she said. "I wonder what Silvia has made today," she grabbed her mobile phone and followed me out and closed the door behind her. We ran down the stairs laughing and joking as we went.

There was an amazing smell drifting up the stairs. Jimmy was standing in front of the fire when we entered the room. I ran over to him and gave him a hug. "Wow, hello beautiful," he said as he scooped me up and kissed me passionately. I heard Maree say something about getting a room.

We managed to pry ourselves apart to go back to the kitchen and join Maree at the bench while she read Silvia's note out loud. It said 'Dear Amber and Maree, I have left a chicken casserole in the oven on low heat. There are dinner rolls to go with it, there is also a lemon curd cheese cake and cream in the fridge for dessert. Love Silvia' we all moaned with appreciation just thinking about it.

I got the plates and cutlery out and Jimmy took the pot out of the oven and put it onto a chopping board in the middle of the dining room table with a ladle inside to serve it with. Maree put the dinner rolls into the oven to bake for five minutes, two each and three for Jimmy.

She put the butter with a bread knife on the table. When the bread rolls were ready, she put them into a basket and put them on the table. We sat down to eat and filled our bowls with the piping hot casserole. "Your Mom really knows how to cook," I was saying to Jimmy.

"Yes, her mother, my grandmother and her grandmother before that taught her well."

Maree asked, "Do you know the police here in town, Jimmy?"

Jimmy stopped eating and looked up at Maree, "why do you ask?" he said.

"Maree got pulled over," I chimed in.

"Which one was it, the young fella or the old guy?" He asked. We both burst out laughing. Maree was turning red.

"Obviously the young one," I said, "Maree has a date with him on Friday night. Do you know him, Jimmy?"

"Yeah, I've met him a few times, he's quite new to the area. He's only been here a few months, just a kid really. Came up from down south somewhere, Blue Mountains, I think. Not a bad fella, easy to get along with. Now the old bloke, he's another story. He didn't like my father, which makes it hard for me but just doing his job, I guess," he trailed off with his thoughts and went back to his dinner.

Maree and I looked at each other and went back to our dinner as well. After dinner, we stacked the dish washer and cleaned the kitchen. Maree went to her room to study. I was laying around with Jimmy for a while on the lounge in front of the fire.

Just chatting and cuddling, he was asking me about my job. "I used to get some satisfaction out of it, like when I won a case but lately, I couldn't care if I never went back to it. It was a whole other life and not one I was happy with.

I've just been going through the motions but not enjoying it for a while now," I said.

"Have you thought about what you would want to do?" he looked at me expectantly. That's when it hit me, things had got a little serious between him and me.

I looked him in the eye and said, "Honestly, I don't know, I would have to think things through a lot longer. Don't get me wrong. I love it here and I'm really liking you but it's a big decision and I haven't even discussed any of it with Maree yet. Who knows what she'll want to do but I would rather give it at least a month or so and then see how we feel." Not long after I said that, Jimmy got up to leave. Giving me an excuse as to why he had to have an early night.

I was still wide awake and it was only nine o'clock. I couldn't have planned it better if I tried. I made myself a coffee and found a cinnamon bun in the bread bin. I took them upstairs with me ready for a long night. I went straight to Alice's room.

Chapter 6

I entered the room and turned the bedside lamp on and looked around the room; she was not in front of the doll's house like last night nor was she anywhere else. I sat cross legged on her bed and waited. I enjoyed my coffee and the bun. It was 11 o'clock on the digital clock beside the bed. The first thing I noticed was a light came on in the doll's house.

I got off the bed and went over to have a look and see where the light had come on in the replica house. It was on in Alice's bedroom I felt slightly paranoid for a minute while I scanned the room looking for Alice. She was sitting on the bed smiling back at me.

"Hi sweetheart, how are you?" As soon as the words fell out of my mouth, I regretted it. Her smile turned to a frown and she left the room through the bedroom door. I opened the door and she was still there. I followed her down the hallway and down the stairs.

She went straight through the front door and went right down the side of the house. She was waiting for me at the tree line. I had a look around when I got to the corner, all was quiet but it was a half size moon. It was bright enough that I could see. I did have a flash light in my pocket but I didn't need it yet.

I got to where the path began and saw Alice move slowly through the woods making sure I was able to keep up. All the way to the river and along the path that led to the bridge. She waited for me to catch up when I needed to. We went past the bridge and followed the path beside the river around another bend. Then we came across a huge log that went from one side of the river to the other side. She floated across the log and up to the track that led to a bit of a clearing.

I caught up and found Alice as I got closer, I could hear her crying. "Alice," I said as I came up behind her, "what's wrong?" She looked up when I came up beside her, puffing a little.

"I went in a car from here."

"Oh, OK, whose car?" I asked.

"I don't know," she cried.

"What color was it?"

"I can't tell, I'm asleep." She disappeared again.

I walked back through the woods and across the lawn back upstairs and put my pajamas on and climbed into bed. The digital clock beside the bed said 2:44 am just before I drifted off. The next day I enjoyed just going to the pool and watching another movie and hanging out around the house. Then Monday morning came and the alarm woke me at 7:30 am, Maree and I had agreed to meet downstairs about 8:30 am the night before. So I rolled out of bed and had a nice hot shower.

We were leaving at 10 am to drive to Murwoolinbah. We had to go to the bank and check out the safe deposit box and make an account up for housekeeping for Silvia. We had agreed on a $5000 limit. Any bigger than that would need to be discussed.

I enjoyed my morning shower and washed and dried my hair. I put a nice pink dress on that had tiny flowers on it. I could smell the bacon and eggs cooking as I jogged down the stairs. Silvia handed me a coffee as I took my usual seat at the kitchen bench. I was surprised I beat Maree up for a change. She arrived ten minutes later just as Silvia was passing me my breakfast.

"Good morning," she said as she sat down beside me. "I was up late last night studying," she accepted the coffee Silvia handed her, took a sip and sighed.

"So, big day?" Silvia asked.

"Just going to the bank and we have some clothes shopping to do. Don't we, Maree?" She was miles away. I bumped her arm to get her attention. "Don't we, Maree?"

"What?" she said looking slightly annoyed.

"Have some clothes shopping to do."

"Ah, yes, we do. I have a date on Friday to shop for," she told Silvia.

"Anyone I know?" she asked raising her brow.

"Only the young gorgeous local town cop," I teased. Her mood started to improve as she drank more coffee. I was on my second cup.

After we finished our breakfast, we took a water bottle each out of the fridge and headed out onto the veranda toward the garage. Of course, we had to take the Mustang. The garage door whirred to life when Maree pressed the button on the key ring.

Then she pressed the button to start the car. We sat there for a while waiting for the motor to warm up. I had a small grocery list that Silvia had given me to get while we were in town. I put my sunglasses on and checked I had everything as Maree put the car in reverse and backed out of the garage.

The gate swung open with another button. Maree drove slowly down the lane and put the indicator on to turn right. We drove to town, talking most of the way. I told her what happened last night with Jimmy and our conversation and how he got a little worried about us leaving.

She agreed with me that we needed more time to make those kinds of decisions. I also told her about my hike out in the woods and where it ended and why.

"So it sounds like she was taken by somebody who parked their car in that spot," she said.

"She also said she was asleep at the time so she didn't know who or what kind of car it was."

"Yeah, I feel like we have come to a dead end. I know why Aunt Mary couldn't help if she couldn't leave the house." We both let our thoughts drift with that thought for a minute.

We arrived at the bank and parked in the parking spot out the front. We got out of the car. Maree was in jeans and a pretty blue top with a butterfly made from sequins on the front. She walked ahead and held the door open for me. "Thank you," I said as I entered. There were only two people serving and only one other customer in the bank.

We stood at the beginning of where a line would start and got directed to come straight through to the teller that wasn't busy. It was a young girl dressed in her work uniform, early twenties I would say. She opened the account in both our names and set up an automatic way of topping it up if it went below $4000.

We were then directed to a door to the right. The lady came and opened it from the other side. We were led down a hallway and into another room to the left. She said, "Just let me know when you girls are finished, I'll come back and let you out. If I'm busy," she said, "just ask the other lady out the front." We agreed and waited till she closed the door.

The key had the number 315 engraved into it. I put the key into that number and it gave way. I slid the drawer out. It was quite large, big enough to fit a manila folder in and about four inches deep. I had brought a spare reusable shopping bag in with me. I got it out and put the folder in. It looked like it was full of old paper clippings and photographs.

We didn't want to spend too much time in there. There was a bag with some jewelry in and another bag with God knows what. We put it all in the same bag and left the room. We put it under the seat on the driver's side and got back in and drove to the big Westfield shopping center down on Main Street. It had an undercover parking area which is where we went and parked not far from the doors to where the escalators were.

Maree managed to get straight into the first hairdressers we saw. It didn't take long, then we went to Best and Less and brought some bras and underpants. Then we went to cross roads and brought a couple of outfits each, we went to just about every other store and the car was packed by the time we left.

We also went to Woolworths to get the few things that were on Silvia's list. Then drove over to Harvey Normans so Maree could buy herself a new laptop. We had literally shopped till we dropped, our feet were so sore and we stopped at KFC drive through again on our way home.

Maree ordered a chicken wrap meal deal so she could eat while driving and I brought a three-piece dinner pack because I liked their bread rolls. We put the radio on 97.3FM and listened to it all the way home.

When we arrived home, we parked near the front door and unloaded the car. So much stuff. Jimmy must have heard us drive in because he came out to give us a hand. We took it all to the front room on the lounge so we could sort out whose clothes were whose.

Maree was only a size eight and I was a size 10 which made it easy to sort through. Then we took them upstairs to our rooms to put them away. I had bought two pairs of denim shorts and two pairs of jeans, one black pair and a light denim pair with holes in the legs.

I also bought three summer dresses, five tops and enough undies and bras to last a whole week. I went to Billabong and got myself three new sets of bikinis and two one-piece togs as well. I also brought five new pairs of shoes.

A white pair, a black pair and a silver pair and a tan colored pair, they were all just casual ones that would go with anything and a new pair of runners. I felt like I had a whole new wardrobe.

I went downstairs to find the stuff we got from the safety deposit box in the car. I opened the front door and saw Jimmy had already put it away in the garage. I went back through the house and out the veranda to the garage. I went to the third bay down and opened the door and turned the light on.

The motor was still making noises as it cooled down. I opened the back driver's side door and reached in under the driver's seat and pulled out the reusable shopping bag I had put there earlier.

Jimmy had already taken the groceries into the kitchen to Silvia, who was putting them away. She was in the cool room when I came through earlier. Now she was stirring a pot on the stove on my way back. Jimmy must have gone back to his chores.

"Hi Silvia, what you cooking?"

"Pea and ham soup, I hope you like it."

"Hmm yum," I said, "It smells divine." I kept going and went upstairs to find Maree.

She was still putting her clothes away; she had two outfits laid out on the bed. "Which one do you think, Sis?" I looked at them both, one was a denim skirt with a top that crossed over at the front and tied together on the side. It had loose three-quarter sleeves. I loved the colors blues, pinks and purples. It had a real boho look about it.

The other one was a gorgeous apricot colored dress with a lacey V neck, a built-in belt at the waist and flowers around the scalloped hem just below the knee.

"I reckon the apricot dress but I do love that top though. It would be nicer with denim shorts for a more casual look but not really for a dinner date," I said, "unless you put it with jeans instead, like the black ones you bought." Maree finally decided on the dress and put them away into her wardrobe.

I just remembered what was in my hand. "I brought the bag up out of the car, are you ready to have a look?" I asked as Maree came back into the bedroom. We both were so excited; we hopped onto the bed and emptied the contents.

The manila folder we put to the side; out of the two bags, I opened the one with jewelry first. There were bags inside the main bag and each one had a piece of jewelry in it. The first one had Uncle Tom's old Rolex watch in it, the next had his wedding ring and a dress ring as well, the next bag was a really pretty sapphire and diamond necklace.

Then a few different gold and silver bracelets and quite a few pairs of earrings with different stones and a pearl necklace that must have been worth a fortune and pearl bracelet, ring and earrings to match. We put them all back in the bag and got the next bag.

It was made of calico with a drawstring top. It had some weight to it. I opened it and tipped the contents onto the bed. It was a movie recorder, I opened it up and it said the battery was low. There was a power cord with it, so we plugged it in to the outlet beside the bed.

While the camcorder was charging, we opened the manila folder. The first thing we came across was a lot of old photos some black and white, some early time color Polaroids. Mostly of Alice as a baby up till the week before her disappearance and Uncle Tom and Aunt Mary in happier times.

Silvia and her ex-husband were in a couple as well. Either in the photo or in the back ground. There was even a couple of Jimmy when he was a baby and growing up alongside Alice.

"Aww, he looks so cute," I said. After going through the photos, the next thing we came across were the newspaper clippings. 'Little Girl Lost' was the front page on the Local Herald, Alice Sullivan 12-year-old girl missing from Limpinwood in Northern NSW is what they said.

Mother goes to get a jacket and the little girl goes missing, if anyone has seen or knows any information should contact the police on 000. The Sun and The Mirror, the national newspapers had the same photo as the one in the Herald and basically said the same thing. Another story was a reward being offered of $10,000 if it leads to Alice being found. The police report was there also.

We put everything back into the folder and checked on the camcorder. "I'll be surprised if it still works, it's pretty old," Maree said as she picked it up. We both moved in to have a look as Maree opened the screen. It surprised me it was the same scene as my dream that first night I arrived.

Uncle Tom chasing after Alice on the front lawn pretending to be a tickle monster and Aunt Mary joining in laughing and rolling around on the ground with them. The person filming moves the picture to include the side of the house and standing there watching them in the back ground was Jimmy and his dad. The camcorder stopped there.

"That's weird that was exactly what I dreamt about on the first night, remember? I didn't see Jimmy or his dad though. Somebody must be trying to tell me something," I said. "I wonder if it was Aunt Mary from the other side. Unless Alice is doing it, I wouldn't know. I guess it doesn't really matter. What matters is that we help Alice and to do that we would have to solve the mystery of what happened to her and who was responsible." I still didn't know if I could but I would definitely try to do my best.

It was 5:30 in the afternoon, Maree went to unpack her new laptop and load the new office program she brought for it. "I might go find Jimmy and leave you to it," I said as I got up and headed for the door. She waved her hand and went back to what she was doing.

I put the file and the other bags back into the recycle bag and took it to my room and hid them in the back of my wardrobe where Silvia wouldn't come across them.

I stopped by the kitchen on my way through. Silvia worked from 7:30 am till 4:30 pm most days, so she had already left for the day. The note on the kitchen bench said, 'Dear Amber and Maree, there is some pea and ham soup on the stove, just needs to be heated up. There is also a vanilla slice in the fridge for dessert, love Silvia.' I grabbed an apricot out of the bowl when I opened the fridge to check out the slice. Then left the house and headed out the back to find Jimmy.

I found him in the shed getting an arm full of wood to bring inside. I offered to help and he gave me a few pieces to carry. I was telling him about my day of shopping and all the clothes we'd bought. Careful not to include the safety deposit box or my little escapade the night before.

I rabbited on while he got the wood stacked and lit the fire. He seemed happy enough. I asked him if he wanted to stay for dinner but he declined and said he had to go see his dad for some reason. I asked if I could come but he shook his head and kissed me on the forehead.

"No, sorry. Dad doesn't handle anybody coming to the house." I felt like he was giving me the brush off as he left via the veranda. A few minutes later, I watched his Ute drive out of the gates from the front room.

Maree caught me looking out the French doors, "is he not staying for dinner?" she asked.

"No, reckons he's going to see his dad, I offered to go with him but he says his dad doesn't like visitors."

"That's weird," said Maree.

"I know, oh well we have pea and ham soup for dinner and vanilla slice for dessert. I don't think I'd want to meet him anyway, after seeing the way he was carrying on the other day out the back. Even in that video we saw today, he just looked creepy."

We both went into the kitchen. I turned the stove on and buttered a couple of slices of bread each. Maree sat down at her usual spot at the kitchen bench and I got the plates and cutlery out and served us up a bowl of soup.

The vanilla slice was from the local bakery. It was so yummy. I had no plans for the night and neither did Maree, so we decided to pick a movie from the library in the front room.

We chose a girlie one called 'Suddenly thirty' and relaxed in front of the television. When it finished, we called it a night. I told Maree to go ahead and I would lock up. "Goodnight," she said as she gave me a hug.

I hugged her back and went to lock the place up and headed upstairs to bed myself. It had been a long day. I had a quick shower and climbed into bed. I fell asleep as soon as my head hit the pillow and I slept like a log all night.

The sun was just coming up when I opened my eyes and I yawned and stretched as I made my way to the bathroom. I splashed my face and cleaned my teeth and chose a new olive-green singlet top, a pair of black exercise pants that went just below the knees and my new runners.

I felt like going for a run. Nobody was around when I went downstairs and grabbed a water bottle out of the fridge. I left via the front door and headed down the side of the house and across the lawn toward the path that would take me through the woods and down to the river.

I pushed myself because it had been a while and it felt good to be out in nature instead of the city runs I used to go on. Or having to drive 45 minutes to find a place to run.

I was really enjoying the fresh air. It wasn't long before I came to the river, I took the path to the bridge then continued around the next bend to the log I had crossed the night before and climbed the short hill to the parking spot where I had seen Alice sitting the other night. Then I had an idea. I would follow the track to see where it led to, see where the car would have to come from.

I thought it may just lead to the main road but I'd see. I ran and the track was pretty well worn, so it wasn't hard. About five kilometers later, I came to a house but not just any old house. It was Jimmy's parents' house. I came in through the back of the property though and I saw a big semi-trailer parked on the far side.

There was no landscaping done here, I thought. The only thing I could see was a bit of a hedge garden that surrounded a tree and the rest of the ground was just leaves and dirt.

The newspaper was still on all the windows and upstairs the veranda looked well-kept with hanging plants and a jasmine vine was covering the railing so you couldn't see much else. I turned around and headed back the way I came. By the time I got home, Maree was up and talking to Silvia in the kitchen.

I stopped on my way through to refill my water bottle and put it back in the fridge. Maree said, "Did you go for a run? I was wondering where you were," it was nine am already. I had been gone for three hours.

"Yeah, I'm going for a shower, I'll be back shortly." I ran upstairs and had a nice long hot shower.

I couldn't stop thinking about where the track had taken me. I wondered if Jimmy's Dad had something to do with Alice's disappearance and ultimately her death and if he did, how I could prove it.

I came out of the bathroom after drying my hair with the hair dryer and put on a pair of denim shorts and a maroon-colored top with 'it's cool to be kind' written in white letters on the front; I had bought it yesterday.

I went back downstairs and Silvia handed me a coffee and a plate of scrambled eggs with bacon tomato and onion and a couple of pieces of toast on the side. "This is really yummy," I said, "what's in it?"

"The secret ingredient would be chicken stock cube. I always put a little in," Silvia said, "I'm glad you like it." Maree was on her second cup of coffee.

She turned to me and said, "Have you got any plans today?"

"No, none at all, why's that. What would you like to do?"

"I was thinking if Jimmy's not busy, we could get the motorbikes out and go for a ride."

"You know they scare me, Maree."

"Jimmy could double you, then you wouldn't have to worry," she said with a pleading look on her face. She used to go riding with Danny, an old school friend she used to go out with.

"I guess that would be OK," I said as I put another fork full of egg into my mouth. The intercom was just next to where we hung our keys. Maree got up and pushed the button that had Jimmy's name underneath.

"Hi Jimmy, are you there?" she asked.

After about thirty seconds, his voice sounded back. "Yeah, I'm here, what's up?"

"I was wondering if you could take me and Amber on a motorbike ride today. Please, please, please," she begged.

"Yeah, I guess I could do that. When do you want to go?" he asked.

"Well, Amber's just having breakfast, so after that would be good," she said.

"I'll just get a couple of things done and meet you girls in about an hour or so, if that's OK?" Jimmy said.

"That sounds great, thanks Jimmy," Maree answered.

Maree said she was going upstairs to get changed out of the shorts she was wearing. I finished my breakfast and drank a second cup of coffee. Silvia was busy loading the dish washer.

"I'll pack you guys up a lunch if you like," she was saying.

"It's OK," I said, "Maree was telling me the other day when that young policeman pulled her over that out the other side of Limpinwood was a few little towns she had wanted me to see, we might have lunch at one of the pubs out that way. If you want to pack a backpack with some fruit and water that would be nice, thank you."

Silvia went to find a backpack and I went upstairs to get changed. I put my new black jeans on with a white T-shirt and a brown leather jacket and some brown boots. I put my hair into a low plait at the back so the helmet would go on easily and my hair would not get in the way. I put my visa card in the inside pocket of the jacket. Left the bedroom and headed for the garage.

Maree and Jimmy were there already; she was sitting on a red Honda XR 250 and he was going over the controls and giving her a general run down. He turned to me.

"Hey, so your sister tells me you don't ride. Are you happy to jump on the back with me?" he said, his was a red and white Yamaha IT 490, he handed me a black helmet the same as Maree's.

"Where were you guys thinking of going?" I turned toward Maree and said, "Remember where you got pulled up? Let's go see these little towns you were talking about, maybe we could stop and have lunch at one of the pubs?" I looked over at Jimmy, "What do you think Jimmy, you know the area?"

He had more of a motor cross helmet on and faded denim jeans and a black leather jacket. *He looked hot,* I thought. He gave me one of his gorgeous smiles and said, "I know where I will take you girls, it is out that way though. Come on jump on," he said.

I was a bit nervous but hopped on behind him and held tight to his waist. We took off slowly so the white gravel wouldn't get too wrecked and headed off. Jimmy pressed the button for the garage door and then the gate.

Chapter 7

We rode through town. As we passed the police station, we saw Eli out the front. He looked up to see who was riding the bikes. Maree waved and he waved back with a big grin on his face. Maree was right, he was quite cute but too young for me. Perfect for Maree though.

I cuddled into Jimmy as we left town and there was nothing but road and greenery everywhere you looked. The first little town we came across was called Swanton; only had a general store which doubled as a garage and a pub, the next one was bigger not much but as you came into town you had to go across an old one lane bridge about one hundred meters in length.

It had a sign at the beginning saying only one car at a time was allowed on it. We rode across the rickety old bridge then we came up and around the bend and there was a pub on the left and a couple of shops; a general store and an antique shop, across the road was an abandoned house with all the windows broken and a man with a horse in the paddock next door.

We kept riding for another hour or so then we came to a town called Ravens worth, it was a funny town. We pulled up in front of the pub and parked the bikes, it was 12:30 pm. We took our helmets off and had a bit of a stretch. We weren't the only ones there, the smell that was coming out of the pub was amazing.

I was looking forward to something to eat. Maree was talking about the bike and Jimmy was listening and talking back. I was looking around just next to the pub was a little shop that had all sorts from souvenirs to clothes and antiques. I wandered off to have a look.

As soon as I entered the shop, the bells sounded; they were hanging on the door itself. It was quite dark and smelled of incense, everywhere I looked there was something to look at. I heard a voice of an old man coming from out the back.

I was looking at a poncho hanging on the wall when he came out saying, "Hello dear, if you need help with anything you just let me know," he went and sat on the seat near the register. I heard the bells going off and I knew it would be Maree and Jimmy coming in.

I was over the back corner looking at some tarot cards that I had found, they looked really old, they were wrapped in a black velvet piece of material and had a little book that went with them and it was all in a little silver box with a price tag of $40 on it. Maree came over to see what I was looking at. I had it in my hand, I was going to buy it.

"Show me," Maree said. "Oh wow, they look cool," she had a quick look then gave them back.

When I went to pay for them, the old guy said, "Those things there," he gestured toward the box of cards. "They know things, sometimes you don't want to know," he said as I tapped my card on the eftpos machine. "They belonged to my wife," he said. "She's not with us anymore, poor dear but she swore by those things and they never let her down, not once. All in the way you ask the questions she used to say. She'll be glad they're going to a good home," he said.

I thanked him and felt the energy of his dead wife. She was happy too, I waved good bye and promised to look after them and left the store. I put them in my backpack and joined Maree and Jimmy in front of the pub.

We went up the ten stairs that led to the veranda and entered the bar. We ordered one coke for Jimmy and two diet cokes for ourselves. I put it on my card and we looked at the menu that was on the bar and the specials that were written on a chalk board on the wall.

I ordered the 250-gram rump steak and Jimmy ordered the 500-gram rump, both medium with mushroom gravy. Maree chose the bangers and mash potatoes off the specials board. I paid for Jimmy's and Maree paid for her own.

We took a number and went and sat on the veranda to chat and enjoy the view. It was a beautiful sunny day 28 degrees, just a slight breeze. Jimmy was talking about a waterfall that was not far from here. Said we could have a look after lunch if we wanted to. Of course we agreed, it was just up the road another thirteen kilometers.

Lunch was fantastic, cooked to perfection, nice fresh salad and beer battered fries. Maree enjoyed hers too. There was not much else in town, just an old store and petrol station all in one. And an old abandoned church with a small graveyard out the back.

We put our helmets and backpacks back on and Jimmy and Maree got their bikes going and when Jimmy was ready, I hopped on the back. The turn off to the waterfall came up on the right after ten kilometers. The sign said Cedar Falls three kilometers.

We took the turn and rode the three kilometers, there was nothing but trees either side of the single lane road, a lot of bends in the road that made me nervous. I must admit though I was really trusting Jimmy's riding by this stage.

We made it to the car park and got off the bikes and took our helmets off but left our backpacks on. You could hear the waterfall from the car park. There was a sign saying it was 200 meters to the waterfall and a track leading down toward it.

We followed the track down to where the waterfall flowed off the cliff edge just to the left. There was another sign pointing to another track to the right saying 500 meters to the pool at the bottom. It was quite high, there was a bit of a lookout with a fence around. Maree and I took some photos and decided to come back another time and make a day out of it.

We made our way back to the car park and enjoyed the ride all the way back home. Maree said she would catch up with us later and stopped in town to visit Eli at the police station. She couldn't wait till Friday and I don't blame her. It was only Tuesday.

Jimmy and I arrived back at the house. While he was putting the bike back where it came from, I thanked him for the amazing day. When he had finished, I gave him a long passionate kiss and asked if he would join me for a drink after the long day of riding.

He said, "Yeah, OK, why not," and followed me into the house. I was so glad he had settled down a bit since last night. I asked him what he would like to drink and he opted for a beer. Silvia was in the kitchen and offered to make us up a platter.

"Yes please," I said as I opened the door that led to the cellar. When I returned with a six pack of beer and two bottles of white wine, Silvia was busy slicing cheese and kabana and adding biscuits and dip to the platter. I passed a beer to Jimmy and put the rest in the fridge. He was sitting at the kitchen bench telling his mom about our day.

It sounded like he really enjoyed himself. I asked Silvia if she would join us when I was pouring the wine. She said she would only have one because she had to drive. I got another wine glass out of the cupboard and poured it for her.

I was telling her about the pokey little shop we went into, next door to the pub and showed her the tarot cards I bought that came in the silver box. She did say that it wasn't really her thing and that she was catholic, so it wasn't really allowed. I understood and took a mental note not to mention them again.

It felt good to be hanging out with decent people who really did care. I was sitting next to Jimmy at the kitchen bench and his mother was looking so happy listening to Jimmy talk about the ride and how well the bike handled. It made me think of the old days when Mom was alive and I could talk to her about anything, before Andrew came along anyway. Then my thoughts went to Aunt Mary, she would have loved the tarot cards and the story behind them.

Jimmy was looking at me waiting for an answer. My awareness came back to the room. "What was that?" I asked.

"Mom said she's going home," Jimmy said. Silvia had gone to get her hand bag out of the pantry where she normally kept it. On the way back through, she gave me a hug and said she'll see me tomorrow. I mentioned the bank account for housekeeping and told her a card was in the mail for it.

"In the meantime, we have put five hundred in the top drawer of the cupboard in the pantry near where you put your bag." She thanked me and went out via the veranda to where she parked her car in the first bay of the garage.

When Jimmy came back from seeing his mom off, he wrapped me in his arms and we kissed and he held me for the longest time. I asked if he would stay for dinner and he said he'd love to. I had told Silvia not to worry. That I would figure something out. We ended up having two-minute noodles with some fresh bread from the local bakery.

We waited up for Maree and I asked Jimmy if he would stay with me for the night. He said he would love to. It was about 10 pm that we heard Maree come home. Then not long after we heard the gate on the veranda and then Maree came in through the French doors near the fire. Jimmy was putting some more wood on.

"Hey Maree, how'd it go?" he asked.

"Really good," she said, "I just hung out at the cop shop for a while, then we had to go check out a burglary," she said. "It ended up being the neighbor's cat but it was good, we got to know each other a bit better. He was raised by his dad in the Blue Mountains who is also a police officer and he joined the police force down there after going to the academy in Sydney."

"Did you have dinner?" I asked.

"Yeah, we got a burger from the corner store. It was really nice, you'll have to try one, one day. I'm going up to bed," she said hugging me on the way past.

"OK, goodnight," I said as I returned her hug. I locked up and headed off to bed myself. Jimmy had taken the time to go and get a change of clothes and came in through the French doors and locked up behind himself.

"Just thought I would go get a change of clothes," he said gesturing to the shorts and polo shirt he held in his hand.

"Good idea," I said, "I'm ready, let's go," we climbed the stairs holding hands all the way to the bedroom. As soon as the door closed, he grabbed me and drew me close; he started kissing my neck and breathing in my ear giving me goose bumps. Taking my jacket off and then his.

Kissing the whole time, struggling to get our jeans off while moving over to the bed. "We should have a shower," I said in between breaths.

"Don't worry," he said as he put his hand between my legs and I felt him put his fingers inside me. I didn't know what he was doing but he was definitely hitting the spot. I was getting so wet. I took hold of his penis and I asked him to put it inside me, he felt so hard and I was so ready.

He moved his hand and put himself inside me. I was laying on my back with my feet up near his shoulders. It felt good as he thrust himself in and out, over and over. Then I asked him to lay down and I got on top and gave him my all. It didn't take long for him to explode inside me. I gave a couple of squeezes and he groaned with pleasure, *those yoga classes were really paying off*, I thought.

When he had finished, I rolled over and we lay there for a little while, while we got our breath back and to wait for our heartbeats to settle down. I was looking at all the callouses on Jimmy's hands and just chatting away. Then I got up out of bed and said, "I'm going for a shower."

He said, "Don't turn it off and I'll go in after you."

It felt good to be clean, after I showered, I stepped aside and called Jimmy in. I watched him washing himself, having a good old perve you could say.

Just when he was about to finish, I went down and I took his penis into my mouth and his eyes rolled back as he groaned; when he got to the stage where I knew he was about to climax, I rubbed the warm liquid all over my chest.

We had a quick wash and got out and brushed our teeth. I put a white silk camisole nightie on and hopped into bed. Jimmy came out with a pair of black silk boxers on. He climbed into bed and he kissed me good night and cuddled in behind me.

We fell asleep like that; I woke up the next morning to Jimmy going down on me then finishing me off energetically. "Wow," I said as I rolled over to kiss him on the mouth. "Good morning, Jimmy, I could get used to that," I said as I got out of bed and headed for the shower.

I put my shower cap on and had a quick wash; when I had finished, Jimmy took over the shower and washed his hair while he was there. He just shook his hair after he combed it and it fell into place.

I got dressed into a pair of denim shorts and a pale pink blouse with buttons down the front. Jimmy came out of the bathroom with his usual black cargo pants and a light blue polo shirt on. "Look at you, looking so hot," I said. He slapped me playfully on the backside and I laughed and returned the sentiment.

We both went downstairs together and gratefully accepted the coffee Silvia handed us, after we settled at the kitchen bench. Silvia asked if we wanted some raison toast. It was an inch thick and just what we needed. I ate two pieces and Jimmy ate four.

Jimmy was just telling us what chores he had planned for the day when Maree entered the kitchen. She was dressed in her workout gear and on her way to the gym before breakfast, carrying a towel. She got herself a bottle of water out of the fridge on the way through. I felt like I had already done my work-out for the day after the way Jimmy had woken me up.

After he finished eating and had the last of his coffee, he leaned in and gave me a kiss and said, "I'll catch up with you a little bit later." I returned his kiss and watched him exit via the veranda.

Silvia turned to me and said, "It's good to see him so happy, it's been a long time," as she packed the dish washer. I asked Silvia what she had planned for the day and she rattled of a list of chores. Then had a doctor's appointment in Murwoolinbah later in the afternoon.

"Nothing serious, I hope?" I asked.

"No, just a regular checkup," she said. "I'm going to visit a friend while I'm in there, so I won't be back today. I'll have to leave about 2pm."

"All good," I said, "don't worry too much about dinner, we can figure something out." I had absolutely no plans today at all. "It would give me something to do."

"I might go upstairs and check out the cards I got yesterday, thanks for everything Silvia, we really do appreciate all that you do for us," I said as I got up to leave.

"I know, thank you. I love my job and I've come to like you girls too," she said with a tear in her eye.

I gave her a hug and said, "We've come to like you too, Silvia," then left to go upstairs to my bedroom.

It was so good to get some time off work and not have to worry about other people's problems. I made my bed so it would be easier to lay the cards out. I was reminded about last night and the intensity of our love making. I got the silver box off my dressing table where I had put it yesterday.

I was excited to see them. I sat cross legged on the bed and my first thought was about the lady who owned them and of the old man from the quaint little shop. Also the things he said about the cards. It's all in the way you ask the questions and some things you don't want to know but he did say that they will tell you things.

The first thing I did was have a good look at the silver box. On the lid, there was a picture of the sun coming out in between two mountains, the front of the box had a picture of a tree losing its leaves, the bottom had a snow-covered mountain and the back had a picture of baby lambs in a meadow.

It had been handmade, the old man in the shop had said it was his wife's cards but a friend of theirs had made the box. I looked again and thought summer, autumn, winter, spring. All the seasons were represented. I loved it even more, it was special. I opened the box and it was lined with red velvet.

I took the cards out and unwrapped them and put the black velvet cloth aside. I opened the little book and it had the meaning of every card written and also how to use them. I quickly read the directions.

It showed how you could ask a question and do a three-card spread or you could do a card for the day or you could do a whole spread for a general reading of whatever time period you deem it to be about. It showed you the positions to put the cards in and what a card would mean in that position.

I started shuffling the cards thinking I would just do a general reading, so I had to lay out five cards in the shape of an arrow. The first card was the present, the second one diagonally above that was what you could expect, the third card at the top was the unexpected, the fourth one below that to the right was the immediate future and the last one diagonally below that was the long-term future.

So I stopped shuffling and put the cards down in that order. The first card I had to look up was the present. The card I got for that was ten of pentacles, which meant inheritance or things passed down through generations such as teaching kids to cook or sew, etc.

The second card was what I expected; I got the ten of cups that meant happy families. I thought of Maree and it made me smile. The next card was the unexpected, I got the nine of cups in that position and I looked it up.

It described a man and woman just enjoying their lives together. *Yes*, I thought, meeting Jimmy was very much unexpected. The next one was the immediate future and I got the king of pentacles, which meant my life would be quite cushy where material things were concerned. *Definitely*, I thought.

Then the long-term future card I got was the fool which meant taking a leap of faith and following my intuition. The book said if I wanted to elaborate on anything I could draw another card, so I did. I did it for the immediate future and I got the eight of cups card, which meant I would be walking away from something that I had put a lot of emotion and effort into.

I picked the cards up and started shuffling them again. I was thinking about everything that was going on in my life at the moment and the apartment in the city. I drew a card for that out of the middle of the deck. The book had said you need to not only look at all the pictures on the cards but to go with what you feel.

It was the eight of cups again. I picked it up and studied the card. There were eight golden cups stacked up over a waterfall in the foreground. A figure in a black cloak had turned his back and was walking toward a mountain in the background.

Looks like I'll be getting rid of the apartment, I thought. I had already been thinking that way but I wasn't totally sure yet. I guess it depended on Maree and what she was feeling. I made a decision to have a chat and see where her head was at. I wrapped the cards back up in the black velvet cloth and put them carefully back into the box.

Just as I went to get up, I heard a knock at the door. "Come in," I yelled as I put the box back on my dressing table where it belonged. It was Maree still in her workout outfit wiping sweat off her brow.

"Do you want to come for a swim?" she asked.

"I'd love to," I said.

"Cool. I'll get changed and meet you down there," she said as she left. I chose a black one piece. It had a pink and purple stripe that went diagonally down the middle at the front. I had a look in the full-length mirror and thought I could do with a bit more of a tan. I still took the sunscreen with me, because I didn't want to get too much sun.

Maree met me at the linen closet in the hallway, we both went to get a towel at the same time. "Good to see you Sis, it's been a while," I said as I passed her one.

"Yeah, I just felt like a workout this morning, I've had a lot on my mind. It gives me a chance to think," she said.

"Yes. I know the feeling, I've been doing a lot of thinking myself lately," I said. "Good time to have a chat." We ran downstairs and out to the pool. We put our towels on two chairs to the left and I went to the shallow end and walked in and Maree went to the deep end and dove in.

It was beautiful, I swam a couple of laps. I was having a rest getting my breath back just where I could stand easily. Maree came over to where I was and said, "So tell me what have you been thinking, Amber?"

"Well," I said, "I've been thinking about living here permanently and getting rid of my apartment in the city. I haven't thought about my work though. All I know is I'm not happy there and it's been like that for a while. It's not just about Andrew anymore. It's genuinely about just me for a change and I'm loving the house and the people. I don't know, how you feel?"

"Well," Maree said, "I've been having a similar thought." I couldn't believe she was saying this.

"What do you mean?" I asked.

She said, "Well as you know, I still live in Mom's house, the one we grew up in and I've been working as a teacher's aide at the same school I went to as a kid. Mom's gone now, so there isn't anything keeping me there anymore. I used to envy you being able to leave home and build a life for yourself in the city. I've never been anywhere or done anything. Honestly, it's been a blast just to get out of that town and now I may have finally met someone."

"Wow Sis, I didn't realize you felt that way. So what's he like?"

She held her hand up and waved it in front of her face, like she was hot and said, "Oo, la, la, he's amazing, we're going out for dinner again tonight. He's on call so we can't go far."

It gave me an idea, I said, "Why don't you invite him over for dinner? Silvia is leaving at two, she has a doctor's appointment in Murwoolinbah and she said she was visiting a friend while she was there. I told her not to worry about dinner, said we would fix something ourselves. What do you think? It will give me a chance to meet this amazing policeman of yours," I teased.

She smiled and went a little pink as she said, "What are we going to cook?"

"I might ask Silvia to put a roast on before she leaves if you like?" I said.

"OK. That sounds fantastic, I'll ask him first and we'll go from there." She got out of the pool and went over to where her towel was on the chair. She was wearing a new pair of togs too, a white crocheted one piece. She dried her hands and picked up her mobile phone and called Eli. After a quick chat, she came back into the pool. She was grinning like a Cheshire cat.

I said, "Looks like that went well?"

"Yes," she said, "He'll be here at 5:30, I thought we could have a few drinks before dinner. Eli can't drink though just in case he gets called in but that won't stop us though," she said with a giggle.

"I better go and find Silvia, so she can organize something. Let's go have lunch and ask," I said. Maree agreed, we left the pool and dried ourselves off. We wrapped our towels around ourselves and went inside.

Maree went upstairs to have a shower and I went to find Silvia. I found her in the laundry at the ironing table. "Hi Silvia, can I ask a favor?"

"What's up?" she asked.

I said, "We've invited Maree's boyfriend over for dinner, would you be able to put a roast on for us before you leave, please?"

"Of course, I can do that," she smiled "What kind of roast would you like? I've got a nice piece of roast beef in there if that's OK?"

"Sounds fantastic, thanks Silvia. Jimmy's right, you are the best." I gave her a quick kiss on the cheek and went upstairs to shower before lunch.

I had a quick shower and put a pair of white cotton shorts on making sure I had white underpants on underneath and I put on another new top; this one was pink and had flowers and a pretty bluebird on the front. I dried my hair and put it up in a ponytail, it was getting so long. I ran back downstairs.

Maree was already in the kitchen chatting to Silvia. I said, "Hello," as I entered and took a seat at the bench beside her. She stopped talking and looked at me and smiled. It was so good to know she was thinking along the same lines as me about moving here.

I'm sure we'd have to give more thought to all the details but at least now I could start planning for the future. At the moment, I didn't have to worry about money, so I could think about work at a later date.

Silvia made us a ham and salad sandwich for lunch and while we were eating, she got the roast beef out of the cool room. She said she had planned to cook it tonight before I had told her not to worry, so it wasn't really putting her out at all, she said she was happy to do that.

Maree was so excited; l was listening to her talking about Eli and how she was getting to know him. It got me thinking about Jimmy, so after lunch I excused myself and went to go find him to see what he was up to tonight.

I found him out the back chopping wood. I yelled out his name to get his attention. He smiled and stopped chopping, "Hey gorgeous, what's up?" he said. I loved the way he made me feel special.

"Hi sweetheart, I was just wondering what you were doing for dinner. Maree has invited Eli and I was hoping you would come to. It will be a good chance for me to get to know him."

"Yeah, I'd love to," he said. He tried to wipe his sweat on me. I screamed and dodged him. "What time do you want me there?" he asked.

"He's coming at 5:30," I said.

"OK, no worries," he replied, gave me a kiss on the lips and went back to his chopping.

I looked at my watch, it was one pm already. I went in to help Silvia with dinner. She was just putting the roast in the oven as I walked in. "Hi Silvia, I've come to give you a hand. What would you like me to do?"

"Oh, OK, you can get some potatoes out of the pantry and peel those if you like, that would be great, thank you," she said. I went into the pantry to get some the potatoes. They were quite large, so I counted one each for Maree and I and two each for the guys.

I put them into a basket and carried them out to the sink. I peeled them all and washed them clean. I cut them into quarter's length ways and did some pumpkin as well. I put them into a bowl of water to cook later. Then asked what else needs to be done.

Silvia told me to get the peas out of the freezer and put some in a pot of water on the stove. Then to get the corn cobs out of the cool room. I got four and removed the husks. I put those in a slightly larger pot of water on the stove. She was peeling the carrots then made some gravy. By 1:40, we had everything done.

While we were busy doing all this, I told Silvia that I was planning to stay here and getting rid of my apartment. She was thrilled to bits because it meant she would be able to keep her job and it also meant I would not be leaving Jimmy.

She screamed and jumped up and down as she hugged me. I didn't realize just how worried she must have been that we would sell the place and she would lose her job. It made me think I would have to tell Jimmy tonight. He too will be relieved.

I had a couple of hours to kill so I went upstairs. Silvia had said Maree had gone off to study, so I didn't want to annoy her. I decided to go visit Alice. I entered her room and found her sitting in front of her doll's house. I was quite surprised because it was the middle of the day. I closed the door and went over to sit beside her.

"Hi Alice," I said, "What are you doing?"

She turned to me and said, "Are you really going to stay?" I hadn't realized that she knew everything that went on around here. Just because I can't see her all the time, it didn't mean she wasn't there.

"I am staying Alice," I said. She was crying again but this time it was happy tears. I should have realized; I am all she's got in this house. Aunt Mary is gone and she wouldn't talk to anyone else but me. I had to try and find out what really happened to her. Then maybe she could find some peace and be back with Aunt Mary and Uncle Tom.

I asked her, "Is there anything else you can remember or think of that might help me find out what happened to you?" I could tell she was trying hard to think.

"There is one thing," she said, "I don't know what it means but I keep picturing a gum tree with a hedge around it."

"Really?" I said. I knew I had seen the same thing recently. That day I went for a run and followed the track from where the car was parked. It was the only thing in Silvia's back yard. I had to ask, "Alice, do you remember Jimmy's Dad?"

"Of course, he used to do the lawns and chop the wood." Then her face started changing like she was remembering something awful.

"What?" I asked.

"He used to do horrible things to me and he always said if I told anyone, he would kill me," she started crying again. I couldn't believe it. I knew there was something about that guy.

"OK, it's alright I'll see what I can do. I might go and have a look at this tree with the hedge." I remembered there was also a picture of Alice standing in front of the tree with the hedge around it. "I'll find out when Jimmy's Dad will be gone again and I will know when Silvia will be working. Then I'll go have a look," I said. She agreed and stopped crying and her attention went back to the doll's house.

I got up and left the room and went back down the hallway to my own room and set about finding something to wear for dinner. I opted for a new dress I had bought; it was yellow, which really set off my skin nicely. I put a little bit of makeup on and put my hair up on each side with hair clips in the shape of a little yellow flower. I bought them especially to go with this dress from a costume jewelry shop in Westfield's at Murwoolinbah.

I was thinking about the apartment and how I was going to get the furniture out. I remembered the ten-ton dual cab truck out the back in the shed. Maybe Jimmy could help me with that and Maree can help me pack. Then we will have to do the same for Maree and work out what we were going to do with Mom's house.

There was so much to do but I felt like it was the right thing for us to be doing. I put some nice little diamond stud earrings on, had one last look in the mirror, then I left to go find Maree.

I found her in her room wearing the gorgeous boho top with her black jeans and black boots. She had a little bit of makeup on and looked really pretty. I told her so and we left to go downstairs. There was a note from Silvia on the kitchen bench.

It said, 'Dear Amber and Maree, Check the roast and put the potatoes, onion and pumpkin on for an hour or so before you would like to eat. The rest just needs to be heated up and don't forget the gravy in the microwave. There is a pecan pie in the fridge. Put some cream with it for dessert, love Silvia.'

I checked on the meat with a long fork, it was perfectly cooked. I got a plate out and I took the tray out of the oven. I put it down on a chopping board and got some tongs out of the second drawer and used those and the fork to transfer the meat over to the plate.

Then wrapped it up in some foil I got from the pantry. I put the tray of vegetables in the hot oven. Silvia had already put cooking oil all over them and herbs and seasoning.

Maree had gone downstairs to get wine and some beer for Jimmy. I still had a few cans of southern comfort in the cool room. So I went to get them, I still had three. I opened one and put the other two in the fridge. As I was coming out of the cool room, Jimmy walked in the French doors.

"Hi Jimmy," I said, he had an arm full of wood and stacked it beside the fire.

He brushed his black polo shirt off and came over and gave me a kiss saying, "Hello, gorgeous," and went back to the lounge to get the fire started. I watched him walk away, and he looked good in his black jeans.

Maree got back with a six pack of corona beer for Jimmy in one hand and two bottles of wine tucked under her arm. "A white for now and a red to have with dinner later," she said as she put the two bottles on the bench. She got a beer out and put the rest of them in the fridge.

Then she got a wine glass out of the cupboard and poured herself a wine. I found a couple of coolers in the bottom drawer and put one on Jimmy's beer and the other on my can. I handed the beer to Jimmy as he entered the kitchen area and I opened my can then we all clinked our drinks with each other's and said, "cheers."

That's when the door bell sounded. I looked at my watch, he was right on time. Maree was so nervous but excited at the same time. She put her wine glass down where she was sitting at the kitchen bench and went to answer the door. Jimmy and I just looked at each other and raised our eyebrows and smiled.

Maree came back ahead of Eli. He took his hat off as she introduced us both and went back to her seat and pointed to the one beside her for him to sit. He shook both mine and Jimmy's hand, *it was a good firm shake*, I thought. The sign of a good character. He was wearing his uniform about five foot seven, brown hair and brown eyes.

He was quite well built, maybe not as beefed up as Jimmy but he still looked fit anyway. I could see why Maree had fallen for him. He was very good looking and had a boyish charm about him.

"Hi, it's nice to meet you Eli," I said.

Jimmy said, "G'day mate, how are you?"

"Yeah good, very good," Eli said. "Shame I'm on call, I would have liked to have a beer with you guys."

"Oh well, another time," I said as I offered him a can of coke.

"Thanks," he said as he pulled the ring at the top and took a swig. Silvia had put them in the fridge earlier that day and told me they were there.

"I hope you like roast beef," Maree said, "Silvia did most of the work though."

"How is Silvia? I haven't seen her for a while. The last time was at your Aunt Mary's funeral. It was a sad day," he said thinking back. "I had never met your Aunt Mary but I was helping to carry the coffin because there weren't enough people at the funeral and the reverend had asked me. Always happy to help," he was saying.

"Thank you," Maree said, "it means a lot." I nodded in agreement.

I turned all the pots on at the stove, the peas, corn and the carrots Silvia had peeled. She had left the honey on the counter top near the stove so I would remember to put some in the carrots. After an hour, I checked the oven. Jimmy was carving the beef and it looked amazing and so was the smell in the kitchen.

Maree and Eli set the table and I served up all the plates and got the gravy jug warmed up and took everything to the dining room table. Maree poured herself a red wine and got Eli another can of coke. I checked that Jimmy and I had a fresh drink, then we all sat down to eat.

We talked and laughed all the way through. Jimmy was right, he was easy to talk to and happy to answer any questions we had. We had finished dinner and Maree and Eli were still sitting at the dining room table chatting away. Jimmy and I said we would do the dishes. That's when I decided to tell him about staying.

"Hey Jimmy," I said.

"Yeah, what's up?" he said looking up from where he was tying up the rubbish bag.

"We have decided to stay," I said with a grin.

He let the bag go. "Really?" he asked. I nodded.

He was so happy he picked me up and spun me around. "Wow, that's fantastic, does Mom know?"

"Yes," I nodded.

"She'll be happy," he said.

After we finished cleaning the kitchen, I got the pecan pie and the cream out. I got four sandwich plates out and served the dessert. It was really yummy. After chatting for another hour or so, Eli got up to go.

"Thanks for an excellent evening. It was nice to meet you and thank Silvia for the amazing food, it really was good," he said.

"You're welcome, Eli, I'm sure we'll be seeing you again soon." Maree walked him out to his car.

I turned to Jimmy and said, "Well that went well, he seems really nice."

Maree came in looking really happy. We all sat at the kitchen bench and talked about what a good night it turned out to be. Maree was happy that we liked him and after a while, she grabbed the rest of the bottle of red and said she was going up to her room. We said goodnight with a hug and a peck on the cheek.

Jimmy and I moved over to the lounge with a fresh beer and a can of southern comfort and coke. "Is your dad still in town?" I asked.

"No, he left yesterday, why's that?" Jimmy asked.

"No reason just making conversation," I said. "Where has he gone this time?" I asked.

"He's gone to Perth, he won't be back for a week or so," Jimmy said.

"Are you staying the night?" I asked.

"If you want me to," he said. He turned to kiss me and I responded.

Jimmy and I were talking about the apartment and when we would go and get my furniture. I said, "I will have to organize things over the phone tomorrow. I think I may have to give two weeks' notice and the same for my job."

"We could go up over the weekend if you like," Jimmy said.

I agreed. "Let's go to bed," I said with a yawn. He couldn't help but yawn as well, funny how they were catchy. We locked the place up and turned the lights off and went upstairs to get ready for bed.

I changed into a nightie and Jimmy stripped off to his jocks and we crawled into bed. Laying in the dark, we cuddled up and talked and kissed. He started playing with my nipples, he was laying curled up behind me and I felt his manhood growing beneath me.

I turned around and kissed him and grabbed his penis and started moving my hand up and down his shaft. Then I went down and put it in my mouth and sucked hard, long and fast. He was moaning then I went to hop on top ready to put him inside me.

"No," he said and rolled me over and kissed me then worked his way down to my breast and sucked my nipples then worked his way down to my vagina. He was licking and sucking and playing with my clit with his finger. It was driving me nuts, after a while he dragged me down to the end of the bed and put himself inside me. He fucked me hard and fast.

I said, "Don't stop," I was still coming and I wanted him to come inside me too. I used my pelvic floor muscles and squeezed on and off, it made him explode and groan as he did.

We both lay in the dark talking and cuddling and then I rolled over and he cuddled me from behind and we fell asleep. I opened my eyes and looked at the clock. It was 7:45 am. Jimmy was already in the shower. I got out of bed and went to join him. He was just finishing so as he got out, I got in.

It was nice and hot a good way to start the day, I thought. I asked Jimmy what his plans were for the day while he dried himself off. "I have to do the lawn and check the gardens for weeds," he said.

I finished my shower and dried myself off then cleaned my teeth and got dressed. I put on a pair of dark blue denim shorts and a plain fawn colored top. I blow dried my hair. Jimmy was sitting on the bed waiting for me, it was really sweet. I thanked him and we both left to go downstairs for breakfast.

We could smell the bacon cooking as we ran down the stairs. We both said "good morning," as we walked into the kitchen. Maree was sitting at the bench eating.

She looked up and said, "good morning."

We took our seats at the bench and Silvia handed us a coffee saying, "good morning. I hear last night went well."

"Yeah, it went really good and the food was amazing as always," I said.

"Aww thank you, it was a joint effort though," Silvia said.

I turned to Maree. "I've decided to give notice on my apartment today. I'm hoping you can come with me on the weekend and help me pack. There is a ten-ton dual cab truck out in the shed. Jimmy said we can use that. I wonder if Eli would give us a hand with the furniture. I guess it depends if he's working or not," I said.

"I think he is on call all the time, it's a small town and there is only him and Earl on duty. If something happens, they might both be needed," Maree said.

"That's OK, I can ask a friend. I'm pretty sure Stuart wouldn't mind. He's one of my customers, I've known him since high school," Jimmy said.

"We will have to go and pack first. It will take all weekend just to do that. If Stuart is only available on the weekend, Maree and I could leave tomorrow but you may have to put your date off till Saturday night instead. You can stay the night Friday and drive the Focus back on Saturday in time for a date on Saturday night. Would you mind doing that Maree?" I asked. "No it's all good I'll give Eli a call. I'm sure he won't mind" Maree went off to the front room to give him a call. 2 minutes later she came back out saying Eli was completely fine with that.

Jimmy took his mobile phone out of his pocket and rang his friend Stuart. After he got off the phone he said, "Yeah that's fine, he'll be here Sunday morning." We finished our breakfast and I drank my second cup of coffee. Jimmy had to go and do the lawn and the gardens. I went to the front room to ring the real estate and put my notice in.

I couldn't believe my life had done a full three sixty so quickly, it had only been two weeks. I still had to put my notice in at work so I went over to the computer. I turned it on and waited for it to load. I brought up my email and typed out my resignation.

I just said I had moved to New South Wales and wouldn't be coming back. It was like a weight had lifted off my shoulders. I didn't realize how much it was weighing me down till then.

I went looking for Maree, she was still in the kitchen talking to Silvia. I went in to join them. Maree was just asking about the school in town. Silvia was saying that she knew a couple of the teachers who worked there and she would find out if they needed a teacher's aide before the start of the new school year.

"That would be fantastic, thanks Silvia," Maree said, *she looked really happy*, I thought.

That would be perfect if she could get a job here. I guess I will have to think about what I was going to do for work. It could get too boring in this massive place day after day all by myself. *I needed something*, I thought. I'll pack my place up first and go from there. *At least, there is plenty of room in the attic for the furniture I don't need*, I thought.

Silvia was chopping up vegetables of all kinds, she was making a stew for dinner. Maree was planning to go and hang out at the police station with Eli. So it would be just me and Jimmy if he wasn't too busy. I looked at my watch, it was only 11 o'clock.

I asked Maree if she would like to go for a drive. I knew Silvia had some washing and ironing to do. So I knew she would be here busy all day.

I was glad Maree didn't really question and jumped up off the chair and grabbed the keys for the Mustang saying goodbye to Silvia. I followed her out to the garage waving goodbye as we left. Down to the garage and into the third bay. We were sitting in the car waiting for it to warm up.

Maree turned to me and asked, "So, where to Sis?"

I told her about Alice and what she had said about Silvia's ex and what he had done to her. I told her about the tree with the hedge and she remembered the photo in the manila folder. "I spoke to Jimmy and his dad has gone away on a job to Perth. So I know nobody is home. I just wanted to have a look around," I said.

She reversed out and drove slowly down the lane, "oh well, no harm in looking," said Maree. She already knew the way. They arrived at Silvia's house and parked in the driveway. They didn't have close neighbors so nobody was around. They got out of the car and went down the left side of the house.

We went over to the windows to see if we could see anything other than newspaper. We went around the back of the house and about fifty meters away was the gum tree with the hedge around it. We walked over to it. The hedge was a bit taller than me and I was five foot three. It wasn't really that well-manicured just years of neglect I'd say.

In the photo, it was only about knee high. I walked around it not really seeing anything out of place. I couldn't see the tree through it because it was so thick. Maree and I went back over to the house and tried to see if we could see anything where the newspapers were.

There was one window down the right-hand side of the house where there was a little gap in the paper but it was so dark inside and the sun outside just made it too hard to see anything. We went back to the car and drove home.

On the way home, I asked Maree. "Would you like me to help you pack up Mom's house after we get mine sorted?"

"Yeah, I'm not looking forward to that though. That's going to take more than just a weekend," she said. We grew up in the house, our parents had bought it not long after they married 30 odd years ago.

"We will have to have a garage sale," I said.

"Yes, definitely," she agreed.

"Maybe go for a week or so to sort through and pack everything. It won't be so bad if we both do it," I said.

"We will miss the guys," Maree said.

"Sure will," I agreed.

It was about lunch time. I asked Maree if we could go and try one of those steak burgers from the corner store. So that's what we did. While we were waiting for it, Maree went across to the police station to see Eli. She knew he was there because there were two police cars parked in the carpark and there were only two policemen in town.

She came back and ordered one for Eli and Earl as well and asked if I could drive the Mustang home and Eli would drop her home later tonight. I wasn't going to say no to that. I got my burger and gave her a quick hug goodbye. "Have fun," I said.

I hopped into the driver's side and put my bag and my burger on the passenger's seat. It was a nice black leather interior with thick black woolen seat covers. So comfortable and still smelt new. I put my seatbelt on and pressed the start button, it was weird not to have a normal key to start it.

We were parked diagonally at the front of the shop on the main road through town, which meant I could drive straight out. There was no traffic so I pulled out and headed home. It was quite an exhilarating drive. I put my foot down after I turned down the lane leading to the house.

I could see why Maree loved it. The motor made a lot of noise and you could feel the vibration go through your body with the g forces. I went slowly through the gate and around the white gravel driveway and into the third bay garage.

I took my burger up to my bedroom and sat at the table. The corner of my bedroom had a kitchenette which had a table and four chairs. It also had a kettle, toaster and a microwave. I ate in silence. Then I took the time to pack a bag and get ready to leave in the morning.

I came out of the bathroom and through the wardrobe into the bedroom and was surprised to see Alice sitting on my bed. "Did you find anything?" she asked.

"No Alice. I'm sorry I didn't. I looked everywhere around the tree. There was nothing there," I said. Alice disappeared again. I felt bad about not being able to help her. *I didn't even know what I was looking for*, I thought.

I went downstairs to find Jimmy; he was out in the shed giving the truck a once over and making sure it had all its fluids topped up and checking the air in the tires and cleaning out the back. He put a furniture trolley in as well as a few blankets to protect the furniture and ropes to tie things down.

"Are you available for dinner tonight, Jimmy? It'll just be us. Maree's down at the police station again. Eli is bringing her home later," I said.

"Yeah, OK, what's for dinner?" he asked.

"Your mom was making a stew earlier; I don't know about dessert though. I drove the Mustang home today," I said.

"Did you like it?" he asked.

"I can see why Maree loves it. It makes my BMW seem plain," I said.

He laughed and said, "You'll have to get something different to suit your new life, maybe an MG might suit you better."

Now I laughed and said, "Yeah maybe." It was good just to be spending time with him, watching him do the things he had to do. He even got me helping him with a Ute load of wood. He gave me gloves to use so I didn't mind. It was like a natural workout.

We kept busy till about five o'clock, he said he was going home for a shower before dinner. "Would you like to join me?" he said.

"Why not?" I said and followed him back to his place. We went straight through to his bathroom. I couldn't help but notice how clean things were and I said, "Does your mom clean your place too?"

He smiled and said, "I'm too busy most of the time, of course she does, she always has."

"Fair enough," I said.

He showered first and when he was nearly finished, I stepped in beside him. It was a big open shower with no glass or curtain. The tiles were slate. I took the soap out of his hand and started washing his back and then my hands got a little carried away.

He grew hard within my hands. He got the soap and turned me around to wash my back and then he got carried away with his hands. He picked me up and started thrusting himself into me. I kissed him and he was kissing me back.

He leaned me back and sucked on my nipples and bringing my head back up, kissing my neck and kissing me on my mouth again. He was directing my body up and down till we both came together. He washed himself and left the shower so I could have a good wash too.

I washed my hair as well after all the sweating I did loading the wood. I wrapped myself in the towel Jimmy had left next to my clothes. I found another one hanging up and used it to wrap up my hair.

Still wrapped in my towel, we left his place to go back to the main house. While he got the fire going, I ran upstairs to get dressed and blow dry my hair. I put a red silk nightie on and went back downstairs. I went straight to the kitchen bench and read Silvia's note.

It said, 'Dear Amber and Maree, as you know there is a stew on the stove to be heated up and a custard tart in the fridge for dessert, love Silvia.'

I turned on the stove and got a big spoon out of the second drawer and put it on the counter top ready to stir. I got some bowls out and a couple of spoons. Then I got the bread out of the bread bin. It smelt so fresh, I buttered three slices of bread for Jimmy and two for myself.

I got a coke and a diet coke out of the fridge and gave the stew a stir. Jimmy came up behind me. He moved my hair to one side and kissed my neck, my body was reacting and I got goosebumps. "Jimmy," I pleaded as I tried to concentrate on stirring the stew. He stopped and gave me a reprieve. The stew was ready so I dished up a bowl each. We sat at the kitchen bench and enjoyed our dinner.

We chatted for a while and then we ate a piece of Silvia's custard tart. We decided to have an early night. Just as we went to climb the stairs, I heard a car pull up in the driveway. *It must be Eli dropping Maree home*, we thought. We kept going so she wouldn't think we were spying on her.

I was glad she got home early because I knew she still had to pack for tomorrow night. We had already agreed to leave about nine am. I set the alarm for 7am and we laid down to sleep. I sent Maree a text message saying, 'Goodnight Sis, love you.'

I got one back saying, 'I love you too, goodnight.'

I kissed Jimmy and said, "Goodnight."

He returned my kiss and said, "Goodnight sweetheart." We were both tired after all the work we had done. He cuddled up behind me and we went to sleep.

Chapter 8

We woke up when the alarm went off. Jimmy rolled over and said, "Good morning, beautiful."

I kissed him and said, "Good morning to you," I rolled out of bed and Jimmy did too. We cleaned our teeth at the double sink and got dressed. I had a spare toothbrush put in my bathroom for Jimmy and everything he would need for a shave. He was quite impressed when he saw it.

I was glad I could make him a part of my life and make him feel happy. He was already dressed in the usual black cargo shorts and a white polo shirt. It reminded me of the day we met when I had seen him emerge from the woods. I had to stop and take a breath.

He was watching me as I was stepping into my denim shorts and putting a bra and a white T-shirt on. I was smiling back at him. I said, "I'm going to miss you," as I went to kiss him and then grabbed the brush to do my hair.

He said, "I'll grab your bag and meet you downstairs," I couldn't help thinking how lucky I was to have met this guy while I put my hair up. Then ran downstairs with a smile still on my face.

I entered the kitchen and took my seat at the bench. "Good morning, everybody," I said, everybody said it back. Silvia handed me my coffee cup and I thanked her. She had made pancakes with butter, maple syrup and freshly whipped cream. I ate three and Jimmy ate about six. Maree had put her bag with mine near the front door.

After breakfast, Jimmy went to get my car. He parked it out the front and put our bags in the boot and warmed it up. As Maree and I drove out of the driveway, Jimmy and Silvia waved from the front steps. I beeped the horn as we drove through the gate. I couldn't believe it had only been a couple of weeks since we arrived and I was giving up my apartment in the city already.

We listened to Spotify all the way to Brisbane; we sang, talked and enjoyed the view all the way. I parked downstairs next to the Focus and we took the lift up to my apartment. I walked in and looked around. I went through each room taking mental notes of what I would need to do. Then went to put the kettle on. We had brought our bags up with us. I found an Eski in the boot that Silvia had put together for us and found the makings of a coffee out of it.

Jimmy had also put about a dozen packing boxes and a roll of heavy-duty garbage bags and a sticky tape gun with a spare roll of tape on the back seat. He was so thoughtful; I was thinking when the kettle boiled and my awareness came back to the room.

Maree came into the kitchen saying, "There's not really that much, is there?"

I handed her a cup of coffee and said, "no, not much at all really." She noticed I nearly went to tear up as I said it.

"It's OK, Sis, what we do, we do it together."

After our coffees, we went and got the boxes out of the car and started packing. Maree started in the kitchen and I started in the bedroom. After a while, we stopped for lunch. Silvia had packed the makings of ham, cheese, tomato and onion sandwiches. We sat at the dining room table and ate our sandwiches and washed them down with an orange juice.

After lunch, we decided to get some air so we took the lift to the ground floor and went for a walk to the nearest bottle shop. It was only two blocks down. We brought a bottle of vodka and some lemonade and a ten pack of southern comfort cans as well. We got enough supplies to see us right through the week-end.

Then struggled to carry it all home. We got back to the apartment and put the alcohol away. Then I made us a fire engine, which was made up of vodka and red lemonade. I put the stereo on and my eighties music on random play. I handed Maree a drink and I said, "Cheers to moving out and moving on," we clinked our glasses together and went back to our packing.

When I noticed the sun going down, I rang the local Chinese shop and ordered a home delivery. When I told the old Chinese guy at the other end my address, he remembered me from the night I ran. I had been going there for years and I had left my order behind.

"Amber," he said, "Are you OK, I seen you run and I haven't seen you since, what happened?" I told him about Andrew and about me moving away and leaving my job. I thanked him for his yummy food and he wished me luck for the future.

The food arrived 45 minutes later. I got some plates out and dished it up; sweet and sour pork, Mongolian beef, fried rice and Singapore noodles. Maree poured us a fresh drink and we sat down to eat. "Well the kitchen is almost done," Maree said, "I've got the oven soaking too, I thought if we soaked it overnight, it will be easy just to wipe out tomorrow in the morning."

She had put some newspaper underneath it in case it leaked onto the floor. "That's great I'm going to do the same with the bathroom, so after our showers we'll spray everything with Exit Mold then just wipe things over tomorrow," I said.

I washed the dishes after we finished eating. Then went back to packing. I had almost finished in the bedroom and started on the bathroom. That didn't take long. Maree had a shower then I had one and after I put my nightie on, I sprayed the shower. We settled into the lounge to listen to music and talk with our drinks in hand.

We were both starting to feel a little bit drunk. We got up and danced for a while then sat back down with a sigh. I said, "I guess we better make the lounge up for you to sleep," I went to the linen closet to get Maree some sheets and a blanket. I made the lounge up for her and sat back down to chat for a while.

"So how's things going with Eli?" I asked.

Maree smiled just at the thought. "Yeah, things are going well, he's taking me out to the pub in Swanton. He reckons they do a really good seafood basket there. He also said they have another policeman coming to join them at the station, so they can take time off sometimes, so that will be good. Supposed to be coming next week some time. How are you going with Jimmy?"

"Amazingly fantastic," I laughed. "I can't believe how much everything has changed over the last few weeks for us both. It would be good if you got a job at the school in Limpinwood, wouldn't it?" I said.

"That would be a dream come true. What are you going to do, Amber? Would you start your own practice, do you think or have a look into something at Murwoolinbah?" Maree asked.

"I have mainly done family law and domestic violence but I haven't liked it for a while. It's depressing really, people either arguing over their possessions or fighting each other. You don't want to know what I've been thinking," I said.

"What, tell me?" she asked.

"Well, you know how the house is so massive and we are only using two of the bedrooms. I was thinking we could turn it into a bed and breakfast. Not straight away but when things settle down a little and we finish moving and everything," I said and watched for Maree's reaction.

"Wow," Maree said. "That's a fantastic idea and if I don't get the job at the school, I won't have to worry so much."

"Yeah," I said as my thoughts drifted thinking about how much I would need to do. Maree's thoughts drifted to. We finished the last of the drink in our glasses. Maree got settled on the lounge and I thanked her for helping me with the packing as I gave her a kiss on the forehead and said "goodnight," cleaned my teeth and hopped into bed.

I had got Jimmy's number off him before I left. I rang it and he answered straight away. "That was quick," I said.

"Yeah, I just got into bed and I was about to ring you but you beat me to it," he said.

"I've just got into bed too, we got a lot done today," I said.

"That's good, I'm missing you already, you know," he said.

"Me too, what time are you coming on Sunday?" I asked.

"What time would you like me to be there?" he asked.

"Is nine too early? I don't really want to be here any longer then I have to," I said.

"Yes, that's fine, can't wait to see you. This place is pretty quiet without you girls. No one to light the fire for. Oh well, get some sleep and we'll talk again tomorrow," he said.

"OK, goodnight sweetheart, I love you," my heart caught in my throat and I stopped breathing for a second. I couldn't believe I had just said that.

Then he said, "Goodnight Amber, I love you too," and hung up the phone. *Oh my god*, I thought as I stared at the phone for a minute thinking, is this all too soon, it's only been two weeks. I put the phone down on the bedside table and plugged it in the charger. Then laid down and drifted off to sleep.

I slept well and woke up as the sun shone through the cracks in the blinds. I made my way to the kitchen stepping over garbage bags as I went. Maree was still asleep, I put the kettle on and by the time the kettle was boiled, Maree had woken up and came and sat at the table.

I made the coffee and handed one to Maree as I came and sat down to drink it and wake up a little. We were both a little hung over so it was unusually quiet. I got up to refill our coffees and cook some toast. After we had something to eat and a second cup of coffee, we were ready to continue with the packing. Maree was right about the stove, it cleaned up really easily. The bathroom didn't take much to clean either.

We made a toasted sandwich for lunch with the ingredients Silvia had packed and poured ourselves an orange juice. Maree left not long after we had eaten. I asked her to text me when she got home so I wouldn't worry and waved goodbye as she drove out of the downstairs carpark.

I took the lift back upstairs to the 9th floor and walked in to survey each room to see where I was at with the packing and cleaning. The lounge room had been fully packed, the photo albums were boxed out of the side board and the drawers had been emptied and boxed, also all the ornaments and photos I had around.

The pictures I had hanging around the walls were down and the walls had been washed. I just needed everything out of there to vacuum and that reminded me I better get somebody in to do the carpets and pest control.

I made a few calls, one for the carpets, and another for the pest control and also the electricity company to organize getting the power turned off. I managed to get everything organized for Monday and the power disconnected on Tuesday. I had a blow-up mattress in the cupboard in the spare room. I was going to just use that after the guys took the furniture.

I gave Jimmy a call, he answered on the fourth ring. "Hey gorgeous, what's up?" he said. I loved the sound of his voice over the phone.

"Hi Jimmy, I just remembered I have to get the carpets and pest control done. I've rang and booked them in but I'm going to have to stay till they come on Monday, so it's not going to matter what time you get here tomorrow," I said.

"OK, no worries. I'll see what suits Stuart and I'll talk to you tonight then. How's it all going anyway?" he asked.

"Yeah good." I was just wandering around having a look while I was chatting. "I've only got the cupboard in the spare room and the linen closet in the hallway. I've got to wipe over all the walls in the hallway and the bedrooms and do the vacuuming yet but the kitchen and bathroom have been done and the lounge and dining room are all done too," I said.

"You've been busy then," he said.

"Yeah, I may use the extra time to visit a couple of friends while I'm in town. I haven't really spoken to anyone about anything since I left," I said.

"OK," he said.

"It's Saturday afternoon now so I know exactly where everyone would be; down at The Vibe, it's a little pub three blocks down. Maybe come a little later in the day if you like. Just in case I have a few drinks tonight. I'll give you a call anyway," I said.

"No worries, all good," he said. We said our goodbyes and I went to have a shower and get dressed.

I remembered which garbage bag I had put some jeans in and got a nice top out of my bag that I had brought with me. It was a black short sleeved top with a crocheted V neck line. I had a couple of friends I worked with but outside of work, there wasn't really anyone besides my sister.

My life had kind of revolved around work and Andrew. I'd never been one to have close friends. Even in school, I was a bit of a loner. If I did have any close friends, they would end up teasing me for having psychic abilities and being different to what was considered normal. I pretty much didn't confide in anyone in the end.

My sister Maree was probably the only one that never made fun of me and rarely judged me about it. Knowing what I know now, I wish I had known Aunt Mary way back when. I put a little makeup on and a pair of flat black shoes. I left my hair out after blow drying it.

I grabbed a small black shoulder bag and put my card and phone in it. I noticed Maree had texted while I was in the shower, so I texted her back. I was glad she had got home safely and grabbed my keys and left the apartment. I took the lift down to the street level.

It was a beautiful afternoon weather wise and not too much foot traffic either. It didn't take long before I walked into The Vibe. There were tables and chairs out the front and half of the tables were full of diners. The smells were amazing as I entered and headed further past the other diners inside to the back of the room where the main bar was.

I spotted my work mates sitting at a table to the right. When they spotted me, they started waving for me to come over. The three amigos were there as well as Steven from accounts. The three amigos were Trudy, Bridget and Barb; they were the office grapevine all hanging to get the gossip. They had heard about me putting my resignation in and wanted to know all the details.

When I told them about Andrew, they were not as shocked as I thought they would be. They all thought it was going on anyway, they just didn't know who with. I was surprised that nobody had said anything to me though. I kept most of the details of my new life to myself in case things got back to Andrew. *I didn't need him looking for money*, I thought. I only stayed for two drinks then made an excuse to leave.

I arrived home with pizza in hand from the local Domino's. I sat at the dining room table feeling slightly pissed off and washed my pizza down with a can of southern comfort. I felt like an idiot. I was obviously the only one at work who didn't know about Andrew and his floosy.

I looked at my watch, it was 8pm. *I better give Jimmy a call*, I thought before it gets too late. He picked up on the second ring. "Hey gorgeous, how's your night going?" he asked.

"Not good," I said. I told him about my night.

"Well," he said, "you won't ever have to see them ever again now, will you?" I agreed and with that thought, I totally cheered up.

"Thanks Jimmy, it's just what I needed to hear," I said.

"OK, well, I will see you tomorrow so we can empty this place out and I can get to the vacuuming," I answered.

"All good, we will be there about lunch time," he said. "Are you feeling a bit better?"

"Yeah, I am. I'll get the linen closet and the cupboard in the spare room done then I'll go to bed," I said. We talked for a little longer and then said goodnight and hung up.

I grabbed a garbage bag and headed for the linen closet. It was 11:30 before I laid down to go to sleep. I laid there for a while pondering my life and how much I didn't know about the people in it. Or how little I had meant to people I actually thought cared.

Then I pictured Silvia and Jimmy waving good bye from the front step in Limpinwood and the love that I felt from them and my sister Maree. It made me smile and not long after I fell asleep.

I slept in till 10 o'clock in the morning and then went into the kitchen to make a coffee. I felt fresh and ready for the move. Jimmy and Stuart turned up while I was on my second cup. I'd just finished my toast. I went and pressed the button that opened the door and let them in.

They had parked in the street and had little witches' hats on the road to divert the traffic, so we had to hurry up and load it. The guys concentrated on the furniture and I just kept bringing boxes and garbage bags down. Jimmy packed it all in properly with ropes and blankets.

Stuart was a nice guy, a real salt of the earth type person. Between the three of us, it was all done by 2:30 and the guys were back on the road home by three. I finished cleaning the apartment walls and cupboards and vacuumed the whole place.

Jimmy had inflated the air mattress with a foot pump. It was only a double bed one but it was quite comfortable when I made it up with the linen off my bed.

He rang me when he got home to tell me they had arrived safely. He said they'd stopped at KFC for dinner in Murwoolinbah on their way home and asked if I wanted the stuff from the apartment put away in the attic so I could go through it in my own time down the track.

I agreed that would be a good idea and we said our goodnights. We hadn't mentioned the L word since that first night but we knew we would talk about it when I got home.

Monday morning, the pest control guy came at nine am and the carpet guy came at 10 am. By lunch time, I walked into Ray White real estate and gave them my keys. I got back in my BMW and left the city and my old life behind. I stopped once for fuel and again at red roosters drive through at Murwoolinbah on the way home and arrived at 4:30 pm.

I drove my car straight into the second bay of the garage and walked inside via the veranda. I was carrying my hand bag and my luggage bag. I was about to put them down to get my key out when the French doors opened and Jimmy grabbed my luggage bag off me and stepped aside to let me in. He followed me in with my bag.

He put it in the foyer and came back to the kitchen where I was filling the kettle. "How was the trip?" he asked as he came up beside me. I put the kettle on the stove and turned it on.

Then turned toward him and gave him a huge hug and said, "I'm so glad to be home." He said he was glad to have me home.

Maree must have heard me come in, she came into the kitchen and gave me a hug too and said it was good to see me home. We all sat down and had a nice cup of coffee and talked about the last few days. "It's been a long day and I still have stuff in my car that needs to come out." I got up to go.

Jimmy came with me to give me a hand. He got the Eski and the blow-up mattress out of the boot. He dropped the Eski into the kitchen and took the mattress up to the attic. I followed him in to the kitchen and emptied the Eski and took it out to the laundry to put it upside down over the sink to dry out. I got a garbage bag of dirty clothes out of the back seat of the car and put that in the laundry too.

Maree had gone back upstairs. There was a note on the bench from Silvia. I hadn't noticed it till now, it said, 'Dear Amber, hope you got home safely, there is a meat pie in the oven and vegetables on the stove. There is also a chocolate log in the fridge for dessert. Love Silvia.'

I love my new life, I thought as I took my luggage bag upstairs. I went via the lift so I didn't have to carry it. It had rollers so I only had to wheel it in, down the hallway and into my room.

I picked it up and put it on my bed. I emptied the contents and then put the bag under the bed so it was handy for next time when we had to go clean out Mom's place. I heard a knock on the door. I yelled out to come in, it was Jimmy. He walked in and locked the door.

"Hey babe, I've missed you," he came over to where I was standing near the bed and we hugged and kissed. His voice was husky when he said, "I do love you, I know we haven't been together long but I really missed you when you were gone and I couldn't imagine my life without you now."

"Me too," I said. It was good to be home, he was kissing my neck then took my denim shorts and under pants off and bent me over the bed and gave himself to me. Afterwards, we laid on the bed talking for a while.

Then I heard another knock at the door. I had already dressed so I went to answer. It was Maree. "I hope I'm not interrupting anything," she said.

"Not at all," I said looking at Jimmy lying on the bed on his side leaning on his elbow. I sat on the side of the bed and Maree hopped onto the lounge kneeling with her arms over the back of the lounge. Asking if we are ready for dinner yet. I looked at the time on the bedside clock. It was seven o'clock already.

"Yes, we are coming," Jimmy got up and we all went downstairs. Maree had already heated up the vegetables on the stove. She just had to serve it out, we all sat at the kitchen bench to eat.

"So how did your date go, Maree?" I asked. She went all dreamy eyed and smiling.

"Dinner was amazing, definitely loved the seafood basket and the company was outstanding," she laughed. "He even came home for a night cap and ended up staying the night, we talked till 3am, and it was fantastic."

"Good. I'm happy for you Sis, you deserve the best. I definitely missed this one," I said poking Jimmy in the ribs. He grabbed me and started tickling me. I tried to tickle him back, then begged him to stop. Maree was dishing out the dinner. I went to get the cutlery out and the tomato and barbeque sauce out of the pantry.

The pie was amazing, it had big chunks of rump steak and onion in it. I couldn't eat it all because I'd eaten earlier but Jimmy cleaned his and my plate up. I was telling Maree about the girls from work and what they had said. "I felt like crap, I'm so glad I left, at least here I'm with people that care."

Maree got up and gave me a hug. "I'm sorry you were made to feel that way, they are just a bunch of bitches anyway," she said and went to put the dishes into the dish washer. "So you've done everything and even handed the key in, hey? You shouldn't have any problems getting your bond back," she said as she wiped over the surfaces.

I went over to put the kettle on, "does anybody else want one?" They both said yes and we all sat at the kitchen bench and talked for another hour or so. I looked at my watch and it was 9:30 already. "What is the plan for tomorrow then?" I asked.

Jimmy said, "There is still some stuff in the truck that needs emptying. Stuart and I did all the big furniture pieces but there are still the boxes and garbage bags to go. I wasn't sure if you needed to go through it for clothes or whatever first, so I waited for you to help."

"You're so thoughtful Jimmy, I do have some clothes and stuff to go through, thank you. I'm going to skip dessert and leave you guys to it. I need an early night, it's been a long day, goodnight, and I love you guys, thanks for all your help with the apartment. I'll see you in the morning." I kissed them both goodnight and went up to bed.

I woke up and noticed Jimmy in bed beside me, he must have come after I'd fallen asleep last night. I looked at the alarm clock, it was 6:30 am. Jimmy was still asleep snoring softly. I lay there for a while staring at the ceiling thinking about the day. I thought there was no use going to the gym this morning.

I'll have enough to do with the unpacking. Jimmy opened his eyes and looked over at me and smiled. We cuddled up for a while and just talked about things in general. I got up to shower. I couldn't be bothered last night so I felt like a grub. Jimmy said he had showered last night so he got up and went downstairs. He said he had a couple of things to do before breakfast.

It was nice just to stand under the hot water and wash all the grime off from the day before. I'd have to ask Silvia to change my bed linen. I washed and blow dried my hair and put it up in a type of messy bun and dressed in denim shorts and a black T-shirt and I put my runners on too, just to protect my feet. Then ran downstairs for breakfast.

Silvia was happy to see me and I had missed her too. I sat at the kitchen bench and she handed me my coffee. I thanked her and told her about the last few days and how good it was to be home. Jimmy came in when I was half way through my scrambled egg.

Silvia gave him a huge plate full and then Maree arrived. Silvia handed her a coffee and made me another as well. I was asking Silvia about washing my sheets. She didn't mind, she said she was happy to have other things to do. She was always busy and we were lucky to have her and I told her as much.

"Thank you," she said, "it means a lot," she left to go to the laundry.

Maree and Jimmy were chatting, they got along really well. He'd just finished eating and Maree was eating and talking at the same time. Jimmy had his elbows on the bench over his empty plate, listening intently. I got up and put mine and his dish into the dish washer and went to get a water bottle out of the fridge.

Jimmy gulped the last of his coffee down and put his cup in the dish washer. Maree had offered to help with unloading the truck. "Yes, that would be great," I said, Maree got up and put her plate and cup into the dish washer and turned it on. Silvia had done the rest of the cleaning already.

We followed Jimmy out the back to the truck, which was back where I had seen it parked in the shed last time. It didn't take long before we had it unloaded. Jimmy was standing in the back of the truck and passing the boxes and bags down to Maree and I. From there, we made two piles.

One for the attic and one for my room. We used the stairs at the back of the house and all got a really good workout. After that, I went to sort out my wardrobe. Maree went off to study and Jimmy went to do some lawn mowing. It felt good to have my whole wardrobe back and I had it all sorted. Jeans in one spot, dresses in another, etc.

I was getting hungry so I went to find Maree, she was still in her room studying and listening to her music as always. At least, she saw me coming this time. She was happy to take a break, so we went down to the kitchen. Silvia wasn't there but she had left a note.

'Dear Amber and Maree, there is some zucchini slice in fridge for lunch, love Silvia.'

"Oh yum," I said as I opened the fridge to retrieve it. It was a whole baking tray; we sat down and ate till we were full and put the rest away. We got a diet coke each out of the cool room and washed it down with that.

I asked Maree if she wanted to go for a swim after lunch. She said she could do with the break, we both could. We went upstairs to get our togs on. I put a sky-blue pair of bikinis on and met Maree at the linen closet in the hallway.

Maree was wearing a lime green bikini with white palm trees on. We grabbed a beach towel each and ran downstairs to the pool. We put our towels down in the usual spot and as usual, Maree went straight to the deep end and dove in and I went to the shallow end and walked in. The pool temperature was the usual thirty degrees Celsius.

When it reached my thighs, I dove under and swam a few lengths. I was going down the left side of the pool and Maree was doing laps on the right-hand side. It felt good to switch off for a while and not have to worry about my apartment or my work in the city anymore.

I stopped where I could stand and floated for a while and looked up at the sky and watched the clouds slowly drifting across, it was so relaxing.

I got out and asked Maree if she wanted something to drink. She said not to worry that she would go and have a look. We both got out and wrapped ourselves in our towels. I went and got a couple of cans of southern comfort from the cool room.

The ones I had bought in the city. I grabbed two coolers from the bottom drawer in the kitchen and went back to the pool. Maree went down to the cellar and brought a four pack of pineapple vodka cruisers back to the pool with her. We put the towels back on the chairs and our drinks on the edge of the pool.

We sat around in the spa drinking, chatting and enjoying the rest and relaxation. The subject came up about Mom's house and what they wanted to do with it. It was located in the town of Tin Can Bay about three hours north of Brisbane in Queensland. It was a four bedroom with two and a half bathrooms.

It was on two acres and had a nice size in ground pool and a front and back veranda. It was also wheelchair friendly now too after needing to do that for Mom when she went downhill. We both agreed that we were probably best off keeping it.

At the moment, it was a quiet place with an elderly population but we both felt that down the track, it would be worth something. So we decided it would be good to go there and clean up and pack everything. We would rent it out for now, it could be a constant income.

"We only have another three weeks off before school is to start, although it's different down here, they go back a week earlier, I think. I'll have to ask somebody," Maree said.

"It would be good to take Jimmy with us," I said.

"Yes, definitely, that would make it so much easier," said Maree. "We'll have to ask and see when it suits him, I guess." We heard the pool gate open and looked over to see Jimmy coming in with his towel, he was only wearing a pair of board shorts with a surfer surfing a wave on one side.

I realized I was staring and looked up to see his bare brown muscular chest and caught his eyes sparkling as he was grinning. He put his towel down near ours and came over to join us in the spa.

We told him about Mom's place and what we were thinking of doing with it. He accepted the can I offered him and said he would be available any time. He said, "I work for you girls, so whatever you need, I'm happy to help. I'll just make sure my clients have as much wood as they need and then I'm all yours," he said as he smiled and put his arm around me and pulled me closer to his side.

Maree took that cue to hop back in the pool and have a swim. I had another swim too, we all did, it was getting late so we got out and dried ourselves off.

Jimmy went to start the fire and we went upstairs to change. I put my new jeans on, the light denim ones with the holes in and a nice maroon T-shirt with a picture of the Statue of Liberty and New York City written on the front. It was time for the news by the time I came downstairs, so I put the television on in the lounge and caught up on what was going on in the world.

I turned it off and put the stereo on instead. *The news was always so depressing*, I thought. Jimmy had gone back outside. *Probably went to have a shower and get dressed in time for dinner*, I thought.

Which reminded me, I wondered what was for dinner. I went and got a six pack of southern comfort from the cool room. I opened one and put one in a cooler for Jimmy. I put the rest in the fridge. Then went to see what Silvia had written on today's note.

It read, 'Dear Amber and Maree, there is a pot of Bolognese on the stove, just need to cook some pasta to go with it. There is some cheesy garlic bread in the oven, just needs to cook and there's a trifle in the fridge for dessert, love Silvia.'

I put a pot of water on the stove for the pasta and turned the dial for the Bolognese to just reheat it slowly. Then waited till the water boiled before I put the oven on for the garlic bread. I loved not having to worry about meals or the cleaning, washing or ironing.

But I must admit I would have to do something; in the end it could get boring. I made a mental note to go through each room and think about turning it into a bed and breakfast. *That would keep me busy*, I thought.

I put the spaghetti into the pot. Sipping on my drink and dancing to the music, I didn't hear Jimmy come in till he came up behind me and scared the holy shit out of me. Maree came in not long after. I kept my eye on the pots and got three plates out and another for the cheesy garlic bread.

When the pasta was ready, I dished it up and sat down at the kitchen bench to eat. Silvia had put a little bit of chili into the Bolognese. It wasn't too much just enough to make our lips tingle a little. "So what's the plan for tomorrow?" I asked to nobody in particular.

Jimmy said he had some chores to catch up on and Maree only had her study. "Would you like to go kayaking with me, Maree?" I asked.

"Why not that sounds like fun," she said. "Jimmy said we can use the Ute if we wanted to, we could put the kayaks on the back and drive it to the spot near where the boat ramp is on the other side of the river."

"That sounds fantastic, thanks Jimmy," she said. "We could ask Silvia to make us a picnic lunch again too. We won't rush, we'll just head off after breakfast."

After dinner, Maree went up to her room to study. Jimmy and I watched a funny movie with Eddie Murphy in it on the television then he kissed me goodnight and said he had an early start. That he was going home because he didn't want to wake me in the morning. It was 10:30 already when he left, so I locked the house up and turned the lights off and went to bed myself.

I woke up at 7:30 am and went to have a nice hot shower. I blow dried my hair and put it up in a ponytail and put a new bikini on, this one was purple with black lace around the edges of the top and along the top of the bottoms. They were really pretty. I put black shorts and a black crop top on and my thongs. I grabbed a beach towel on my way downstairs.

Maree was already half way through her breakfast. Silvia handed me a coffee. "I packed you girls a picnic lunch." She turned to me and said, "don't worry, Maree told me you were going kayaking so I've made it into a backpack so it won't be too heavy for you both."

"Thanks Silvia that's fantastic," I said.

Jimmy came in when I was half way through my breakfast, he handed me some keys and said, "I've parked the Ute out the front. The kayaks are already in the back. I tied them down with a bungee cord so it won't be too hard to undo and tie back down after you finish."

He gave us directions. He didn't know I had already been there before and I wasn't going to let on either. I finished my second cup of coffee and got up to leave. Maree was already out the front checking out the kayaks. I put my backpack in the back where Maree had put hers. I got in behind the wheel and started the engine to let it warm up. Maree jumped in and we both buckled up.

Jimmy waved goodbye as we drove out of the gates and down the lane. We had to drive as if we were going to Silvia's and then there was a laneway right next door on the right-hand side. As we turned into the lane way, we noticed Jimmy's Dad out the left-hand side of the house washing his truck; it was blue and had a Kenworth sign on the side of the bonnet. He was staring at us as we drove past toward the river and we couldn't help but stare back.

I was thinking that I would love to see him go to jail for the awful things he had done to Alice. I knew I was going to do everything in my power to prove it was him who killed her. We got to the boat ramp and carried one kayak at a time down to the boat ramp.

We put them into the water and hopped on board with our oars in hand, and our back packs on we set off. It was a beautiful day; the woods were thick on both sides of the river. As we came around the first bend in the river, we came across the bridge that Jimmy had built. Then the next turn in the river we passed under the huge log that went from one side of the river to the other. I told Maree this is the log that I told you about.

We continued paddling down the river and we came across a little pebbled beach after a couple of hours of paddling. It also had a nice little grassy spot where we could sit to have our lunch.

It was so peaceful out here. Nobody around for miles or so it would seem. What the girls didn't know was that they had been followed. Jimmy's Dad was hiding on the other side of the river, watching.

Silvia had packed a few different lunch boxes; one had a ham and cheese sandwich each and she had put some sliced tomato in a separate one. Another one had a few different stone fruits in and she had a flask of fruit cup cordial made up in a cold furnace.

There was a packet of chips each and two Mars bars as well. We ate what we could then went for a swim. It felt like we didn't have a care in the world and after we finished swimming, we sat down on our towels to dry off for a while before it was time to paddle back.

Maree had stepped into her kayak and was sitting waiting for me to get into mine; as I went to step into mine, I heard a noise come from the woods on the other side of the river. It kind of sounded like somebody stepping on a twig. We both looked up but couldn't see anything. I let it go and hopped into the kayak and we slowly paddled back up the river under the big log, the bridge and back to the boat ramp.

We carried the kayaks one at a time back to the place where the Ute was parked and tied them down the same way Jimmy had it before. As we drove down the laneway, we noticed the stuff was still there for washing the truck but there was no sign of Jimmy's Dad.

"You would think he would be finished washing the truck by now, wouldn't you?" I said.

Maree nodded her head in agreement. "You don't think he would have followed us, do you?" she said remembering the noise we had heard down the river where we had our picnic. We drove home in silence, not sure what to think.

When we got home, we washed the kayaks off with the hose out the front of the garage and left them out in the sun to dry. Then we went into the kitchen to put away the left-over food that we didn't eat from our backpacks. Silvia came in and asked how our kayaking went. I took the chance to ask her about her ex-husband.

"I noticed your ex-husband's truck at your place, he must be back home again, aye?"

Silvia's face changed and so did her carefree mood. "I want you girls to stay away from him, he's not a well man. He is on medication but he doesn't always take it though," she said, "now what do you girls feel like for dinner?" She was changing the subject, as she obviously didn't want to talk about him any longer.

We didn't want to upset her so I just said, "anything will do, thanks," and we left to go upstairs.

On the way up the stairs, Maree and I looked at each other with raised eyebrows. Then went off to our rooms to get changed. By the time we went back downstairs, Silvia had gone home and the house was quiet. The note on the bench said, 'Dear Amber and Maree, I have made up some mince for tacos on the stove, just needs reheating and everything else is ready in the fridge. There is also a caramel tart and cream to go with it for dessert, love Silvia.'

Jimmy had already been in to light the fire. That's weird, I thought it was only 4:35 pm when I checked my watch. I went down to the cellar to get a bottle of wine to go with dinner. Maree was at the kitchen bench when I got back. I poured a wine for us both and we sat down to have a chat about Silvia and the way she acted when we brought up her ex-husband.

I wondered if Jimmy was going to come for dinner. I pressed the intercom button that said Jimmy underneath it and waited for a reply. When one didn't come, I went out the back door and I checked the shed. He wasn't chopping wood either.

I came back to the kitchen and told Maree, "I can't find Jimmy, I guess it's just us tonight," and took a seat back at the kitchen bench.

"You could ring him if you wanted to," she said.

"Nah, I'm not worried; he might be visiting his dad now that he's back in town or busy elsewhere."

We enjoyed a quiet dinner then decided to have an early night. It was only 7:30 pm when we locked the place up, turned the lights off and went upstairs. Maree was going up to study so I went to my room. I wanted to have another look at the photos, especially the one with the hedge around the gum tree.

I locked my bedroom door just in case Jimmy walked in and went to my wardrobe. I reached in and got the recycle bag out from where I had hidden it before. I went over to my bed and sat down cross legged and emptied the contents carefully onto the bed. I opened the file and went through the photos.

When I got to the one where Alice was standing in front of the hedge, I looked at the photo again more closely this time. The hedge just behind Alice had a bit of a gap in it. I didn't remember seeing a gap in it the other day when I checked. It must be just overgrown.

I looked again, just between Alice's legs in the photo it looked like something was catching the sun under the hedge where the gap was. It could be nothing but it could also be something. The least I could do is go back and check it out. *I might have to wait till Jimmy's Dad goes away again though*, I thought.

I put everything back into the recycle bag and put them back into the same spot in the back of my wardrobe. I was surprised not to hear from Jimmy at all, so I decided to have an early night. I went downstairs in my nightie to the front room to pick a book from the library so I could read for a while before I went to sleep.

Instead of putting the main lights on, I just used a torch and turned the lamp on that was on the computer table. I noticed headlights coming in the driveway. I looked out the window and it was Jimmy's Ute. It was 9:30 pm. I chose a book and turned the lamp off and used the torch to get back up to my room. Reading helped to get my eyes tired and I fell asleep.

I was following Alice through the woods and she disappeared when I got to where Jimmy had parked the Ute, that's when I woke up. It was already morning; the strange thing was in the dream; Jimmy's Ute was there and Alice disappeared into the car.

It didn't make sense. I dressed in my workout gear and went to work out. I took my headset so I could just tune out and really push myself. I had just finished when Jimmy popped his head in to see if I was up for breakfast.

I accepted his offer and headed for the kitchen. I left him with Silvia and Maree while I ran upstairs to have a shower and get dressed. I went back downstairs and had sausage and eggs for breakfast. Maree was asking Jimmy about the log over the river and he said it was the old bridge that they had used for years before he had built the new one.

I asked him where he had been last night and he said he had to see his dad. "Yeah, sorry I should have called," he said then talked about a certain tree that somebody had put him onto that he had to go and chop down. So it was going to keep him busy for the next couple of days so he wouldn't be around as much.

He said he would still come and light the fire at night but he wouldn't have much time to just hang out. He was heading off after breakfast. I kissed him goodbye and he left via the veranda.

Chapter 9

Jimmy left the house via the veranda and headed back to his place. He grabbed his keys and left. He drove straight over to his dad's place. "It's about time," his dad said as he opened the door.

"I had to stay for breakfast. I told Amber and Maree that I would only be available to light the fire in the afternoon and the rest of the time I can help you out here for the next couple of days anyway," Jimmy said. He followed his dad through the front room and down the hallway to the right. His Dad opened the bedroom door.

Rachel Gibbs was lying naked on the bed; she couldn't move her arms or her legs. She was tied up and kept falling in and out of consciousness. She had a dark colored pillow slip over her head so she couldn't tell where she was and there was masking tape over her mouth. So she couldn't scream.

All she remembered was doing some food shopping for her family at the local shopping center at Norseman in Western Australia. She was putting the groceries into the boot. Then everything went blank. She woke up in what felt like a truck cab sleeper. It felt like days had gone by; she couldn't see where she was but she had seen the truck driver each time he made her sit up to eat.

He would remove the tape and afterwards put it back on. She was given some sedatives as well so she would slip in and out of consciousness. She woke up and she felt like she was on a different bed in a house and her arms and legs were tied to each corner of the bed.

She heard the door open and she could hear the voices of two men. "I like this one," Jimmy's Dad was saying. "She's a fighter."

"Good," Jimmy said as he removed his pants and he took his time to rape the woman. His Dad watched his son. Then they untied her and led her down the hallway by her wrists to the bathroom. Jimmy told her she had to wash herself well then took her back to the bedroom and tied her back up to the bed.

His Dad took his turn raping Rachel and this time Jimmy watched. She tried struggling both times but it just made her wrists and her ankles hurt more.

They made her a sandwich and Jimmy sat with her while she ate it and gave her a drink of water. He threatened to kill her if she made any noise. Then replaced the tape back over her mouth. She was crying and begging him to not do this but knew it was a waste of time.

He wouldn't even talk unless it was to urge her to hurry up and eat. He didn't bother drugging her again. Nobody was going to hear her here. He and his dad had put some extra sound proofing material into the ceiling.

Jimmy and his dad had been doing this ever since Alice. She was the first one; his dad had taught him more than just how to fix things. He had taught him how to please a woman and also how to kill but they had a special place for that.

His Dad had secretly built a bunker under the property. It was so well hidden that not even the police could find it. They had kept Alice down there for months before his dad had killed her; he did it right in front of Jimmy then watched while he made Jimmy have sex with the corpse.

Jimmy walked back into the kitchen and sat down with his dad to have a beer and talk about their new toy. Then his dad was telling Jimmy how he had got to follow the girls down the river in their kayaks.

"Don't worry, they didn't know I was there," he was saying.

"Yeah, well just remember I have to live there. You can't go scaring them, remember the youngest one is with that young copper too, so you don't want to draw any attention to yourself, which reminds me; have you taken your medication today?" Jimmy asked. "You don't want Mom on your case either."

"Yeah, yeah, I'll take them," he said as he grabbed the packet off the table and took one.

"I won't stay too long, there is a tree that needs chopping down. I've got the chain saws in the Ute. I'll be back later tonight after I start the fire at the house. Can you fix us some dinner?" Jimmy asked as he got up to leave. His Dad just grumbled something to himself under his breath as his son left the house.

Maree had decided to go and visit Eli at work. I had decided to have a look around the house and evaluate each room upstairs in case we felt like turning it into a getaway retreat down the track, after we've got Mom's house sorted. We would have to put off doing that till Jimmy could come and help. I knew

Maree had got a neighbor to do the lawns till she got back, so we didn't have to worry too much.

I was busy till the sun started to go down, then went to find Maree. She wasn't in her room so I went downstairs. I found her watching the news in the lounge room near the kitchen in front of the fire. It reminded me I had missed seeing Jimmy.

I made a mental note to make sure I caught up with him tomorrow afternoon when he came in to light the fire. There was a story about a missing woman from somewhere in Western Australia on. I put the kettle on and went to read the note Silvia had left on the bench.

It said, 'Dear Amber and Maree, there is a tray of braised steak and onions in the oven on low and vegetables on the stove. Just need to heat them up. There is also a fruit cocktail parfait in the fridge for dessert, love Silvia.'

Maree turned the television off and came in to see what I was up to. I turned all the vegetables on and finished making the coffee. She was sitting at the bench when I handed her a coffee and asked what she had been up to. "I just hung out with Eli at the police station. Earl's wife, Wendy brought in a nice casserole for lunch, so it was good to meet her and have a chat."

"She was telling me about the old days and how busy this house used to be before when Uncle Tom was alive. They had even held big ballroom dances in the front lounge back then. She said people used to come from all over the country to attend. Could you imagine this place in full swing?" she asked.

"Yeah, it would have been amazing," I said as I sipped my coffee.

After dinner, I made myself a milo and took it up to bed with me. I had a quick shower but used a shower cap, so I wouldn't have to wet my hair. Then settled in with the book I had started reading last night. It was 10 pm when I saw Jimmy's lights come in the drive. I didn't know what to think. I knew he was busy cutting the tree down but you couldn't be doing that this late. At 10:30, I turned my lamp off and went to sleep.

I woke up early and dressed in shorts and a T-shirt. I put my runners on and ran downstairs and grabbed a water bottle out of the fridge. Nobody was up yet so the house was dark and quiet. I took off out the front door and headed toward the path to the woods.

It was so refreshing; the early morning dew was still on the foliage as I ran through the woods and down to the river. I washed the sweat off my face in the water and had a bit of a rest.

Jimmy was right, it was a good place to think. I sat just looking at the view and thought about my life and Jimmy and how different things were now with a decent guy that treated me so well compared to how Andrew was with me. *Not to mention my sex life*, I thought.

I couldn't even remember the last time I had sex with Andrew but I do remember having to fake an orgasm most times. Oh well, good riddance to him and his floozy. I didn't know how I lasted six years.

I decided to go and see if Jimmy's Dad was still in town just out of curiosity, so I went down the path beside the river. Instead of taking the new bridge across that Jimmy had built just for something different, I followed the path further around the next bend and came up to the log that I followed Alice over the other night.

I carefully navigated my way across and up to where the car would have been parked then continued to the right along the track and ended up near Jimmy's Dad's place. I kept out of sight but I could see that Jimmy's Dad's truck was still parked in the yard. I thought about checking out the hedge again but I changed my mind when I saw Jimmy turn up in his Ute. I ducked down a bit further behind the bush that I was hiding behind.

I looked at my watch, it was eight o'clock in the morning. I turned around and headed back to the house but took the bridge that Jimmy had made on the way home instead of the log. I got home about 9:30. I was looking in the fridge when Silvia came in.

"I put some bacon and eggs in the microwave. I'll make you some toast to go with it if you like. Have a seat and I'll put the kettle on," she said then busied herself at the stove. I was happy to sit at the kitchen bench and wait. Two minutes later, I was enjoying a late breakfast.

"What's Maree up to?" I asked.

"She's up in her room, I think," she said.

After breakfast, I enjoyed another coffee then went upstairs to shower and wash my hair. I put some black denim shorts and an orange T-shirt on after I blow dried my hair. Then went to find Maree. I knocked on her bedroom door and heard her yell out to come in. I opened the door and she was at her laptop as usual.

"Good. I could do with a distraction," she said looking up at me while spinning back and forth on her office chair. "Did you go for a run?" she asked.

"Yeah, it's such a beautiful place for it." I sat down on the edge of her bed to talk. "I stopped down at the river and did some thinking and then I thought I would see if Jimmy's Dad was still in town. I took the old log across the river just for something different, instead of the bridge that Jimmy had built."

"And was he still there?" she asked.

"Yeah, the truck was there, then Jimmy turned up so I made sure he didn't see me," I said. "He didn't come home till late last night. I saw his Ute come in the drive about 10 o'clock. I wonder if that's where he's been," I said.

I changed the subject. "Would you like to go for a drive or something?" I asked.

Maree jumped up out of her chair and said, "Yes, I could do with some shopping therapy," and went into her wardrobe to change. She was still rattling on when she walked back out two minutes later wearing a knee length olive green dress and casual black flats on.

I certainly didn't have to twist her arm. I said we would have to make a detour to my room first. I put a purple dress with blue flowers on and some leather sandals. Carrying our hand bags, we ran downstairs and Maree grabbed the keys for the Mustang off the hook in the kitchen. On our way through, we told Silvia where we were going and she wrote a quick list for us to pick up while we were in town.

Maree went ahead to warm up the Mustang and five minutes later, we were on our way out of the drive. Down the lane, Maree put the indicator on to turn right toward Murwoolinbah. It was great, the music was blaring all the way and Maree loved the way the car handled.

We parked in the carpark underneath the shopping center close to the escalators. We bought a few clothes and had a kabab and a thick shake at the food court for lunch. Then went to Woolworths and got the list of groceries for Silvia. Maree loved driving the Mustang all that way and gave it a little more of accelerator on the way home.

Not all the way, just a couple of kilometers till I screamed and said, "No more." Then she apologized and came back to the speed limit. "Lucky no police cars are around in the middle of nowhere," I said.

We arrived home around 3:30 in the afternoon and unloaded the car out the front before Maree parked it in the garage where it belonged. We sorted everything out in the front room on the lounge just like we did the first time.

Size 8's for Maree and mine were the size 10s. We had gone berserk again. "Lucky we have nice big wardrobes to fit it all in," I was saying as I carried everything of mine through the door and up the stairs to my room.

I wanted to be there to meet Jimmy when he came to light the fire tonight. I dressed up a little in a really pretty red sundress I had bought and ran downstairs in case he came early. By 4:30, I was sitting at the kitchen bench waiting for Jimmy to come.

Silvia had put the groceries away and gone home early. Maree was still upstairs sorting her clothes out. She knew I was hoping to catch up with Jimmy. So I knew she wouldn't be coming downstairs in a hurry. We had talked about it on the way home and I was going to be romantic by seducing him with alcohol and a pretty dress and hoped that he stayed for dinner.

Silvia had left a note saying, 'Dear Amber and Maree, I have cooked satay chicken and fried rice for dinner on the stove, just need to heat it up and there is a chocolate cake and custard in the fridge for dessert, love Silvia.'

I was sipping on a can of southern comfort. Jimmy arrived at 5:45. He came in through the French doors with an arm load of wood. He unloaded it and brushed off his pale-yellow polo shirt. I waited till he finished then wrapped my arms around him.

"Hey gorgeous, how are you?" he said while he returned my hug, I kissed him on the neck and grabbed his crotch and tried to get him going. I was surprised when he pushed my hand away and removed himself from my arms and said he had to go. Said he didn't have time for that.

He kissed me on the cheek and left. I watched him drive out of the gate 10 minutes later from the window in the front room feeling very confused.

I climbed the stairs and knocked on Maree's bedroom door, she answered straight away and followed me downstairs while I told her about what happened with Jimmy. "That's weird. Did he say where he had to be?" she asked.

"He mentioned something about his dad and medication," I said. We had our dinner then went upstairs. Maree wanted to study and I was going to go to bed and continue reading my book. I was going to stay up till I knew Jimmy was home. He got home a little after 10. Then I drifted off to sleep.

I dreamt about Alice again. I followed her through the woods across the log and up the hill to Jimmy's Ute again and when she disappeared, I woke up. It was already 7 o'clock and I rolled out of bed and into the shower. I was contemplating the dream while the water cascaded over my body and as I dressed in jeans and a dark blue top and headed down the stairs, I still felt none the wiser. If Alice was trying to tell me something, I really wasn't getting it.

Maree was already in the kitchen talking to Silvia when I arrived. Silvia stopped and handed me my coffee and asked me if I wanted some savory mince on toast for breakfast. I said "I would love some, thanks." I looked over at Maree, she was busy eating and reading the local paper at the same time. Silvia was busy in her own world and I was thinking about Jimmy.

I asked Silvia, "Is Jimmy still busy cutting down that tree today?"

"I don't know," she said. "I haven't seen him this morning." I went back to my thoughts. I was wondering what I was going to do with my day. After I had finished eating, Silvia took my plate and refilled my coffee.

"The markets are on today," Silvia said.

"Oh, I forgot about that," I turned to Maree, she was already packing the paper up and gulping down the last of her coffee. I finished my second cup then we both went upstairs to grab our hand bags and Maree took the keys for the Mustang from the hook in the kitchen.

"Would you like us to get you anything, Silvia?" I asked.

"No, I already went down before work, thanks anyway," she said. I waved goodbye on my way out.

It was nine o'clock already, so it was hard to find a parking space. Maree ended up parking in the police station carpark. "The perks of dating a cop I'd say," she said grinning from ear to ear. We got out and headed across the road first. The church always held a baking stall. Silvia said she always supplied a few cakes and biscuits.

I bought some white Christmas and some jam filled lamingtons. Then looked at some jewelry and bought a couple of pairs of earrings. So did Maree, we also brought some pretty wind chimes to hang on the veranda and listened to a three-piece local band playing old eighties music.

I put a twenty dollar note into the guitar case they had open on the ground. They were very appreciative. It was good to see the little town come to life. There were people everywhere.

We ended up going to the police station after putting our goodies in the car. Eli and Earl were just sitting around not doing too much. "Hi guys," Maree said then turned to Earl. "Earl, this is my sister Amber."

I shook his hand and said, "Hello, nice to finally meet you and put a face to a name."

"Maree may have mentioned you a few times too," he said looking at Maree with a big cheesy grin.

"Yes, I'm sure she did." I went a little pink.

"All good though," he said.

"So what are you girls up to?" Eli said. Maree was sitting on his desk swinging her legs.

"Not much, just checking out the markets," Maree said.

We stayed there chatting till about lunch time. Then Maree and I went and got some fish and chips for us all from the general store across the road for lunch. "So what's the go with Jimmy's Dad?" I asked Earl.

"The whole family is a bit weird if you ask me," he said.

"What do you mean by that?" I asked.

"Jimmy's Dad Reg, short for Reginald, he is nothing but trouble. He is a paranoid schizophrenic, if he takes his medication, he's OK but if he doesn't, he can be a pain in the ass. Especially toward women. Jimmy usually helps him when he's at home. I don't know how he holds down a job." His thoughts trailed off.

"What about Jimmy and his mom?" I asked.

"Jimmy covers for his dad and his mother covers for them both if you ask me."

"What do you mean by that?"

"Don't get me wrong, Jimmy tries his best to keep his dad in line. But at the same time, there is something not quite right with that one either. I don't know what it is but I don't trust him or his mother. She tends to baby him a little, he's a grown man, for god's sake," he said as he came out of his thoughts.

"If I was you, I would be very wary of that lot. Even when Alice disappeared, Reg was my number one suspect. I just haven't been able to prove anything. I'm not giving up though, I told your Aunt Mary the same thing. So if you ever hear or see anything unusual, don't hesitate to call. You know where I am."

"I will, thanks," I said. "Do you believe in ghosts?" I was asking no one in particular, Earl was the first to answer.

He said, "My wife Wendy said she had seen one once. I don't know myself. I'd have to see it myself to really believe it," Eli agreed. We stayed for a little while longer and then headed home. On the way home, Maree asked me about Alice.

"Have you been seeing Alice again?" I told her about the recurring dream that I kept having and told her how I went into her room and talked at times. Maree listened intently.

When we got home, we hung the wind chimes up on the veranda, one had fairies and the other one had butterflies. They looked really pretty and sounded good too. Silvia was in the kitchen cooking a shepherd's pie for dinner and peeling the vegetables to go with it.

We stopped to show her what we'd bought. She said she was the one that made the lamingtons and the white Christmas and she was happy that we had bought some. I put the kettle on to have them for afternoon tea. Silvia joined us but had a cup of tea instead.

Not long after she finished the pie, she put some cheese on top and put it in the oven on low. She cooked all the vegetables and then turned everything off. Wrote a note and left it on the bench and left via the veranda. She always parked her little red Tesla in the first bay of the garage.

Maree and I had gone downstairs to find something to drink. We settled on a couple of bottles of white Moscato wine and went back to the kitchen. Jimmy was in the lounge room lighting the fire. I was surprised and happy to see him. I put the bottles on the kitchen bench. I went over to where Jimmy was crouched down, putting the smaller bits of wood in to get it started.

I said, "Hi Jimmy, it's good to see you."

"Yeah," he said, "good to see you too, what have you been up to?" he asked. I told him how we had been to the markets and what we had bought. I also mentioned that we finished off having lunch at the police station and how I finally got to meet Earl.

I detected a bit of sarcasm in his voice when he said, "well that would have been nice."

I couldn't help myself. I had to ask. "Can you stay for dinner or does your dad need you again?"

He looked at me with a bit of a frown and said, "I know I haven't really been here for you," he stood up and cupped my face in his hand, "but I've got to make sure he has his medication and that he's eating well and looking after himself. He has another job coming up in Melbourne so he has to leave again tomorrow and I've finished with that tree now. So I'll make it up to you tomorrow."

I smiled and said, "OK, I'll look forward to it," we kissed and he finished lighting the fire and left.

I went back to Maree in the kitchen and poured myself a glass of wine. We talked about our day and enjoyed the shepherd's pie and vegetables. I loaded the dish washer and wiped over the counter tops. We talked for a little while longer then we headed up to our bedrooms to settle in for the night. I went into the bathroom and decided to run a bath so I adjusted the water to suit me.

Then went to get a nightie out of my wardrobe and I took my earrings out. I returned to the bathroom and got undressed. I put some bubble bath in and stepped into the tub. I had brought a bottle of wine up with me and had a glass sitting on the side of the bath. I put my hair up and laid down. I turned the spa on. It was so relaxing; I nearly fell asleep.

It was getting cold so I got out. I dressed in my nightie and was about to crawl into bed when I had an idea. I put my dressing gown on and walked down the hallway to Alice's bedroom. I had my torch in hand so I used that instead of turning on the lights.

I opened the door and went over to the bed and put the lamp on. I scanned the room looking for Alice. She was in the teepee. I could just make out her silhouette. "Alice, I have an idea," I said with a bit of excitement in my voice. She crawled out of the cubby house and came over to where I was sitting on the bed.

She sat down beside me, ready to listen. "I know you have been giving me dreams of us going to the spot where Jimmy parks on the other side of the river but you keep disappearing. I wonder if we go there in my car to that spot and see if you can remember the drive or anything about that night. What do you think?" I asked.

"OK," she said, "it might help." I told her that Jimmy's Dad was leaving again soon and then it would be safe again. I wanted to take her to the tree where the hedge grew and see how she reacted. *There had to be a reason I kept thinking about that photo*, I thought.

"We may not find anything but it's worth a try to see if we can jog your memory," I said.

I said goodnight and left to go back down the hallway to my bedroom. I got into bed and laid down. A million things were running through my head.

About Jimmy most of all and what Earl had said about being wary of him and his mother as well. In the end, I decided to turn my lamp on and get back to my book.

I knew it would make my eyes tired and take my mind off everything. I saw Jimmy's lights come in the drive about 10:30. I was thinking it wouldn't take that long to make sure his dad was taking his medication and eating properly.

Then I thought it could just be me being paranoid after Andrew playing up on me. I went back to my book and finally about midnight, I drifted off to sleep. I slept in till 9:30. I put my dressing gown on and went downstairs for coffee. Nobody was around so I put the kettle on. I noticed a note on the kitchen bench.

'Good morning, Amber. I've left your breakfast in the microwave; Maree told me to tell you she is out with Eli and won't be back till late. I had to go to Murwoolinbah for the day. I have left a pot of stew on the stove for dinner. You will need to give it a stir every now and again till it's cooked. There is an apricot pie in the fridge, you can put some ice-cream with it for dessert, love Silvia.'

I went to the microwave and had a look; it was bacon, egg and baked beans. I turned the microwave on for two minutes and made my coffee. The microwave dinged and I got my breakfast out using a tea towel, so I wouldn't get burnt.

I sat at the kitchen bench and ate. I made some toast and I made a second cup of coffee and stirred the stew on the stove. I was still tired from my late night so I didn't really feel like doing too much.

I took my coffee to the lounge and turned the television on and the news came on and I knew there was a good midday movie about to come on after that, so I sat on the lounge to watch. The story the news lady was talking about was the lady that went missing from a carpark at her local supermarket in Norseman in Western Australia.

The family was pleading for somebody to come forward with any information. She had three little kids under the age of 10. I felt sorry for them and also wondered if the father had something to do with it. The police were looking into him.

I got up to light the fire and make the most of a lazy day. After that, the sport and then the weather came on. I took off to go to the bathroom and stirred the stew again. Then settled in to watch the movie. It was an old thriller with Sally Field as the main actor.

I had seen it years ago but I couldn't remember what happened so I still enjoyed it anyway. After the movie, I stirred the stew again and went into the front room and chose another movie to watch. This one was another thriller with John Travolta in it.

I turned the stew off and stocked the fire up. Halfway through the second movie, I fell asleep. I didn't wake up till Maree came in about six. It was just getting dark. Jimmy came in not long after to light the fire. When he saw it was already lit, he restocked it and came over to where we were sitting at the bench waiting for the kettle to boil.

He kissed my cheek and asked if I was having an early night. I didn't register for a second then remembered I was still in my pajamas. "No," I said. "I just had a rough night getting to sleep last night, so I've stayed in my pajamas and watched movies all day." He sat down at the bench with us and had a coffee.

"Are you staying for dinner?" I asked.

"What is it?" he asked.

"Just stew," I said. I got up to go and turn the stove on to heat it up. He said he would and chatted for a while. I got the bowls out and buttered some bread. I stirred it again and when it was hot enough, I dished it up. We all enjoyed the stew and I enjoyed seeing Jimmy again.

It felt like we had had a huge love affair and then nothing. Maree knew I needed to talk so after she finished dinner, she said she was going upstairs to shower. I told Jimmy how I felt and that I had seen him come in late every night.

I said I was trying not to be paranoid but after what Andrew had just put me through, I couldn't handle it. He told me he was sorry and said it was because he was looking after his father. Making sure he was eating and taking his medication.

I was a bit cranky so I couldn't help saying, "It shouldn't take all night to do that."

"Yes, you're right, it doesn't, I did stay for a few beers," he said.

"You shouldn't be drinking and driving then, Jimmy," I said raising my voice a little.

He got up and said, "Well on that note, I'll catch up with you tomorrow when you calm down. I finished cutting that tree down today so I'll be here doing my chores most of the day." He said as he left.

Well that didn't go well, maybe it's just me, I thought. I went upstairs to see Maree. I knocked on the door and then I opened it, she was at her dressing table doing her hair when I walked in. She could tell I was upset.

"Hey," she said, "what happened?" I told her how things went and she told me not to worry. She said, "Maybe he is just tired after looking after his dad and things will get back to normal again soon."

"Maybe," I said with a sigh. I talked for a little while then left her to go to bed.

Chapter 10

Jimmy went back over to his dad's place after dinner. "Hi Dad," he said as he let himself in. His Dad was at the kitchen table with a beer in his hand.

"Hi Jimmy, how'd you go?" he asked.

"Oh, Amber's getting the shits with me being away too much. Fucking woman, always got to complain," he said, getting himself worked up as he grabbed a beer out of the fridge. He sat down then he got up and went down the hallway to the bedroom to take his mood out on their latest victim.

Rachel was asleep when he got there. She woke up when Jimmy ripped the pillow slip off her head. He undid the rope that she was tied to the bed with and dragged her by her hair down the hallway and into the bathroom to the shower.

He turned the faucets on and made her get in and wash herself. She still had the tape over her mouth so she couldn't scream; he could see the fear in her eyes. Then he dragged her back to the bedroom and tied her arms and legs back to each corner of the bed.

He started biting her nipples with no mercy, just enough that he didn't break the skin, then shoved his fingers up into her vagina, first one and then three in and out and around at the same time. Then he got a torch that he had beside the bed and shoved it up inside her, it was 10 inches long and an inch and a half wide.

She finally passed out from the relentless pain he inflicted as he kept shoving it in and out. He had his penis in his other hand and was tugging himself at the same time. When she passed out, he stopped and slapped her till she woke up then raped her to finish off.

He was in a much better mood by the time he came back out to the kitchen. He grabbed a beer out of the fridge and handed another one to his dad. "Feel better now, son?" he asked with a grin on his face.

"Fuck yeah," he said as he took a swig of his beer. "I can't stay long, that bitch Amber is keeping tabs on me. You can get rid of this one though," he gestured toward the bedroom, "she's not much good anymore, too much blood, you'll have to make sure you clean up before you go."

"You know I struggle on my own. I'm not as young as I used to be," Jimmy's Dad said.

"Alright, I'll come early and give you a hand so Mom doesn't see. How long do you think you will be away?" Jimmy asked.

"Probably about five days, I guess," his dad answered. Jimmy finished his beer and said goodbye.

He drove in the driveway about 9:30 and looked up at Amber's window and noticed her standing there, watching. He felt a bit trapped by this one. He didn't know what to do with her yet. But he knew he couldn't keep this up. He just had to be more careful, he thought.

Amber was still wide awake after sleeping half the day, so she waited up to see Jimmy drive in at 9:30 and saw him looking up at her in the window as he did. She didn't know what to think anymore.

He seemed so perfect to begin with but she was starting to think she may have rushed into something way too soon. Or Maree could be right and he was just tired due to looking after his dad. I got into bed and finished the book I was reading then laid down to sleep.

I woke up early before the sun came up. It was only 4:30 am. I got up and dressed in my work out gear and headed for the gym. I took my flashlight and stopped at the linen closet to get a towel. The house was dark and quiet and the sun wasn't even up yet. I heard a car outside on the way downstairs.

I went to the window in the front room and saw Jimmy's Ute driving out the driveway. It made me wonder where he would be going at this hour. I made a mental note to ask him about it later on and kept heading toward the gym. Stopping at the fridge for a water bottle on the way through.

Jimmy turned his lights off as he pulled into the driveway at his parents' house. He let himself in downstairs and went to wake his dad. While his dad was getting up and dressing, he went to check on the woman in the spare room.

She was awake when he pulled the pillow slip off her head. She was bleeding between the legs and covered in bruises. He decided to rape her one last time, then he hit her on the head with the torch beside the bed. His Dad walked in and gave him a hand to carry her naked body out the back and they threw her down the hatch that opened up to the bunker. They covered their tracks and went back inside to clean up.

"Next time try getting someone who won't be missed so much, like that last one. Get a prostitute or someone that has no family. Take time to research a little first," Jimmy said.

"Yes, OK, I'll try," Jimmy's Dad said. "Just means I'll be gone a little longer though. I'll need time to research."

"Try getting someone a bit younger this time too," Jimmy was saying.

Jimmy left before his mom's alarm clock was due to go off. He rolled the Ute out of the driveway with the lights off and didn't start the engine till he was far enough away from the house for her not to hear. He was cutting it fine; he knew but he couldn't help himself from doing her one more time before he had to kill her.

What he didn't know was that his mother had been watching them the whole time out of the dining room window. He drove home and took a shower to wash any trace of Rachel Gibbs off him. He dressed in his black cargo shorts and light pink polo shirt and went to chop wood. It always soothed him to think of what he had done while chopping wood.

I really pushed myself in the gym and by about 6am, I was on my way back to the kitchen when I heard Jimmy chopping wood out the back. That's keen. *He must have extra to do with the tree he had to cut down*, I thought. I kept going through the kitchen and went upstairs to have a shower.

I was thinking about Jimmy and what I should say or do and the answer that I came up with was to do a reading and see what the cards said. I dressed in jeans and a T-shirt and sat down cross legged on the bed with the silver box in hand.

I took the cards out and put the black velvet cloth to the side. I started shuffling while I was trying to think of a question. I didn't know what to think so I was just thinking of Jimmy and drew a card. It was the lovers' card; I didn't bother to look it up.

I just thought it was pretty self-explanatory. As in, Jimmy and I are lovers but I didn't think to look at the card. If I had, I would have seen there were two women on the card and not just one.

I put the cards back away and went back downstairs in a lot better head space. "Good morning, Silvia," I said as I entered the kitchen. I sat down at the bench and watched Silvia put the kettle on. "Jimmy's chopping wood early this morning," I said as she handed me my cup of coffee.

"Yes, well he should have a pretty good stock pile after cutting down that big tree he's been working on lately," she said.

"Yeah, he'll be happy. I hope I get to see him a bit more now that his dad is going away again," I said.

Maree came in through the French doors after her work-out. "Good morning," she said and continued upstairs to have a shower and get ready for the day. I was secretly hoping Jimmy would come in and join us for breakfast but he didn't.

I had some raisin toast and a second cup of coffee. Maree came down and joined us. After my coffee, I went to look for Jimmy; *maybe he could do with some help*, I thought.

He was just putting the axe down as he came into my view. "Hi Jimmy," I said waving. "I thought you might want a hand," he said he could do with one. So I got the gloves from the bench in the shed where I had left them the last time I was helping.

I helped him load his Ute; it was sweaty work. I asked him if he would like to come in for a cold drink. He accepted and followed me through to the kitchen. I stopped at the gym to grab a couple of towels and handed one to Jimmy. I got a can of coke for Jimmy and a can of diet coke for myself out of the cool room and took a seat at the kitchen bench.

We both appreciated the refreshing break. "How's your dad, Jimmy?" I asked.

"He's fine, he's gone away again. Got a load to take to Melbourne today. He won't be home for about five days or more. I'll be able to catch up with my chores around here a little. I'm sorry I haven't had much time for you while he's been here but I just need to make sure he takes his meds and stays out of trouble when he's in town. It saves Mom worrying too much," he said.

"Does that mean you will be available for dinner then?" I asked hopefully.

"Yes, it sure does, what time would you like me to be here?" he asked.

"Come at 5:30 if you want to have a few drinks first. What would you like to drink?" I asked putting my hand on his knee.

"Jack Daniels would be good. I do have a lot to do with the gardens and heaps more wood chopping needs to be done. Especially if we are going away to pack up your mother's house. I'll need to get ahead, this tree will help with that," he said.

"At least I've got one load done, thanks to you for helping, I'll have to go and deliver that now and get back to do some more."

"Well, I'm happy to help as much as I can if you like, just give me a call," I said.

"Thanks," he said and gave me a kiss, this time it wasn't just a quick peck on the cheek. He gave me a really good pash and his voice was husky when he said goodbye.

I felt so much better now that Jimmy was acting normal again. I ran upstairs to find something nice to wear for dinner. I chose a skirt and an aqua blue top that would accentuate my bust. I laid them out on my bed and went to find Maree.

She was at her laptop with Spotify playing on her head phones again. I got her attention and told her about Jimmy and how he was back to normal. "You were right, he must have just been tired from looking after his dad," I said.

"What are you guys doing tonight?" I asked. Maree knew I was talking about her and Eli.

She eyed me suspiciously and said, "Why, what would you like us to be doing?" I went bright red. Maree said, "Don't worry, we will make ourselves scarce."

I thanked her and asked if she would like to go have some lunch and then maybe a swim. She said yes to both. I left to go get changed and meet up in the kitchen. I put another new bikini on, this one was rainbow colored. I wore a light cotton jacket over my swimmers and tied it up on the side.

I entered the kitchen with a beach towel I got from the linen closet and put it on my seat then took the lift down to the basement. I got a six pack of Jack Daniels from the boxes to the left in the wine cellar and made my way back to the kitchen. I went and put them in the cool room to get cold for Jimmy later.

I took my seat at the kitchen bench and Silvia was making us a salami and cheese sandwich for lunch. Maree was talking to her about her assignment that was due in and I was happy to listen. She said she had almost finished it so she wasn't too concerned.

Silvia said, "That reminds me Maree, I had a talk to Julie Dutton, she's one of the teachers at the primary school in town. She gave me the number for the principal, Tracey Reeds is her name." She went to get the number out of her bag in the pantry. Maree was so happy but at the same time a bit nervous. Silvia came back and handed her the piece of paper with the phone number on it.

She went to the front room for a little privacy. She came back 10 minutes later. She was excited, she said, "The principal reckons they would love to have me onboard but she just has to run it past the Board of Education first and with a bit of luck, she said she should know by next week."

"How exciting," I said and gave her a hug.

"I hope so," she said. We enjoyed our lunch then went to chill out in the pool for a while. We swam laps and floated and sat in the spa and chatted. We both felt pretty good about our lives. Maree was telling me all about her and Eli. She was so happy; *I could see those two getting married down the track*, I thought. She laughed when I told her.

She said, "And don't go getting all psychic on me either," wagging her finger at me and splashed as she did a bomb dive back into the pool. I got out and relaxed on one of the chairs for a while. I turned over after 20 minutes and done the other side.

Maree had followed me out and was doing the same. When I had done both sides, I got up to go and get us a cold drink. I went to the fridge and got us both a diet coke and went back to the pool area. I gave one to Maree and put mine down beside the pool.

I went into the pool house and got a couple of floating animals. One was a swan and the other was a unicorn. Maree got up off the seat when she saw what I had. I gave her the unicorn and we had a lot of fun trying to stay on top of them.

About 4:30 we got out and went to have a shower and get dressed. Maree had rung Eli earlier and they were going out for dinner to the pub in Swanton where they had the seafood baskets last time. By 5:30, they were back downstairs. Eli came to pick Maree up and I waved goodbye.

Jimmy came in the French doors. He lit the fire while I got us a drink, a Jack Daniels can for him and a southern comfort can for me. I got two coolers out of the bottom drawer. There was a note from Silvia on the bench, it said, 'Dear Amber and Maree, there is a roast chicken and vegetables in the oven on low, peas and corn are on the stove to be heated up and don't forget the gravy in the microwave. There is fruit cake in the pantry to go with custard in the fridge if you want dessert. Love Silvia.'

We sat down on the lounge in front of the fire and talked for a while about Maree and the job at the school and then I went to switch the television on to watch the news at six o'clock but Jimmy talked me into checking the dinner instead. He said he was starving so I got up to turn the stove on.

I got the trays out of the oven and Jimmy went and put some music on. I put the chicken onto a plate and cut it in half then in half again. "Would you like a leg or the breast?" I asked Jimmy, he opted for the leg and so did I. I got all the vegetables out of the pan and onto a plate. The peas and corn were ready so I heated up the gravy and made us both a plate full.

We just sat at the kitchen bench to eat and it was really yummy. Half way through, I asked Jimmy. "How will your father go when we go to clear Mom's house out?"

"Well I guess we could do it while he's gone," he said.

"Wow that's pretty short notice but I don't see why we can't," I answered.

"Well, I have enough wood in stock and I've pretty much already stocked up most of my customers. I could do the rest tomorrow and we could head up there on Wednesday, if you like," he said.

"That would be fantastic, at least Maree will be ready to start school when it goes back the week after next. I know she is pretty well up to date with her studies so she won't mind," I said.

We finished dinner and Jimmy helped me clean the kitchen while I loaded the dish washer. I was telling Jimmy that I would probably have to have an early night after being up so early this morning which reminded me of seeing him up that early too.

She didn't want to upset him again though. He had already seen her looking out the window last night. Let alone this morning. "Are you going to stay with me tonight?" I asked.

"Yes, I could do that," he said.

We decided to go into the front room and pick a movie to watch while lying in bed. It was only 7:30, we picked an action movie hoping that would keep us awake long enough to watch it. We locked up downstairs and turned the lights off.

"I'll leave the outside light on for Maree," I said. As we made our way up the stairs, Jimmy got the movie going while I put a nightie on. Then he stripped off to his jocks and gave me the remote. When we were settled in bed, I started the movie. It was nice to lay back in his arms and we both fell asleep like that.

The next morning, I woke up to Jimmy wanting to make love. I rolled over and gave myself to him as he explored my whole body again; only this time I was ready and enjoyed every second. I went down on him as well and got him to cum in my mouth.

He didn't stop there though, he fucked me again and blew his load again this time inside me. I gave a few squeezes with my pelvic floor muscles and made sure I got every single drop. He looked a bit surprised, so I told him that was what I was doing. Which made him groan even more.

Afterwards, it took a minute for our breathing and heart rates to get back to normal. We cuddled for a while then Jimmy said he would have to get up and get things done so we could be ready to leave for Tin Can Bay the next day. I got up and put my dressing gown on and went downstairs with him to put the kettle on.

He stayed for a coffee but left before Silvia arrived. I went back upstairs and had a nice hot shower. I was in a really good mood after my wake-up call. I dressed in denim shorts and a black T-shirt. I dried my hair and put it up. I put my diamond stud earrings in and went downstairs for breakfast.

Maree was already at the kitchen bench reading the morning paper and Silvia was at the stove cooking pancakes. I said, "Good morning," maybe a little too chirpy because they both stopped what they were doing and looked up at me.

Maree couldn't help herself, she said, "Somebody got a bit last night," I went bright red and Maree, realizing Jimmy's mother was there, said, "Woops sorry," laughed a little with her hand over her mouth. Then went back to reading her paper.

Jimmy's Mom smirked, trying not to laugh then quickly turned back to making her pancakes. I sat down and Silvia made me a coffee then put a pile of pancakes in front of me. I put one onto my plate and started buttering it then got the maple syrup and poured some on. Then added some freshly whipped cream.

I turned to Maree and said, "would you be ready to go and do Mom's house tomorrow? Jimmy wants to get it done while his dad is away."

"Um, yeah, we could do that," she said.

"I'll get some packing boxes and stuff ready if you want to help me," I said.

"There is a stack up in the attic," Silvia said. "They're under a gray blanket on the left-hand side. If you can't find them, I'll help you. There is a couple of dozen so don't worry too much."

"Oh good thanks, saves me unpacking the others from my apartment. I wasn't sure about all those yet," I said. Maree finished with the paper.

She put it to the side and said, "Amber, I'll give my neighbor Jason a call, the guy that's mowing the lawns. He might be able to help Jimmy with the furniture and the heavy lifting."

"Really?" I asked.

"Yeah, I'll go and give him a call," Maree said. She went to the front room and gave him a call. She came back five minutes later. "Yep, he can help us out over the week-end he said."

"That's fantastic, Jimmy will be happy he has more than just us to rely on," I said. They both agreed.

After breakfast, Maree and I went to the attic to get the boxes. It took a couple of hours to just get them all down and out the back to the truck. Jimmy was out there and helped us put them into the back of the truck with the trolley and blankets that were already there from the last move.

I told him about Maree's neighbor who would be there to help. We could have everything done by Monday with a bit of luck, I said. Maree and I also gave him a hand to load his Ute up with another load of firewood that he needed to deliver to a client before he went.

When we finished doing that, we all went inside for lunch. Silvia had made us a bread roll with corned beef and salad. We said good bye to Silvia and told her to have some time off while we were gone. Then after lunch, Maree and I headed upstairs to pack a bag for ourselves and Jimmy went to deliver the wood.

When I'd finished packing, I went to see what Maree was up to. She was trying to get her assignment done before we left. I told her I'd see her at dinner then. I went back to my room and got my togs on and ran downstairs to go for a swim.

It was nice to just take some time out and do a bit of a chakra cleansing meditation while I was in the pool floating. I had learned how to meditate in my yoga classes I used to go to at my old gym in the city. They would do a 10 minute one at the end of every class. I hadn't felt this relaxed for as far back as I could remember.

My thoughts went to Alice. *I guess she could wait,* I thought; she's been stuck here for this long now. Another week's not going to matter, I told myself. I finished off with a few laps before I got out. I dried myself off and went upstairs to get ready for dinner.

I had a shower and washed my hair and blow dried it again. It was getting so long I was starting to think it was too much effort at times but I did like to keep it long. I left it out this time and got my nightie on. I put my dressing gown on and went downstairs.

Jimmy had lit the fire and was sitting at the kitchen bench. I said, "Hello gorgeous, fancy seeing you here," and put my arms around him.

We kissed and he said, "I was waiting for you, I thought you would be down here already."

"I went for a swim then had to have a shower. What's Silvia made tonight?" I asked as I peeled myself off him and had a look for the note. I read it out aloud, it said 'Dear Amber and Maree, hope all goes well with the move. Give me a call when you get back. I have made some curried sausages and some rice on the stove; it just needs heating up. There is some fruit salad and cream in the fridge for dessert. Love Silvia. PS: There is an Eski in the cool room I made up for your trip, enjoy.'

"Hmm yum, I love the way she looks after us," I said to Jimmy. "You are very lucky to have such a good Mom, aren't you?" I said as I went in for another kiss. I put the stove on and got some bowls out of the cupboard and asked Jimmy what he would like to drink.

He said, "A coke would do fine," I got him one out of the fridge and a diet coke for myself. Maree turned up just in time so I got her a diet coke out as well and dished dinner up.

Before we went upstairs to bed, we all agreed to meet in the kitchen for breakfast at seven in the morning. Maree went first, she said she had nearly finished her assignment. Said it would only take one more hour then she was going to have an early night after giving Eli a call goodnight. I asked Jimmy if he could stay and he said he was happy to do that. We went to bed early still so we would be fresh for the drive tomorrow. It would take about six hours, I guessed.

I got another early morning wakeup call from Jimmy before the alarm even went off. I was still tired and not really in the mood but went through the motions anyway. I fell back into sleep and the alarm went off an hour later. Jimmy was already up and gone.

I got showered and dressed in tracksuit pants and a maroon T-shirt. I wanted to be comfortable on the trip. I cleaned my teeth and did my hair up in a ponytail. I grabbed my bag and went downstairs. It was 6:45 am and I was the first one there.

I put my bag near the front door and put the kettle on. 10 minutes later, Jimmy and Maree turned up and they put their bags near the door as well. I handed them both a coffee and made some toast for breakfast. We had a furnace of coffee for the trip and Jimmy went to bring the truck around the front.

He put the Eski in the back and all of our luggage. We had both chosen a book out of the front room library on the way out for the drive and locked the door behind us. We climbed up into the cab, me in the front with Jimmy and Maree sat in the back.

The trip up to Tin Can Bay was quite uneventful; we stopped for lunch at Morayfield at KFC and put more petrol in and stretched our legs. We had music from Spotify going all the way and arrived at 3:30 in the afternoon. Jimmy parked the truck in the driveway near the ramp that led to the veranda out the front.

We unloaded our luggage and the boxes. Jimmy and I stayed in Mom's old room because it had a queen size bed and Maree stayed in her room across the hall. Jimmy put the Eski in the kitchen and I emptied the contents into the fridge.

We all had a piece of fruit cake and coffee for afternoon tea and got stuck into the packing. Jimmy started in the garage and I started in the kitchen and Maree started in her bedroom. We didn't stop till the sun went down. We had left over curried sausages and rice for dinner then went back to packing. We went to bed around nine; after such a big day, we all slept really well.

I got my usual wakeup call from Jimmy; I didn't mind though; it was time to get up anyway. I headed for the shower. Then put my hair up in a messy bun and got dressed into dark blue shorts and a dusky pink top. Maree was already up when we went to the kitchen for a coffee.

Maree made us some porridge for breakfast and we all sat at the table to eat. Jimmy said he was making good head way with the garage and Maree and

I were making a dent as well. Maree and I did a lot of reminiscing when it came to photos and awards that we had from growing up.

By Friday night, we had got fish and chips from the local takeaway and sat around the dining room table assessing what else needed to be done. Jimmy had nearly finished the garage and Maree had finished with her room, the spare room and the bathroom.

I had finished the kitchen and my old room. Now we were both halfway through Mom's room and still had to do the ensuite. We were planning to have that finished tonight and clean the whole house over the weekend while the guys were loading the furniture.

Everything went smoothly over the weekend and we gave Jason a carton of his favorite beer to thank him for helping us. The carpet and pest control got done by the same company on Monday morning. Maree and I went to the local real estate agent and organized for them to look after it as a rental property.

By one o'clock, we were back on the road and headed home. We arrived home at 6:30 that night. I had rung Silvia earlier in the day and asked her to have dinner waiting for us. It was good to arrive home to a yummy roast lamb with all the trimmings. I put the kettle on and read the note Silvia had left on the kitchen bench.

'Dear Amber, Maree and Jimmy, hope you had a good trip. There is a roast lamb and vegetables in the oven on low and beans and carrots on the stove. Just needs heating up, there is gravy in the microwave, mint jelly is in the fridge and an apple pie in the fridge for dessert. Love Silvia.'

It was good to be home. Jimmy parked the truck out the back in the shed. He was going to get Stuart to help him unload it in the morning and came back to get the fire going.

I put the beans and carrots on to heat them up and got some plates out and we all really enjoyed the meal and afterwards, Jimmy went home and Maree and I went to have an early night. I had a nice hot spa bath with some Epson salts to help with my aching muscles from all the cleaning and lifting we had to do. I topped it up twice to stop it from going cold. In the end, I had to get out, I put a nightie on and hopped into bed. I pretty much fell asleep straight away.

Chapter 11

Jimmy went home after dinner because he wanted some privacy to ring his dad. He lit his own fire then gave him a call. His Dad answered straight away. "Hey son, how are you? I've got some good news. I'm watching the target as we speak, she's talking to her pimp at the moment but he has to leave soon. I'll let you know when I've got her contained," he said.

Jimmy asked, "How old is she? You know I don't want her to be too old." His Dad said, "Don't worry, she only looks about 16 at the most. Might just be a runaway, looks like it anyway."

"Alright Dad good work, let me know how things go," Jimmy said and hung up the phone.

He grabbed a beer out of the fridge and sat down to wait. He put the television on and the news came on. They were still looking for Rachel Gibbs and now they were offering a fifty-thousand-dollar reward but still had no leads. It was only an hour later that his dad rang. He sounded really excited.

"I've got her, son," he was saying. "She's tied up in the back."

"OK, Dad, when are you expecting to be home?"

"Probably Wednesday night, Thursday morning at the latest," he said.

"OK, well give me a call when you get back and Dad, don't forget to take your medication."

"Yeah, yeah, I'll take it now, goodnight son, we'll talk again soon."

Jimmy had one more beer then he was feeling horny after thinking about the 16-year-old girl he had coming. He looked at his watch, it was only 9:30 pm. He decided to go back to the house and stay with Amber. Her bedroom door was unlocked and he let himself in. He wasn't expecting her to be asleep but he needed her.

He slid in beside her; she was snoring softly. He put his hand up between her legs and removed her panties. Amber was woken up and felt slightly annoyed by Jimmy helping himself. She realized he wasn't stopping; she groaned and tried to push him away but he came up and starting kissing her and saying, "come on, please," in the end she relented and let him go. She couldn't help the amount of orgasms he was able to make her body have. Afterwards, Jimmy cuddled up behind her and they both fell asleep.

He was gone when I woke up. I went in and ran the shower and thought about last night, thinking Jimmy was pretty forceful. I didn't feel good about that side of things but I also hadn't been so pleased sexually before. It confused me somewhat.

My body still ached from the move so I stayed there twice as long as I normally would. I didn't need to do my hair so I just put it up and put a pair of denim shorts and a pink T-shirt with a white heart on the front of it and went downstairs for a coffee.

Maree was already in the kitchen reading the paper and eating her breakfast. I said "good morning," as I entered the kitchen and Maree and Silvia said it back. I sat down and Silvia handed me my coffee.

"I hear the move went well," she said.

"Yeah, I will feel better when it's all finished, we still have to unload the truck yet," I said. I had scrambled eggs on toast and a second cup of coffee. Then we were ready to get stuck into it.

Jimmy and Stuart were out the back chatting when we arrived. "Oh good, here comes the help," he said.

"Ha-ha, very funny," I said and we all laughed. We spent the next couple of hours helping to unload the truck and put it all up in the attic. We thanked Stuart and gave him a bottle of his favorite scotch, Johnny Walker black label. When Maree and I finished, we decided we were going to go for a swim, clothes and all.

We were so hot and sweaty we didn't care. Afterwards, we had a shower in the changing room near the pool and wrapped ourselves in towels. Then went upstairs to get dressed.

Maree was hanging to see Eli; he was picking her up at three in the afternoon to go and spend some time together. The new policeman had settled in over the weekend and today was his second shift, so Eli finally had the afternoon off.

She was waiting on the front steps when he arrived, she jumped up and ran to hop into the car. She leaned over to get a hug. With all the computer stuff in the middle, it wasn't that easy.

He hadn't really made any plan so he asked Maree what she wanted to do. She said she would love to go and see where he lived. He was a bit embarrassed because he hadn't had a chance to clean so he asked her to sit out the front for about 15 minutes. She agreed to let him take whatever time he needed to clean.

It gave her a chance to look around outside. He lived in a two-bedroom house out the west side of town. It was surrounded by trees and had a carport out the front. She heard him vacuuming and giggled to herself thinking how sweet he was to be doing the cleaning first.

Fifteen minutes later, he was opening the door and making a grand gesture to come on in. Maree entered the kitchen first. There was a dining room table in the middle of the room and it led into the lounge that only had the bare necessities.

A lounge, television, fire place, coffee table and a plant in the corner that had seen better days. He asked if she wanted a cup of coffee and she accepted. While the kettle was on, Maree went and checked out the rest of the place. Then came back and watched him making the coffee.

"What's the new guy like?" Maree asked.

"He's about 30 years old, his name is Frank, I guess you would say he is average in build and looks. He's from Murwoolinbah so he kind of knows the area. What else, um he's married and has two little girls, primary school age. I haven't met the family yet but he seems pretty down to earth and seems to take his job pretty seriously too. I think he will fit in really well; he's even got a pretty good sense of humor. You'll get to meet him soon enough." She put her arms around him and said she had really missed him. He picked her up and took her down the hallway to his bedroom. They made love and cuddled and talked till it was dark.

Then they went for a drive to grab a steak burger and chips from the general store. They sat at one of the tables out the front of the shop to eat. Then he dropped her back home and kissed her goodnight. I'll stay another night, he was saying. He said he had a Skype meeting with his sister and her kids at 8:30 that he wanted to be home for.

Amber heard the car in the drive, she was sitting at the kitchen bench having a glass of wine and Jimmy was beside her, drinking a beer. So she got another wine glass out of the cupboard and handed it to her sister when she entered the kitchen.

She was in such a good mood and told them all about her afternoon. Then she went to check her email in the front room. There was one from the Department of Education; it said, 'Dear Miss Maree Stokes, Limpinwood state primary school is quite a small school with only 63 students so as you could imagine we do have to combine our classes into three groups. Kindergarten and grade one are together, two, three and four are together and five and six are also combined. We would be happy to have you on board beginning at the start of the school year. Kind Regards, Minister of Education James O'Grady.' Maree was ecstatic.

She came flying into the kitchen and said, "I can't believe it, I got the job," we congratulated her and celebrated long into the night. We didn't get to bed till about 2 in the morning and I didn't wake up till 11. Jimmy had left already. I didn't have anything to rush out of bed for so I just went to clean my teeth and get the taste of alcohol from the night before out of my mouth.

I put my dressing gown on and went downstairs. My calves hurt as I did the stairs which brought back a vague memory of dancing to my mind. I also had a vague memory of Jimmy and I having pretty full-on sex as well. My head hurt. I went straight to the fridge to get a drink of water.

I said "hi," and sat down heavily at the kitchen bench with my head in my hands. Silvia handed me some Panadol which I gratefully took. She handed me my coffee. "Thanks, where's Maree?" I asked.

"She went to see Eli down at the police station. She's pretty happy about the job," Silvia said, she put a plate of bacon, egg and tomato on toast in front of me. I didn't think I would be able to eat much but I picked away to begin with and by the time I was onto my second coffee, I was starting to feel human again.

"Yes, we definitely celebrated it last night. We went through a few bottles of wine too," I said. Silvia knew as she had taken the trash out earlier. She was pretty sure Jimmy had drunk at least a half a carton of beer as well.

After breakfast, I went upstairs to think about getting dressed. On the way, I changed my mind and headed for Alice's room instead. I opened the door and when my eyes adjusted, I noticed Alice was lying on the bed. I went over and sat on the edge of the bed.

I said "Hi Alice," she was just looking at me waiting for me to say something. I didn't know what to say.

Then she said "I miss my mummy," and rolled onto her stomach and cried into her pillow. I knew I had to do something.

I said "alright, I'll see what I can do. I'm not sure if Jimmy's Dad is back yet or not though."

I was a bit scared of Jimmy's Dad after watching him carry on out the back that day out the laundry window and Earl had warned me to be wary of him as well as of Jimmy and his mother. So I felt I really needed to pick my time to be checking out the hedge around the tree or using the road that led from the river to Jimmy's parents' place.

I didn't want them to think I was suspicious of any of them at all. They could all be totally innocent and I could be barking up the wrong tree completely. I left the room and went back down the hallway to my bedroom.

I had a shower and got dressed in some track suit pants and a black T-shirt. I didn't bother with a bra because I wasn't going anywhere. I had so many boxes to sort through up in the attic. I just wanted to go through and keep what was precious and store the rest.

I stopped for a sandwich at about three then got back into it. When the sun went down, I went back downstairs to the kitchen. Maree was there with Eli stirring a pot on the stove. I walked in from the back of the house.

"Hello, you two love birds," I said and went to look at the note on the bench that Silvia had left. 'Dear Amber and Maree, there is some spaghetti Bolognese on the stove, just need to cook the spaghetti. There is a vanilla cheese cake in the fridge for dessert. Love Silvia.'

I took a seat at the kitchen bench after I cracked open a can of diet coke I got out of the fridge and waited for it to be ready. I hadn't heard from Jimmy this afternoon so I didn't know whether his dad was home yet or not. The last time he was, I didn't see much of him, so I wasn't expecting to see him if he wasn't here already. I asked if either of them had seen Jimmy and they both shook their heads.

After dinner, I went to pick a movie from the DVD library in the front room and took it up to my bedroom to watch while I was in bed. It was a chick flick called 'The Notebook' it was a bit of a tear jerker and it finished at about 10 pm. Tonight I decided to lock my door, I didn't want Jimmy coming in, waking me up and hassling me again.

Jimmy's Dad rang about 6pm and said he was in Sydney and would be home tomorrow night. Jimmy went out and using the light from the shed, chopped wood till about 9:30 then went to have a shower. He got dressed and couldn't stop thinking about the girl he had coming.

He had told his dad not to touch her because he wanted to be the first. After his shower, he opened a beer and put the television on. The late-night news was on. They mentioned Rachel Gibbs but saying they didn't hold much hope because it had been over a week.

Jimmy turned the television off and thought about going over to the house to have sex with Amber. Then he thought about the way she reacted to him waking her up last night, it was 10:30 already and he knew that she had been busy all day up in the attic.

Which means she'll probably be tired and maybe had gone to bed early, so he decided against it. He went to bed and fixed himself up instead while he thought about the young girl that was on her way to him.

I slept till eight and felt a bit better today not as sore as yesterday, I went in to shower and get ready for the day. I dried my hair and put a pretty blue dress on and some earrings to match and went downstairs for breakfast. Silvia had made a breaky wrap with bacon, egg and cheese on and barbeque sauce, I really enjoyed it.

Maree said she was spending the day with Eli going up to the waterfall that we had seen that day we went on the motorbikes with Jimmy. They were going on the bikes. They asked if I wanted to go with them but I didn't want to be a third wheel. I also thought it would be romantic for them to go alone. After breakfast, I waved as they rode out the drive. One on each bike.

I went back into the kitchen and had a second cup of coffee while I read the paper. Afterwards, I went to go looking for Jimmy. He wasn't chopping wood so I went to check his house, he wasn't there either; his Ute was still parked in its usual spot beside the house under the carport. I ended up finding him out the side of the house working on the gardens.

He was hot and sweaty and even had dirt on his face from where he had wiped the sweat. I went inside to get him a cold drink, I grabbed a can of coke out of the cool room and a diet coke for myself. I walked back out the front door because it was closer. He had the wheel barrow there and was pulling the weeds out. He was two thirds of the way along so he had been out there all morning.

I chatted to him for a while and he seemed a bit distant. I asked if he knew when his dad was coming home. He said he would be home tonight and not to expect him to be around much for the next week or so but promised to have all his chores done regardless. I left him to his gardening and went back into the house.

I went upstairs to Alice's bedroom and she was in front of the doll's house chatting away. I didn't think she heard me come in. I called her name to get her attention. She turned to me and smiled and said, "Hello Amber."

I said, "come on, we're going now."

Alice got up and followed me out of the bedroom, down the hallway to my room. I grabbed my hand bag and ran downstairs. I didn't see Silvia as I walked through the kitchen where I grabbed my keys off the hook and went out through the French doors. Through the gate and into the second bay of the garage.

I got into my BMW and looked around for Alice. She had disappeared. I pressed the button for the garage door and warmed the engine up for a while before I drove out of the drive. Jimmy was still working in the garden beside the house. As I drove down the lane, Alice had reappeared in the passenger seat.

I said, "Hey you, I thought you had left me."

"No, I didn't want Jimmy to see me," she said. We turned right at the end of the lane, drove five kilometers then turned right again then five minutes later. Just as I was coming closer to the driveway of Jimmy's parents' house, I noticed Silvia's red Tesla in the driveway.

I pressed my foot on the brake and quickly did a U-turn and went back the way we came. Alice disappeared as soon as we noticed Silvia's car, she got scared. I did too, I wasn't expecting that.

I drove past our place on the way back and went to the bakery in town. I parked out the front and bought a chunky steak pie and an apple turnover and sat out the front on the table and chairs they had out there. There were another three tables, an old couple were sitting at one and the other two were empty.

It was quite peaceful really, a couple of cars went past and I watched a young couple with a baby coming out of the general store with an arm load of groceries and struggling to put the baby, the pram and the shopping all into their brown station wagon they had parked beside me. It was nice to just sit back and watch the world go by.

When I got home, Jimmy was still working on the gardens down the side of the house. I ran up to my room and put my hand bag away. I got changed into a one piece and headed down to the pool. Silvia must have still been out, I thought because I didn't see her on the way through. I did at least thirty laps having a rest in between when I needed to get my breath back.

Then did a bit of a meditation before getting out. I laid down in the sun for a while and turned over after 20 minutes. After another 20 minutes, my swim suit was dry. I grabbed my towel and put it in the laundry on my way upstairs.

I went straight to my bedroom to get changed then spent the rest of the afternoon going through two of the rooms upstairs, reorganizing the furniture and putting different linen on in one of the rooms. I was thinking I may have to number the rooms maybe, so I could keep track. I made a list to get some and organize key numbers as well. There is a lot to think of, I thought but kept plugging away.

I rang Harry Goldman and told him about what I was planning to do with the place and asked for his expertise in what I needed to do for insurance purposes as well as a liquor license and anything else that needed to be done. He said he would look into it all and he also offered to come down and do both our wills and have everything else sorted.

He promised to get his secretary to organize an appointment and redirected the call back to her. His secretary came on the line and lined up an appointment for the following Tuesday at one pm. I thanked her and hung up.

When it started to get dark, I went downstairs to the kitchen to see what was for dinner. Maree and Eli were already there. I said hello and went to look at Silvia's note, it said, 'Dear Amber and Maree, there is some sweet and sour pork and fried rice I've made in the microwave, just need to heat it up and there is a custard tart in the fridge for dessert. Love Silvia.'

"Yum," I said as I went to get a six pack of southern comfort out of the cool room. I took one out and put the rest in the fridge. Maree was telling me about their day at the waterfall. It sounded like they had a ball. She was sitting on the bench and Eli was standing between her legs. Maree had a wine in her hand and Eli was having a beer.

I asked if he was driving, he said, "hell no, I'm staying over, I hope you don't mind."

"No, not at all. You're welcome here anytime, Eli," I said. I turned the microwave on for four minutes and got three plates out. Maree was still excited about getting the job and Eli was so proud of her. You could tell by the way he looked at her as she spoke. He was very much in love with her and so was she.

The fire was already lit so I guessed Jimmy wouldn't be home for dinner. We sat at the kitchen bench, ate dinner and had custard tart for dessert. After dinner, I grabbed a movie from the front room and went upstairs. I had a shower and settled in bed to watch the movie. It was another chick flick called 'The Holiday' with Cameron Diaz in it.

Alice came and laid beside me to watch it with me. Which I felt was so sweet. After the movie, she went back to her own room. I switched the television off and went to sleep. I didn't see Jimmy's lights come in.

Jimmy's Dad rang when he arrived at six o'clock that night. Jimmy answered the phone and his dad said he was home but the girl would have to stay in the truck till he was sure that Silvia was asleep. Jimmy didn't go over till 10:30 that night, that way he could be sure.

He turned his lights and engine off as he rolled into the driveway. All the lights upstairs at his moms were off, so the place was in darkness.

He let himself in to his dad's place downstairs. He walked in through the lounge to the dining room where his dad was sitting with a beer. "Give me your keys," he said as he entered the room. His Dad threw him the keys to his truck. Jimmy went out the front door and down the left-hand side of the house to the Kenworth.

He opened the door and climbed up and in. The girl was asleep in the cab. She had a black pillow slip over her head and her mouth taped up. Jimmy picked her up and heard her try to scream but not much noise came out. He carried her in through the front door and down the hallway to the first room on the right. Her arms and legs were tied but she still tried to fight.

He plonked her down onto the bed and told her to settle down or he would kill her. He took the pillow slip off her head so he could see the fear in her eyes.

Lisa Redding hadn't been with many men before. She had run away from home because her stepfather had tried to rape her and her mom wouldn't believe her. She met Adam while she was hitchhiking around Melbourne. He had offered her a place to stay and a way to make some easy money.

She was scared but agreed to give it a go. Her first client was a truck driver. He had offered her five hundred dollars for the whole night. Lisa rang Adam to tell him that she would be at a certain motel just outside of town and she would catch up with him tomorrow.

Jimmy's Dad had some chloroform on the hanky he had in his pocket. He got it out while she was talking. As soon as she hung up, he put it over her mouth from behind. Took the phone off her and tied her up. He put some tape over her mouth and a dark pillow slip on her head. Then put her in the sleeper's cab.

He gave Jimmy a call when he had the girl contained. Then started the long drive home and drove as far as Sydney. He had to stop halfway to have a sleep. He just stopped at one of the roadside truck stops on the side of the highway. The only other time was to fuel up near Newcastle.

Lisa was worried that nobody would even know she was missing for at least 12 hours or more. That's if Adam even tells anyone, she thought. She knew she was doomed. The truck finally stopped after 2 full days of driving. She didn't know where she was but the truck driver had gone inside and left her alone in the truck.

She was so tied up she couldn't do anything and with the pillow slip on, she couldn't see anything. She didn't even know if it was day or night anymore either.

She kept drifting in and out of sleep. She heard the driver's door open and felt somebody grab her and carry her over his shoulder and into a building and put her down on a bed. Jimmy took the pillow slip off her head. Then he said he was going to untie her legs and take her to the shower.

He threatened to hurt her if she made any noise. He led her into the bathroom by her wrists and ran the water. Then made her take her clothes off and get in and wash herself out properly. When she was done, Jimmy led her back into the bedroom and tied her naked body up to the bed.

Jimmy took his time and kissed and caressed her whole body. He licked her vagina and put his finger in and kept licking while moving his finger around inside her body; she was bucking and she was trying to get out of the ropes around her wrists and her ankles.

The more she tried, the more she felt pain and the more she fought, the more Jimmy liked it. He got on top and put himself inside her, he fucked her slowly at first then he got more and more carried away; he was licking and sucking her nipples and guiding her body up to meet his till he finally exploded.

He collapsed on top of her and he was heavy. She had trouble for a minute till he realized he was squashing her. He put the pillow slip back on her head and pulled a blanket up over her and told her to sleep.

Jimmy turned the bedroom light off and went back out to where his dad was sitting at the kitchen table with his beer. Jimmy went to the fridge and got himself one. "You did good Dad," he said, "we will try not to damage this one, I want this one to last. Have you taken your medication today, Dad?" he asked.

His Dad reached over and got a tablet out of the packet on the table. He took a swig of his beer to wash it down. They sat there and talked for a while then Jimmy got up to leave. It was already 1:30 in the morning. He went in to have one last feel of his new toy before he left. He knew his dad would be in there next pleasing himself but he had told him to be gentle and he knew he would.

Lisa was terrified, she could hear them talking but couldn't make out what they were saying. After the one called Jimmy, the big good-looking guy left, the truck driver came in, he took the pillow slip off and he smelled disgusting like he hadn't showered for a week.

His hair was oily and had his fingers inside her and kept playing with himself while he was doing it then got on top and put himself inside her. It only took about a minute before he came and then rubbed himself all over her face. Then he untied her and made her take a shower. He tied her back up to the bed and put the pillow slip back on and the blanket back up and left the room.

This would be the third night that she would be missing and she was praying that Adam would tell somebody. She didn't know where she was but she knew she was at least 2 days drive away. She slept on and off.

She thought even if Adam did get help, he wouldn't know anything anyway. The older guy with the oily hair, he obviously lived here. She noticed all the windows had newspaper on them, which she thought was a bit weird but it stopped her seeing anything else.

Chapter 12

I woke up at 6:30 in the morning, dressed in my workout gear and headed for the gym. I cranked the music videos up out the front and did an aerobics workout that lasted nearly an hour. Then cooled down for the next 15 minutes. I had taken a set of clean clothes with me and had a shower at the gym afterwards. I put my hair up in a towel and headed for the kitchen.

Silvia had only just arrived and was putting her bag in the pantry. I was surprised when I looked at my watch, she was never normally late. I asked if everything was alright because she looked a bit flustered like she hadn't gotten enough sleep or something.

"I'm fine," she said. "Just had a shit of a night, that's all," she had stayed up last night and turned the lights off about 9:30 like she would normally do. But instead of going to bed, she waited to see Jimmy arrive and carry a young girl out of the truck. I said I knew the feeling and told her to go home and have a rest. She declined and put the kettle on instead.

I told her not to worry if she wanted to take off a bit early, she was welcome to do what she pleased. She cooked me some bacon, eggs, tomato and onion with toast. When I was halfway through my breakfast, Maree and Eli came in. They both sat down at the kitchen bench and Eli said, "We'll have what she's having, please."

"No worries," Silvia said, "coming right up." She made them coffee and me a second cup. We were just talking about what we had planned for the day while we were eating. Eli had to go to work at nine so he was dressed in his uniform. Maree was asking me about the house and where I was up to with getting the place ready for the bed and breakfast.

I told her about my phone call to Harry Goldman and how he would be out here on Tuesday afternoon at one pm. "He's going to go through the insurances and licenses I will need to sell alcohol and run this place as a retreat. He is also going to do both our wills as well. I know you start school that day but by the time you get home, he'll be ready to do your last will and testament."

"Yeah, no worries, that sounds great," she said.

After breakfast, Maree went out to say goodbye to Eli. He had the police car parked out the front. She gave him a kiss goodbye and told him she would catch up after work. She was planning to surprise him by cooking for him at his place tonight and wanted my advice on how she could go about it. I said she would have to either cook something that wouldn't take long or ask him for his keys and tell him that she wanted to surprise him.

She ended up asking Silvia for a good recipe and she had a few ideas. Maree thought she would like to try a lasagna. She thought if she cooked it here, she would have Silvia to help and she could easily make a salad in a bowl and just take the dressing with her.

They also made some cheesy garlic bread to go with it. She decided to meet him at work with all the dinner things. I agreed to drop her off at the police station just before 5:30 when he was due to knock off.

I left them to it and went upstairs to keep going through the bedrooms turning them into rooms for people to stay. I had almost finished the whole left side of the building. That was the room next door to mine.

It had the same design as Aunt Mary's room with the front room that the door opens up to but then it had a kitchenette on the left-hand side and the wardrobe and ensuite was on the far wall and a dressing table on the right. It had some really pretty bedside lamps too. They were in the shape of a moon. I almost took them for my room but I decided against it.

The one next door to that I had finished and the other two rooms across the hall were just about finished. I wanted to change the linen and I had asked Silvia to make sure she cleaned them thoroughly. I made sure all the kitchenettes had the right amount of cutlery and crockery.

Kettles, toasters and microwaves. A spare blanket, pillows, ironing boards and irons in the cupboards. A luggage rack and towels, I put soap, shampoo and conditioner on the list. I was going to have to buy things like that off line. I only had four rooms to go through now.

I had been busy all morning and was starting to feel hungry, so I went downstairs to get something for lunch. Maree and Silvia were making the lasagna, they were making one each. Maree was copying what Silvia was doing.

So I knew what I would be having for dinner. Silvia made me a ham and tomato sandwich. I washed it down with a diet coke and went back upstairs to continue my work.

Jimmy got his chores done early and went to his dad's. He let himself in, Jimmy's Dad wasn't home; he must be down at the shop, he told himself. He didn't care though that's not who he came to see. He went through the front room and right down the hallway and into the bedroom.

Lisa was asleep but not for long, the big guy was back, he took the pillow slip off her head and said, "Good morning, I've missed you." He bent down and kissed her cheek and started working his way down from there taking his time. Making sure he was gentle enough to really turn her on.

He licked and sucked her nipples and down the side of her breast and across to the other one then down further to her navel. His need for her was strong and he wanted her to want him too. He kept one hand on her left breast and used his fingers to part her flaps then started licking her clit. He let go of her breast and concentrated more on her vagina, making her squirt and go into orgasmic spasms.

Lisa didn't want to like it but her body was reacting to everything this guy was doing. He was so gentle, she almost enjoyed it. When he was finished pleasing her with his tongue, he climbed onto the bed and put himself into her wet pussy which turned him on even more.

He rode her for at least an hour stopping to lick her vagina every now and again, he was relentless. He finally blew his load inside of her and laid down beside her till his breathing and heart rate returned to normal. He caressed the side of her face and then said, "Thank you."

Jimmy got up and pulled the blanket back up over her. Then went out to the kitchen and grabbed himself a beer. After a couple of beers, he went back into the bedroom and untied Lisa and led her into the shower and made her wash herself out.

Then took her back to the bedroom and tied her up. His father was still out when he left. He must have gone to Murwoolinbah to get some supplies, he thought.

He left to go home and start the fire in the main house. Nobody was there and he was glad he didn't have to deal with anybody. He left straight away after he had a quick shower, he went to get some takeaway from the general store and went back to his dad's place. His Dad was home by that stage and happy to have the burger and chips his son brought with him.

Jimmy told his dad to take his medication, which he did. After he had eaten, he went into the bedroom where the girl was and gently raped her again. This time, he turned her over and fucked her ass as well. She cried and fought but that only turned him on more. So he flipped her back over and this time, he wasn't so gentle.

Then dragged her by the hair to the bathroom and made her wash herself out properly. He tied her back up to the bed and let his dad have a go. He went home and left him to it. After a nice hot shower, he watched the late-night news and there was nothing about the prostitute. He turned the television off and had an early night.

I sat at the kitchen bench by myself reflecting on my day and how much I still had to do. I hadn't seen Jimmy all day and wasn't really expecting to either. I heated up a piece of the lasagna and got some salad out of the bowl in the fridge. I got the chili, lime and mango dressing out of the fridge door and put the cheesy garlic bread in the oven.

After dinner, I went to pick a book out of the library in the front room and went upstairs to get settled for the night. I had a shower first and washed and dried my hair. Then put my nightie on and hopped into bed. I kind of missed Jimmy and feeling a bit horny, I left the door unlocked just in case he came while I slept. He didn't though. I was so tired and fell asleep only a couple of pages in.

The next morning, I woke up early and dressed in my workout gear and put my runners on. I grabbed a water bottle from the fridge and left via the front door. I ran across the lawn and into the woods. I followed the path all the way to the river.

I crossed the bridge and up the small incline and down to the spot where Jimmy's car was parked and out of sheer curiosity, I ran all the way to Silvia's place. I hid where nobody could see me. I could see Jimmy's car in the driveway and his dad's truck was on the far side of the house.

I looked at my watch, it was only 8am. Silvia would have been at work. I really wanted to check out the hedge again but I was just as scared of getting caught by Jimmy as I was by his dad. I turned around and headed back home. Maree and Silvia were in the kitchen when I entered via the front door.

"Good morning," I said as I took my spot at the bench. They returned the greeting and went back to what they were doing. Maree was scrolling through Facebook on her phone and Silvia was busy at the stove. She was making a savory mince to have on toast. She handed me a coffee and I thanked her. I asked Maree how her date went last night.

She said he loved it and that he had only just dropped her home this morning before work. "That's great," I said. I read the local paper while I was eating my breakfast. Then had a second cup of coffee. Silvia went off to do some laundry and I left to go and sort out some other rooms.

I was starting on the room at the top of the stairs. It had a wheel chair in it so it must have been Uncle Kenny's. It had all the hand railings and special shower and toilet designed for a wheel chair. I finished it by about lunchtime.

I went down the hall to my bedroom and put on a black bikini and grabbed a towel out of the linen cupboard in the hallway. I ran downstairs and found Maree and Silvia in the kitchen looking at more recipes. They had half a dozen cookbooks on the bench.

Eli had loved it so much, she just wanted to do more. They ended up settling on a beef stroganoff and a caramel tart for dessert. I made myself a sandwich with corned meat and tomato and sat down at the bench. Silvia poured me an orange juice.

I went for a swim after lunch, just a relaxing one though because I had already done my run this morning and I had been busy upstairs all morning. I did a meditation while I was floating and then went into the spa for a while. I got to thinking about Jimmy and how I didn't really get to see him when his dad was home. I didn't want to nag him about it though. So I decided to try and catch up with him when he came to do the fire.

After my swim, I went upstairs to pick a nice aqua colored dress to wear and went downstairs to wait. I put the music on and got a southern comfort can out of the fridge. Maree was finished with her cooking and got a bottle of wine out of the fridge.

Silvia had already left for the day. We were dancing and singing and I drank a little too quickly. So by the time Jimmy came in to light the fire around five, I was a little drunk.

"Hey Jimmy," I said as he entered the lounge.

He said, "Hi sweetheart," and gave me a kiss. I didn't want to stop there. Maree had taken her cue to leave when he came in. He fobbed me off and said,

"Come on let me light the fire," I let him finish lighting the fire then asked if he wanted to stay for dinner. I was surprised when he said he would. I got him a can of Jack Daniels and he drank and sang and danced with me.

Eli turned up about six. I answered the door and pointed to the stairs and said, "She's up there," he thanked me and climbed the stairs. I went back into the lounge to party with Jimmy. Maree came down to dish dinner up about seven and we all sat at the dining room table to eat. Maree was pleased with the way the stroganoff turned out and we all complimented her on it and the caramel tart for dessert.

Maree and Eli disappeared up to her room after dinner. I grabbed a couple more cans and asked Jimmy to come upstairs with me. After watching her dance half the night, he couldn't wait to get her naked. I carried the cans and he carried me.

I was giggling all the way upstairs. I opened my bedroom door; he carried me through and laid me down on the bed. He was kissing me and I was kissing him back. He pulled my underwear off and disappeared under my dress. He was driving me nuts with his mouth and tongue.

He came back up and lifted my dress off over my head and undid my bra. I undid his pants and pulled his hips toward me. I sucked him till he was close to cuming then while I was doing that, he was fiddling about with his fingers in my vagina then his finger went slightly into my rear.

I told him no not there but he kept doing both front and back and telling me to relax and enjoy it till I relaxed and let him do whatever he wanted. I had a little too much to drink so I was pretty relaxed. He went back down on me again and made me squirt my juices all over the sheets.

I begged him to come back up and fuck me and he did, long and hard. We both got a pretty big workout then lay in each other's arms feeling pretty well spent. I woke up in the morning and Jimmy was still there. I was surprised and watched him sleeping. He was breathing easily and looking gorgeous and relaxed.

Then he opened his big beautiful blue eyes and looked over at me and smiled. My heart skipped a beat and I kissed him; he kissed me back and then fucked me all over again. I got up to go and have a shower. Jimmy said he had things to do so he left and I went and enjoyed a nice hot shower.

My body reacted just from the thought of everything we had done last night. I was floating on a cloud when I got dressed and went downstairs for breakfast.

Nobody was in the kitchen when I entered but there was a note on the bench, it said, 'Dear Amber and Maree, I have gone to Murwoolinbah to get some supplies; if you need anything, just give me a call. I'll be back this afternoon. Love Silvia.'

I went to put the kettle on and looked in the bread bin. I found some raisin toast and put two slices in the toaster and got the butter out of the fridge. I got the milk as well and put some coffee into my coffee mug. The toast popped and by the time I finished buttering it, the kettle was boiling. I made my coffee and sat down at the kitchen bench to eat.

I couldn't get Jimmy out of my head. I didn't expect any of last night. It put me in a good mood for the rest of the day and I managed to get two more rooms sorted. One was a family room with two beds just to the right of the stairs, the other across the hallway from that. I didn't see Maree till she and Eli came to dinner that night.

We had tacos and sat at the table talking till late. We were only drinking soft drink after last night's effort. We were talking about Maree's job and how lucky she was to get something local. She was telling us that she had put her resignation in at the school in Tin Can Bay and how upset they were that she was leaving.

I didn't see Jimmy that night, Maree said he had been to light the fire early and told her to tell me he'll be busy helping his dad tonight. Maree was talking about going kayaking tomorrow. She wanted to take Eli because he had a day off. She had already asked Jimmy if we could use the Ute.

I didn't want to get in the way but she insisted I go. We planned to meet in the kitchen at 8:30 in the morning. I left at 10 o'clock to go upstairs to bed and left them to lock up and turn the lights off.

I had a quick shower, dried my hair and put my nightie on. I set the alarm for 7:30 and fell asleep quite quickly. Not before I had seen the lights on the wall from Jimmy's car coming home around 11. I wondered what they did the whole time. Him and his dad, surely, they were doing more than just drinking beer.

The next day the alarm went off and I got up and got dressed in a pair of black bike pants and a thin pink cotton shirt tied at the waist. I put my hair up into a messy bun and had my aqua bikini on underneath and grabbed a beach towel on my way downstairs. Maree had left a note for Silvia telling her we would need a picnic lunch for four. Just in case Jimmy ended up coming.

Jimmy already had the kayaks tied up in the back of the Ute out the front of the last bay of the garage. It was the first time I had seen Eli in normal civilian clothes. He looked a lot more relaxed. Maree was in a fantastic mood and I was happy to be going out for the day. Jimmy said he had too much to do. The truth was he didn't want to spend the day with the local cop.

We drove out of the driveway and through the gates and down the lane then turned right and headed for Jimmy's parents' place. Another right and another left then we drove down the track that took us to the boat ramp.

I was telling Eli about the dreams I'd been having and he seemed quite receptive. He was telling us about a friend of his who used to dream about things before they happened.

We carried the kayaks down to the water. Eli carried one on his own and Maree and I carried one between us. Then went back for the last one. We put our backpacks on and headed for the river with our oars in hand.

It was so peaceful; the birds were chirping and the sun was shining. We paddled all the way down to where we had gone the last time when it was just Maree and I. We pulled up onto the little beach and laid out a cloth on the grassy area.

Silvia had packed some corned meat, tomato, lettuce, beetroot, a rice salad, a pasta salad and bread rolls to go with it. I was telling Maree and Eli about the rooms upstairs and how far I had gotten with turning the house into a bed and breakfast when we heard the sound of a dog barking.

It was not a normal bark though; it sounded like he was in distress. It sounded like it was coming from further up the river. We all looked at each other and left everything where it was and jumped into the kayaks and paddled further up the river and around the next bend.

We could hear it coming from another two hundred meters up the river, there were a few branches trapped near the edge on the right-hand side, a dog was caught in among them.

As we got closer, we could see it was a little black dog with a white patch on his chest. His foot was tangled in the tree branch. He barked again when he saw us. He kept barking till we reached him. He knew we were here to help. We left our kayaks on the river bank and went to rescue the dog. He was barking and yelping till Eli managed to untangle his foot. I half expected him to bite Eli but he didn't.

He nearly licked us all to death instead. He had no collar on and I didn't see any properties nearby. So we decided he would have to come home with us and we would put an advertisement in the local paper. Eli managed to balance him on his kayak and we headed back toward the spot where we had our picnic.

We gave the dog our left overs and he gulped them down like he hadn't eaten in days. His paw was a little sore to touch but he would be fine. We named him Lucky and packed up the empty containers and folded the cloth up and put them back in our backpacks. We paddled back up the river to the boat ramp and carried the kayaks back up to the Ute.

The dog was so happy when he got off the kayak and onto dry land, he was barking and wagging his tail as if to say thank you. He rode in the back of the Ute all the way home. When we arrived home, I lifted him down off the back of the Ute and he stayed with us while we rinsed the kayaks off with the hose. Then followed us inside.

Chapter 13

We emptied the contents of our backpacks onto the bench in the kitchen and put the dirty containers into the dish washer. Silvia had already gone home for the day. There was a note on the bench that said, 'Dear Amber and Maree, I made some Smokey barbeque chicken wings, they are in the oven on low and a salad in the fridge to go with it. There is also a rice pudding in the oven for dessert. Love Silvia.' Maree and Eli ran upstairs to go and have a shower.

I looked down at Lucky and he just stood there wagging his tail looking really happy. I wondered if he had owners that were missing him. I went out to the front room and turned the computer on and waited for it to start up. Then I went to Facebook and found the buy, sell and swap site for this area and took a photo and wrote up a post and put that up there with it. Then turned the computer off and went upstairs to have a shower.

Lucky followed me upstairs and was waiting for me in my bedroom when I came out of the bathroom after my shower. I got dressed in jeans and a blue, short sleeve top. Lucky followed me back downstairs. Jimmy was there lighting the fire. Lucky growled when he saw Jimmy.

After I settled him down and said he was OK, the dog was fine. Jimmy gave him a pat and Lucky responded happily. I asked Jimmy if he was staying for dinner, he said he would. But said he would have to go out after dinner to make sure his dad had eaten and taken his medication.

I was chatting away telling him about my day and he was listening intently. We were on the lounge and the dog was laying in front of the fire. Maree and Eli came down and got dinner ready. Then we all sat at the dining room table to eat. Maree and I got some wine from the cellar for ourselves and some beers for the guys. I fed the dog some sandwich meat.

Jimmy left after dinner and Maree and Eli curled up on the lounge in front of the fire. I took the dog for a walk. It was already dark and the stars were out. It was a beautiful clear night; the moon hadn't come out yet. I went out the front door and the dog headed toward the lawn. I followed to make sure he did his business. Then we went back inside.

I said goodnight and headed upstairs to go to bed. Lucky followed me up. I got a spare blanket out of the linen closet and put it down beside the bed and I patted the blanket for Lucky to come and told him to lay down there. It didn't take much; he was happy to do what he was told.

It made me think he must be owned by someone. I turned the bedside lamp on and the main bedroom light off. I climbed into bed and read my book till my eyes got tired. I didn't see Jimmy come in. It was well after midnight when he did.

I woke up to the dog whining and scratching at the door wanting to go out to the toilet. I grabbed my dressing gown and took him downstairs and out the front door. He headed straight to the lawn to pee. After that, he was just checking out the gardens and sniffing around everywhere. I called him to come with me and he followed me back inside.

As we entered the kitchen, Silvia was surprised by our new four-legged friend. "This is Lucky," I said, "we found him down the river yesterday. Eli had to save him; he had his foot tangled in a branch."

Silvia bent down to give him a pat. "He's a friendly little fellow," she said. She got some chicken out of the fridge and put it into a dish. I got a bowl out and filled it with water and put them both down on the floor at the end of the kitchen bench. I told her that I had put it out there on social media to try to find his owner.

She handed me a coffee and after Lucky finished eating, he laid down near the dish and just watched us having breakfast. Maree and Eli came in and both said hello and patted Lucky before they took a seat. Silvia had cooked sausages and eggs and baked beans with toast.

Eli had to go to work and Maree and I were going to the markets. We took the dog with us and brought him a lead and some dog food and treats, some doggy toys too.

I checked the buy, sell and swap site on Facebook before we left to see if Lucky's owner had been found but nobody knew of him at all so far. Lucky didn't seem to care; he had made himself right at home. Jimmy was busy doing his chores in the afternoon. I was with Silvia making up menus for breakfast, lunch, dinner and a dessert one too.

She was thrilled to bits to be able to help and having something different to do. We were all starting to get a bit excited and nervous about the place being turned into a fancy place to stay. It took a few days to get the menus looking the way I wanted them to.

Maree started school on Tuesday morning and Harry Goldman turned up right on time at one pm on Tuesday afternoon. Lucky was by my side when we met Harry in the drive. He gave him a pat and shook my hand. He came in and sat down at the dining room table and got all the paperwork out of his briefcase.

Silvia offered a coffee then went to make it. He said that I would need to do a short course to be able to serve alcohol and apply for the license and we would have somebody coming to assess the kitchen and fridges and cool room. Just to make sure everything was done legally. He also explained all the insurance side of things and what I would need to pay in case anybody hurt themselves or anything like that.

Silvia brought a tray over with coffee and some Madeira cake. After all that paperwork was done, he helped me with my last will and testament. I was glad to get everything done.

Maree got home from her first day at school. She loved her new job and she said everybody was really welcoming. All the staff and the kids. She also got to spend her lunch break across the road at the police station with Eli. Silvia had made a nice lunch for the two of them. Maree shook Harry's hand and said it was good to see him.

She took a seat at the dining room table and Harry helped her with her will too. When all the paperwork was done, I offered him another coffee and a sandwich before the long drive home. He gratefully accepted and used the time to catch up with all the gossip.

Jimmy came in to light the fire while he was there. He came over and shook Harry's hand and said it was good to see him. Harry was glad we had kept Jimmy and Silvia employed. He was also glad to see me and Maree keeping the place and turning it into a bed and breakfast.

He told us our Aunt Mary would be very proud of us both. He also congratulated Maree for getting the job. Silvia had left and we had sat there and talked to Harry for a while. It was like saying goodbye to an old family friend when we waved goodbye.

We walked back into the kitchen after saying goodbye. Lucky had combined it with a walk to the lawn. He followed us back in and checked out his bowl in the kitchen, which reminded me I had to feed him. There was a roll of meat for dogs we had bought. It was kept in the fridge. I had to cut an inch of the dog roll and two hands full of biscuits, according to the lady at the corner store when she asked about our new found friend.

I did that then asked him to sit, which he did straight away. I gave him the food with a bit of a pat and told him he was a good boy. I was surprised the real owners hadn't turned up yet. I checked Facebook again before I went to sleep that night and still no one knew of Lucky.

I was beginning to think we now owned a dog. I didn't really plan for that but I was getting used to the idea and everybody else was getting used to him as well.

Alice loved to come and play with him when I had him upstairs at night when nobody else was around. She was happier than I had ever seen her.

Chapter 14

Jimmy's Dad was going away again. This time, he was going up to Townsville to get a load but then he had to drop it off in Mount Isa. Jimmy decided to keep his toy while his dad was away. Jimmy would just take the time to feed her and look after her while his dad was gone. He still wanted his dad to get another one and bring her back home with him. He just wasn't prepared to wait that long.

Lisa had lost count of how many times she had been raped and abused. She had lost all hope and just wanted to die. Deep down, she knew nobody was even looking. Adam wasn't the type to go to the police. Jimmy's Dad was leaving first thing in the morning.

He fed Lisa and raped her one last time before he made her shower then tied her back up to the bed and left the house. She heard the truck start up and drive away and was somewhat relieved hoping he was going on a long trip. The whole day she slept on and off.

I was sitting at the kitchen bench chatting to Maree about her second day. "I get to float between the three classes," she said.

"That's fantastic," I said as I watched Lucky get up from where he was relaxing on the floor near his bowls and growl toward the door. I knew it was just Jimmy. I told Lucky to calm down and he started wagging his tail as Jimmy came through the French doors with an arm load of wood.

He put it down near the fire and stopped to say hello to Lucky and gave him a pat. Nobody had claimed him so far, so I said 'I would keep him' in the post. That way the owners would know where he was if they ever did come forward. He was too well trained and well looked after to be a stray. I had looked at a map of the area and there didn't appear to be any properties nearby.

Jimmy lit the fire and came over and joined the conversation. Maree was talking about the kids in the grade five and six combined class. She had to help with a computer class they had this afternoon. I loved listening to the way she would talk about the kids and how passionate she was about helping them learn.

When there was a break in the conversation, I took the chance to ask Jimmy if he was staying for dinner or not. He said he would stay for dinner but he couldn't stay long as he had to go over and see his dad again. I told him I understood and left it at that.

Silvia had left the casserole on the stove and just said to have bread and butter with it. She didn't need to leave a note because I was there when she left. Maree went upstairs to have a shower and I stayed in the kitchen talking to Jimmy.

When Maree got back, I served us all a bowl. I was showing them the menus I had finally printed out and laminated. I was calling the place Stokesville and I had hired a guy to come and weld the name on top of the wrought iron gates out the front. They both thought it was a great idea. After dinner, I cleaned up while Maree went upstairs and Jimmy went to his dad's.

After that, I fed the dog and took him outside for a walk. I waved to Jimmy as he drove out the driveway and through the gates. Jimmy hadn't been staying over for nearly a week. I was looking forward to being with him again. I missed his presence but I also missed the sex too.

I was in bed reading a book when Jimmy's lights came in the drive. I looked at the clock beside the bed and it was just after 11. I put the book aside and drifted off to sleep.

The next morning was the first day of my two-day bar course that I had to do to serve alcohol responsibly. I had to go to the local R.S.L. in Murwoolinbah to do it. It wasn't too hard and I got on well with the people doing the course with me. There was eight of us all up. Five woman and three men. At the end of the second day, I received my certificate.

I went home and didn't see Jimmy that night or the night before that. I went down to breakfast and I was talking to Silvia about how much I was missing Jimmy. She said he must be busy helping somebody in town or something then. I said he had told me he was helping his dad. She said his dad had been gone for two days.

"Really?" I said in astonishment. She just realized what she had said then tried to tell me his dad must still be there then. But I could tell she was lying. It made me wonder where Jimmy had really been.

Silvia had left and Jimmy had come in to light the fire. I went to greet him and asked if he wanted to stay for dinner. He asked what we were having and I told him a bacon and mushroom pasta dish. He agreed to stay for dinner but then he had to leave to help his dad. I told him what Silvia had said about his dad being gone for two days.

"Yeah, he had to put his truck into get fixed. Mom wouldn't know, they don't even talk," he said.

"Oh, OK," I said and gave the pasta a stir.

"I have to go again tonight," he said. I didn't want to argue so I just listened without saying too much. Maree came in and I dished up the pasta and Jimmy left as soon as he had finished.

Eli had come over and he and Maree had adjourned to the bedroom. I took Lucky out for a walk and watched Jimmy drive out through the gates. I went to the front room and got a movie then went upstairs to get ready to put the movie on. I had a shower first and put a nightie on. I saw Jimmy's lights come in the driveway about 10:30 pm last night and had the same dream of Alice again and she was still disappearing into Jimmy's Ute.

I had to come up with some sort of plan. Just going over to Jimmy's Dad's place not knowing if he was going to be there or not wasn't working. So the next time Jimmy came to light the fire, I asked how his dad went with getting his truck fixed.

He said he'd gotten it back and he had left to do a job. I couldn't believe it, finally I was going to be able to go and have a look at this hedge. But as part of my plan, I was going to ask to borrow Jimmy's Ute when I knew that Silvia was busy. That way I wouldn't have to worry about him turning up out of the blue.

"How long is he gone for?" I asked.

"I don't know, probably a week or so," he said, "what does it matter anyway?" he asked. He didn't like the way she always questioned him. He was getting pissed off.

"No reason," she said and backed off completely.

Chapter 15

Maree and Eli had gone to the coast for the weekend. They left on Friday afternoon. Silvia went to the markets before work as usual on Saturday morning and I went to find Jimmy to see if I could borrow the Ute. I made out that there was a statue down at the markets that I liked and asked if I could borrow the Ute to get it home.

He didn't mind. He said he had a lot of work to do around the house. At least this way I knew where he would be. I told Alice the night before what the plan was. She appeared in the Ute beside me as we got out of the driveway and onto the lane.

We drove to Jimmy's Moms, the truck wasn't there, and we drove the five kilometers to the spot near the river. Alice was in the passenger's seat. I asked her if she remembered anything. She said she couldn't, so I drove back toward Jimmy's parents' place; as she approached the back of the house from this angle, she started to get scared.

I stopped the car before we got too close, just in case somebody was to turn up. We walked the last two hundred meters to get to the tree where the hedge was.

Alice started crying as we got closer. I asked her if she remembered anything. She was pointing to the hedge and floated toward it. I told her to stop at the spot where I could tell the picture was taken. I could just make out where the gap in the hedge was.

I got down on my knees and felt around under the hedge. It felt like a groove around in a circle about a meter in width in the concrete under the hedge. I couldn't find an opening or anything. I stopped looking for a minute and stood back to have a look and see if anything stood out.

Alice was standing beside me then she floated over to where the gap would have been and disappeared into the ground under the tree.

I didn't know what to think but she didn't come back. I looked around the tree and the hedge for another 15 minutes then I gave up. There was nothing there to find. I went back to the Ute and drove home. I told Jimmy that I had changed my mind about buying the statue.

I went upstairs to Alice's bedroom but she wasn't there. I went to my bedroom and got my togs on and went for a swim. After thinking about things while I was in the pool, I decided to ask the cards. I got them down off the dressing table.

Silvia must have already been in to make my bed. I sat down and thought about Alice going into the ground under the tree and drew a card. It didn't help it was the death card. I drew another card to elaborate and I got the Justice card.

I wrapped the cards back up in the black velvet cloth, put them back into the silver box and back on the dressing table where they belonged. I went downstairs and had some lunch. After lunch, I went back upstairs.

I found a couple of boxes in the maintenance cupboards full of shampoo, conditioner and soaps to put in all the rooms. I had also found some numbers in Bunnings Hardware for the rooms when I was in town doing my course. I had asked Jimmy if he would put them on when he got the chance.

I told Silvia not to worry about dinner and just had some two-minute noodles. I had asked Jimmy earlier in the day and he said he had too much to do. So after keeping busy all day, I went up to have a shower. I read my book till I heard Jimmy come home about 10:30 then turned my lamp off and went to sleep.

That night I dreamt of Alice. I was over at Jimmy's parents' place and Alice was with me and I went to check out the tree with the hedge around it. We were about 10 meters away when Alice floated over to the tree and disappeared into the ground where the gap would have been.

I was looking for her and how to get in to save her. Finally, I looked up and just in the first branch of the gum tree was what looked like a bit of wood that was part of the tree but when I tried to pick it up, it activated the hatch to open. At that moment, I woke up.

It was 4:30 am and I knew what I had to do. I got up and got dressed in denim shorts and a green top and put my runners on. I ran downstairs to get a water bottle out of the fridge and I took Lucky for a quick walk outside to the lawn then put him back inside.

I took off through the woods and across the bridge and up the hill to where Jimmy's Ute was parked in the dream and followed the track all the way to Silvia's place. I knew she would still be home but I didn't think she would be up this early.

The house was in darkness. I made my way to the tree and went through the gap in the hedge, which wasn't much of a gap anymore. When I got to the middle, I looked up at the branch and it was exactly like it was in the dream. I pulled on the knob of wood and the hatch opened.

I must have fallen about 10 feet down and the hatch automatically closed. I remember seeing a ladder on the way down till everything went black. I must have hit my head when I landed. I don't know how long I was out but when I came to, I could hear Alice crying.

I took my phone out of my back pocket where it always was and looked at the screen. I had no reception. I used the light of my phone to look around.

I realized I was laying on top of dead bodies all in different stages of decay. I screamed and tried to get up but my ankle got twisted in the fall. I could vaguely make out Alice over in the corner. I managed to pull myself through the dead bodies and over to the corner where Alice was.

I could see a mattress in the corner. There was the skeleton of Alice lying with her arms and legs tied to each corner of the bed. The reason I knew it was Alice was she had the blue and white checked tunic dress on but there wasn't much left of the material.

It had decayed over time but the leather shoes were still in one piece on her foot bones. I said, "It's OK, I'm here Alice."

She stopped crying and said, "this is me, Amber," and started crying again. I managed to calm her down again.

I looked at the battery on my phone and it was on 58 percent. Alice sat there in silence and for a moment, I did too. Then I heard another noise, it sounded like somebody breathing but very softly. I put the torch light on and started making my way over to the sound. There must have been at least a hundred bodies, and the stench was overpowering and disgusting.

I was breaking bones and my hand was sinking into slimy rotting flesh. On the top of the pile below the stairs was a lady, she had blood down the side of her head but she was still breathing. I checked her pulse. It was there but only faintly.

I recognized her face, it was the lady on the news, Rachel Gibbs, the one that went missing from the shopping center in Norseman in Western Australia. I shook her. "Rachel. Wake up, Rachel," I said. She moaned a little. I looked around for my water bottle.

I knew I had it in my hand when I fell. I found it eventually and got back to Rachel. I kept nudging her to wake up and when she finally opened her eyes, I brought my water bottle to her lips and got her to have a drink.

I managed to get up and drag her over to where I could sit her up and she could lean on the wall. As she became more and more conscious, I sat next to her and gave her a little more water. As she regained her strength, she realized what had happened and where she was. She started shaking and crying. I put my arms around her and told her it would all be OK and we would get her back to her kids.

It was a struggle but I managed to climb back up the ladder and tried to open the hatch. I couldn't find any handles or anything that would have helped me open it. So I climbed back down and went back to where Rachel was against the wall.

She was so weak. I really needed to get her out of here and to a hospital. I looked around the whole room and there was nothing but dead bodies. I would have to stop and think, there had to be a way to open it from the inside.

The hours drifted by. I thought nobody would even know I was missing till Maree got home from her weekend with Eli at the coast. Even then she wouldn't know where I was. I had to find a way out.

Maree came home about five o'clock Sunday afternoon. She had dropped Eli off at his place because they had taken the Mustang to the coast. She took her luggage upstairs and sorted it out and put the clean clothes away in her wardrobe and made a pile to go in the wash. She put the luggage bag back under her bed then took the washing to put down in the laundry.

She was surprised that nobody was home. Silvia had left a note on the kitchen bench, it said 'Welcome home Maree, there is some pea and ham soup on the stove for dinner and a cherry pie in the fridge for dessert. Love Silvia.' She went upstairs to find Amber; she wasn't there so she went to the pool. She wasn't there either.

Maree put the kettle on to make a coffee; while she was waiting for the jug to boil, Jimmy came in to light the fire. Maree said, "Hi Jimmy, have you seen Amber today?"

He said, "She borrowed my Ute yesterday morning because there was some statue she wanted to buy from the markets. She said she changed her mind and brought it home and I haven't seen her since."

Maree rang Amber's phone; it said it was either turned off or not in range. She thought that was weird. Then she rang Silvia and she said she had seen her yesterday before she left work but she hadn't seen her all day today. She said she thought she must have gone out in the car because the dog was still there and Lucky was usually wherever Amber was. Maree thanked her and hung up the phone.

She went to the garage and checked every bay and all the cars were all there. She went back inside. Jimmy was on his way out. She stopped him and asked "Did Amber go to the markets first before she borrowed your Ute?"

He said, "No, she saw a statue there last week but changed her mind about it."

"OK, no worries, thanks," she said and let him continue on his way.

She went back outside and took Lucky for a walk; he went straight to the lawn. Maree was trying to think. She would have known if Amber was interested in a statue at the markets last week because they went there together.

There were no statues. She wondered why Amber lied, she thought to borrow Jimmy's Ute maybe. She didn't know what to think. Maree rang Eli, he said he would come over and see her shortly.

They had pea and ham soup for dinner and decided if Amber wasn't home by the next day, they would treat it like a missing person and put a search party together. That night, Maree told Eli everything about Alice and the dreams and the visits and everything that Amber had said about Alice and Jimmy's Dad.

She even went and got the contents of the safety deposit box and the footage and the photos. She also showed him the letter that Aunt Mary had left them.

Eli believed what she was saying but at the same time, they had no proof or evidence. Or even a reason to look at Jimmy's Dad or the house.

Chapter 16

Jimmy spent the afternoon over at his dad's house with Lisa Redding, the young prostitute his father had brought home. He was trying to be gentle when he raped her so she would last long enough for his dad to get another one. Then he would let his dad kill her if he didn't decide to do it himself.

He had spoken to his dad the night before and he said he had been watching his next target for the last two days and was hoping to get her shortly. Jimmy left there before his mom was due to finish work.

I was in the bunker out the back and nobody knew, not even Jimmy or his dad. I was still trying to think of a way out. In the end, I decided if I could clear a path to the bottom of the stairs, there may be a handle or some way to open the hatch from the inside.

I didn't want to die down here with the rest of the corpses that surrounded me and I didn't want Rachel to die either. I wanted her to get back to her kids.

After moving aside bones and bodies and mush, I finally cleared a path. I sat down to rest as my ankle was painful but I had managed to push through and looked at the battery power on my phone. It was down to four percent. I had been using it too much.

Alice was still sitting beside the bed where her bones were, crying softly. I kept checking Rachel to make sure she was still alive and breathing. I told her that I would get her back to her kids.

I made the decision to use the battery power to look and find a way out. I put the light on and looked at the bottom of the stairs and all around them. I wasn't seeing anything. I shone the light as I went up the stairs and as soon as I made it to the top of the stairs, the light went off.

The battery had run out. I swore under my breath and put the phone back in my pocket. I felt around in the dark for a while. I didn't think I would get it but I pressed on the spot right in the middle of the hatch above my head and it sprung open. I yelled out to Rachel that I would come back for her.

I climbed out of the bunker and put the top back down, it was the middle of the night. I could see the light on at Silvia's. I didn't trust her so I had to think fast. It was a new moon so there wasn't much light. I thought if I could just get home, I would be safe and be able to rescue Rachel Gibbs. I knew Maree would be home from the coast and I knew that she would be worried.

I headed down toward the river. What I didn't know was that Silvia had heard me yell out to Rachel and now she was on the phone to Jimmy. Jimmy answered, "Hey Mom, what's up?"

"You are about to come undone, son," she said.

"What do you mean by that?" Jimmy asked.

"I just heard Amber out the back near the bunker. She's headed toward the river; I think she knows something." Jimmy thanked his mom and left his place to head Amber off, so he could find out if she knew anything and if so, how much.

He crossed the lawn making sure there was nobody around and headed into the woods. I was shaking and running through the bush and down to the river across the bridge and into the woods toward home.

Jimmy's phone rang, he stopped to answer it. I heard it to and went off the path to hide among the trees and listen. I could only hear one side of the conversation though. "Hi Dad, how's it going?"

"Yeah, good. I've picked up a girl that was arguing with her boyfriend. I don't think she'll be missed for a while because I also heard her talking to her mom and telling her that she didn't want anything more to do with her," Jimmy's Dad said.

"How old is she, Dad?" Jimmy asked.

"Would have to be around 20," he said.

"OK, Dad, sounds good, how long till you get home?" Jimmy asked.

"I've just left Mount Isa so it'll take a couple of days," his dad replied.

"OK, I'll see you when you get home and Dad, don't forget to take your medication." He hung up the phone and continued walking along the path to the river looking for me.

I had heard Jimmy ask his dad how old she was, so it told me that his dad had found another girl on his travels and that Jimmy was definitely in on it with his dad. I waited till Jimmy had well and truly passed. Then got back on the path toward home.

My ankle was really sore but there was nothing I could do but push through the pain. I finally made it home. It was 2:30 am and Maree and Eli were in the kitchen not being able to sleep because I was missing and legally, they had to wait till morning to report it. I came limping in through the front door and into the kitchen. Lucky was wining with his tail between his legs. I told him it was ok. Poor thing didn't know what to do. So he went to lie beside his bowls.

Maree flew out of her seat to where her sister was standing in the doorway. She and Eli helped her over to a chair. I told Eli and Maree everything. Eli radioed it in and Earl phoned the police station in Murwoolinbah. He told Eli that he and Frank would meet him at Jimmy's parents' house.

Eli asked Maree to lock the doors and stay together. Maree went around and locked all the doors and knew that I needed to have a hot shower and wash the stench of decaying flesh off my body. Maree helped me get upstairs via the elevator and down the hallway to my bedroom.

She ran the water and left her sister to have a shower. She didn't want to leave her so she waited in the bedroom. When I was finished, I dried myself off and put a nightie and dressing gown on. We went back downstairs via the lift and both sat on the lounge in front of the fire and waited. Maree had got some ice out and put it on my foot. Then wrapped it in a bandage to give it some support.

Eli left to meet Earl and Frank at Jimmy's parents' house. Sirens on and lights blazing. They both pulled into the driveway seconds apart. They took Silvia into custody and bashed the door down to Jimmy's Dad's house and found Lisa Redding tied to the bed; she was so grateful to be found, the police untied her and wrapped her in a blanket and radioed for an ambulance.

Then went out to the tree with the hedge around it. Eli remembered what Amber had said about the opening being in the branch of the tree. He stood back when he opened it so he wouldn't fall in and putting his torch on, he looked down into the bunker and there was what looked like at least a hundred bodies. The stench was disgusting so he covered his nose and had to breathe through his mouth.

He looked around when he reached the bottom of the stairs and spotted Rachel Gibbs still seated leaning up against the wall where Amber said she would be. She was barely alive, he radioed for another ambulance and stayed with her till they came. Looking around with his torch, he knew it would take forensics months to work through this place.

There was an arrest warrant put out for Jimmy and his dad. Silvia was arrested for being an accessory to murder. Reginald Slater was picked up one hundred kilometers outside of Mount Isa with 20-year-old Amanda Cornwall from Mount Isa and Jimmy had not been found.

Jimmy was about five hundred meters away from his parents' house when he heard the sirens and saw the lights of the police cars through the bush. He hightailed it back to the river and swam up river and past the log and further still.

He didn't want the police dogs to pick up the scent. He got out for a brief time; he ran along the river then swam some more. He had covered about 30 kilometers when he stopped to light a fire and dry his wet clothes. He built a makeshift shelter and got some sleep.

Chapter 17

Eli rang Maree and told her everything and said he wouldn't be home for at least another 12 hours or so but they did have a policeman coming to stay with them for a while till they could figure out where Jimmy had got to. They hadn't caught him but they managed to save three women.

Maree and I were still sitting in front of the fire having a cup of coffee when the police officer arrived. He introduced himself as Constable Jake Randel of the Murwoolinbah police department. Maree and I left the Constable in the lounge and went upstairs to get some sleep.

While I was there, I reflected on the last six weeks and my relationship with Jimmy and everything that he had obviously been involved in and even Silvia for that matter. It was a lot to take in.

I was having trouble getting to sleep so I got up and hobbled down the hallway to Alice's room. I opened the door and went over to the bed and put the lamp on. I scanned the room first. I was worried she would be still near her body but then I saw her, she appeared at the end of the bed then floated over to where I sat on the edge of the bed and she said, "Thank you Amber, you found me."

"You're welcome darling, we also saved three women's lives thanks to you, Alice," I said. Then in the far side of the room, I saw a light, it grew bigger and brighter. I could make out two shapes coming from the light, Aunt Mary and Uncle Tom.

Alice turned and looked and she squealed in delight, "Mummy, Daddy, you're here." She looked back at me and said, "I love you, Amber."

I said, "I love you too, Alice."

And she went running into Aunt Mary's arms. She and Uncle Tom thanked me and she promised to guide and protect me through my intuition from the other side. She also said that she loved what I was doing with the place and she loved the new name that I was going to call it too. Then they all disappeared into where the light came from originally.

I limped back down the hallway and into my bedroom. I laid down in bed and thought about everything. I was glad to have been able to save those three women and get Rachel Gibbs back to her family and I was shocked to find out about the young girl tied up in the house. They said she was lucky to be alive too.

I couldn't believe I was that close to a murderer. It sent a shiver down my spine to know he was still on the loose. Oh well, at least Alice had finally been set free from this place and was back with Aunt Mary and Uncle Tom. I finally drifted off to sleep but dreamed I was back down in the bunker surrounded by dead bodies. I awoke in a pool of sweat. It was nine o'clock in the morning. I dragged myself out of bed and dressed in jeans and a T-shirt.

Eli called in the dog squad at first light to look for Jimmy. He had also found the bones of Alice in the corner. This case looked like it would be the worst serial killers in the history of Australia. He was just hoping they could track Jimmy down.

Maree had felt like she had no choice but she had to go to work. She didn't want to ruin her new job. She was tired but with that many police out there looking for Jimmy and one at the house, she didn't feel like she had to worry about me.

I went downstairs followed by Lucky. I let him out and left the front door open, went to the kitchen and put the kettle on. Jake was still there from the night before. "Hi Jake, would you like a cup of coffee?" I asked, he came over from where he was standing in front of the fire.

"Yeah, I would love one, just black with one sugar thanks," he said. He took a seat at the kitchen bench. I made us both a cup then put some raisin toast into the toaster. Two for me and two for Jake as well.

I asked if they had caught Jimmy yet and he said no but the dogs were already out and a search party was looking. My ankle was bruised and swollen but feeling a bit better. I rewrapped it again. There was a note on the bench from Maree, it said 'Dear Amber, I had to go to work, ring me if you need to. Love Maree.'

There was a knock at the door. It was Eli. "Hi Amber," he said as I opened the door.

"Hey Eli, did you find Jimmy?" I asked.

"No but we have a lot of man power out there so it shouldn't take much longer," he said. I offered him a coffee which he gratefully accepted. He had been working the case all night. He and Jake were talking about the case and I was drifting with my thoughts. I couldn't believe I was living that close to two serial killers.

I was thinking of Silvia and how she must have known all these years. I would have to look into getting somebody to replace her. I couldn't even imagine her being in jail. Then I started thinking about my bad luck with men and how I seemed to attract the wrong ones. I was still in shock about Jimmy and what he was capable of.

It made me think of my relationship I had with him and how happy we were and what great sex we had had. Then my mind went to the bunker and his dad and the girl in the house and then to the one in the truck. There was nothing nice about any of them really. I shivered even though it wasn't cold. My awareness came back to the room.

I got up to put the kettle on again. There was another knock at the door. Eli got up and said, "That will be Frank, he's taking over from Jake," as he went to open the door. Frank walked in ahead of Eli. Lucky got up and greeted him.

Frank said, "Hello, who do we have here then?" and patted the top of his head. I told him his name was Lucky. He shook my hand and introduced himself. "Hi Amber, I'm Frank, it's nice to finally meet you. I've met your sister Maree; she's working with my kids at the school. She seems like a really nice person. The kids rave about her already," he said.

"She is," I said. He came across as a really nice bloke who seemed to care a lot about people. Eli and Jake said good bye and left us to it.

Frank was telling me about his wife and what a good cook she was. I asked him about what she did for a living and he said she used to be a chef at the Commercial Hotel in Murwoolinbah. He said she hadn't worked since they had moved here.

"We don't exactly have a pub in town, I guess. Do you think she might be interested in working for us?" I asked. I said I would have to run it past Maree first but to ask his wife how she would feel about talking to me about it. I told Frank what I was planning to do with the place. I even took him on a tour of the place. Lucky was happy to follow us around.

Frank loved the idea almost as much as I did. He knew a lot about the area and said it was a much-needed kind of place. I said we would need to stock the wood near the fire, so he came for a walk with me out to the shed to get some wood from the pile. I was telling him about Jimmy and I couldn't help having mixed emotions about him.

Especially when I looked at the axe that was in a block of wood where Jimmy used to chop the wood. It made me think of the very first time when we met him. So much had happened since then.

We grabbed an armful each and turned to go back to the house. Frank was telling me about the house he and his wife had just bought and how eco-friendly it was. "That's fantastic," I said, it sounded really nice. I told him that I looked forward to a tour of his place one day.

He laughed but agreed. We were unloading the firewood and topping the fire back up. I grabbed a coke and a diet coke out of the fridge and went to sit on the lounge. Frank accepted the coke and sat on the lounge himself.

Chapter 18

Jimmy awoke in the bush down river. He had put together a few banana leaves as a blanket and after drying his clothes with a fire, he got a couple of hours sleep. He knew he had to keep moving. He knew he would be all over the news so he couldn't go into any towns. Or anywhere where people would be.

He was desperate, he had to come up with a plan. He remembered when he was a kid, the police with the dogs would go out searching during the day and then rest at night. Then searching again in the daylight. He had a plan but it had to be done at night time under the cover of darkness.

He went back to the river and this time hid in the bush to the right about 10 kilometers further along and made a bit better shelter and spent the afternoon drying his clothes so he could lay down at about 4pm and get some sleep. He woke up just on dark.

He grew up in these woods and he knew the place well. He had to get back to the house before dawn. He knew it was going to take a lot but he needed food and shelter and there was only one place he knew where to get that.

There was a secret room in the house that nobody knew of but him. He thought if he could get back in, nobody would know to look there. He was glad he was a fit man; he ran and swam all the same way on the way back. It was close to midnight when he arrived, he came in through the path to the river.

He ran across the lawn hoping nobody would see him and went to his place first. He changed his clothes and put the wet ones in the drier. He knew that Amber used to sleep with Lucky in her room so he wasn't worried about the dog but he did see the police car in the driveway when he came out of the woods.

He also knew that if a policeman was there for protection, he would be in the kitchen, dining or lounge room area where the fire was going. The entrance to the hidden room was behind the life size picture of their Uncle Tom, Aunt Mary and Alice when she was a little girl in the front room.

He entered the house quietly through the front door. He could hear the television going in the other lounge. He went to the front room and opened the door behind the photo. He closed the door behind himself. This was a place he knew well when he was a kid; he spent a lot of time in there watching the family go about their day.

There was a television screen for every room of the house. It was never used or even talked about after Tom died. Originally made as a panic room. It was a big room with a bed and a kitchenette in the far corner and to the right was a fully functioning bathroom.

There was a fair size fridge and a big deep freezer to the left, both were always fully stocked. It had been made to be sound proof. It also had a lounge with a television and a washing machine and dryer. Jimmy had everything he needed to survive for months. He laid down and slept for a very long time.

I turned the television on and the news was showing Jimmy's parents' house. They were showing it from a helicopter and talking about the murders. It also showed Rachel Gibb's in hospital and her getting ready to go home to her family.

The husband was already there. They said they would give an interview after she got home to her kids. They also showed Lisa Redding covered in a blanket and being put into the ambulance and said she was not up to being interviewed either.

Then they flicked to Mount Isa and they spoke to the 20-year-old lady that was found in Reg's truck cab. She was crying and saying how lucky she was to be found. Her boyfriend was there with her. He came as soon as he heard the news and so did her mom.

It made me feel good to know that I had helped. I knew I had to make a statement soon but they were having a staff shortage at the moment. I totally understood why. Eli said he would do it himself if it was easier. I said it would be.

That way I wouldn't have to go out. There were going to be reporters and cameras everywhere. I already had to turn my phone off. It had been ringing all morning and they were parked outside the gates.

All I could do was sit in front of the fire and drink coffee. The news was saying they had found over a hundred bodies in a bunker just outside of Limpinwood. They were showing Silvia's picture as the ex-wife of the killer

Reginald Slater and showing his picture. He looked like a crazed lunatic and then they showed a picture of Jimmy Slater.

Warning the public that he was still on the run and very dangerous. My heart skipped a beat when I saw the picture of Jimmy, looking gorgeous as always. I couldn't imagine him doing all those hideous things.

I had to get up and do something to take my mind off everything. I asked Frank if he would mind if I went up to where Jimmy lived in the log cabin. He agreed if he could check the place out first. There were police cars parked out the front, they had the dogs here this morning going through the woods from here and headed down to the river.

They had gone through Jimmy's place this morning. When we got to the cabin, there was crime scene tape around it. Frank said maybe we better stay out of there till the police say it's OK to take the tape off.

We went back to the house. Lucky had used the chance to go for a walk. I made us a ham and salad sandwich for lunch and kept the news on in the background. I wasn't looking forward to talking to the press but I knew I would have to.

After lunch, I went upstairs; Lucky followed me up. I laid down on my bed and thought about Jimmy. I pictured him hiding out in the bush somewhere, scared and cold. Tears came thick and fast. I cried for Jimmy, I cried for the missing ladies, I cried for all the families that would now be able to get closure.

I cried for Alice and I cried for me. I felt so alone like my whole world had fallen apart and it had. In the end, I cried myself to sleep surrounded by a million tissues.

Jimmy had woken up after a good few hours' sleep and then watched Amber cry herself to sleep, wishing he could comfort her. Knowing it would be suicide to do anything other than watch.

Chapter 19

When I woke up, it was dark outside. The clock said 7:30 pm. I was still in my jeans and a T-shirt. I went and had a shower. I stood in the shower for a long time hoping all my problems would wash down the drain and washed my hair as well. I still smelt the smell of death on me.

I don't know whether it was just me or I just couldn't wash it off. *At least I wouldn't have to deal with the press tonight*, I thought. Jimmy enjoyed watching her in the shower. He fixed himself up while he watched.

I put a nightie on and a dressing gown and dried my hair. I went downstairs and found Maree and Eli sitting at the bench in the kitchen. "Hello, peoples," I said as I entered and headed straight for the kettle. I needed coffee.

"How was your day, Maree?" I asked.

"It wasn't too bad at school but there was a shit load of reporters about when I left and they followed me all the way here," she said.

"How are you going, Amber? It can't be easy after what you went through," Eli asked.

"No it's been hard," I said. Breaking news was still on in the background. "Have they found Jimmy yet?" I asked maybe a little too hopeful. They both looked up at me. Maree had come into my room while I was asleep and seen the pile of tissues and told Eli.

Maree got up and came over and hugged me and said, "You poor bugger," she knew how much I liked Jimmy. Then we were both in tears.

Jimmy was watching from behind the wall. He was surprised to see how upset Amber was about missing him. He knew he had real feelings for her as well. Which surprised him too. He had never had those kinds of feelings before. This is what being in love feels like, he told himself.

Amber grabbed some tissues off the bench and blew her nose. "I have to stop this, at least I won't run out of tissues. I just bought a heap for all the rooms in the house," I laughed. Eli said it was his turn to be on duty tonight.

He had gone home earlier and had some sleep so he would be OK to be up all night. He also said if I would like to do my statement tonight, I could. He knew I had had a good sleep too, so I would be wide awake for a while.

Maree went to bed around nine o'clock after a quick meal of spaghetti Bolognese and some cheesy garlic bread. She needed to be up to go to work in the morning. Eli got a pen and paper out and went through everything that happened from start to finish.

It was nearly midnight by the time we finished. I got up to put some milk on and offered Eli a hot chocolate. I thought it might help me sleep. He also explained that they were doing media updates and they would like me to appeal for Jimmy to hand himself in and just answer a few of their questions. I agreed to do it.

So Eli was going to arrange a time tomorrow for that. I was so nervous but if it could help catch him, I was willing to help. I took Lucky out for a walk and saw half a dozen news crews camped out down the lane. It was a mild night and I wondered if Jimmy was out there freezing or if he was somewhere else. I called Lucky and went inside. I said goodnight to Eli, he was restocking the fire and went upstairs to bed.

Jimmy had listened to Amber do her statement and he had heard enough for one night. He laid down on his bed and thought about everything. He knew his dad would be looked after with his medication and he didn't have to worry about where he was now. He couldn't imagine his mom in prison though.

He didn't even think she knew about any of it. The television was saying she was being questioned and maybe charged. He couldn't believe it had all come undone and that was thanks to Amber. I knew she was too nosey, I should have kept my distance, he thought.

Now he had nothing and no one. He didn't know what he was going to do but staying here was better than going to jail. He went back to sleep.

Chapter 20

I slept in till 7:30 and let Lucky downstairs ahead of me. He must have been bursting, he headed straight to the kitchen and barked at Maree and she just knew he needed to get out. She opened the door and he ran. I got dressed into jeans and a pink short sleeve cashmere top.

I put a little makeup on and my diamond stud earrings in. I left my hair down and looked at myself in the mirror. I was looking a bit pale and my eyes were a bit swollen from all the crying. But with a bit of makeup, I would be fine.

I went downstairs and into the kitchen. Maree was just on her way out. "Hey, are you going to be OK? I could stay home if you want me to."

"No, you go, I'll be fine," I said. There was a policeman coming in as she was leaving. I said goodbye as she went out via the veranda. Earl came into the room.

"Good morning," he said. Eli had let him in and Lucky came flying in behind Earl. I patted Lucky as he came past me heading for his bowl. While he was having a drink, I got the dog roll out of the fridge and cut an inch off and grabbed two handfuls of dog biscuits out of the pantry. I told him to sit and he did. I gave him his bowl and patted him and told him he was a good boy.

I made my coffee and asked Earl and Eli if they wanted one too. When we all had coffee and raisin toast, I sat down to chat. Earl asked me how I felt about them doing the interview in the front room in front of the photo of Aunt Mary and Uncle Tom with Alice.

They had heard that Alice had finally been found among the 132 bodies and they all wanted to hear how I managed to uncover this decade's old case and another 131 missing person cases being solved and so many victims getting closure for their families. They thought I was a hero and they all wanted to question me. He said if we do this, they will probably back off a little.

The thought of doing this terrified me with all the cameras and such but if I wanted life to return to a new normal, I was going to have to deal with this first. It was arranged to do at 11 am. I stayed in the kitchen while Earl, Frank and Eli helped everybody get set up with all their lights and cameras.

When they were ready, I was ushered into the front room to sit at a table in front of the photo. Jimmy was on the other side watching it all unfold. There was one particular lady that took control and fitted me with a microphone and calmed me down by telling me what I needed to do and sat at the table next to me and said she would be in it with me.

So if I got stuck with anything, I just had to look at her and she would take the lead. When they gave me the go ahead, they asked what happened. "Well, my sister and I inherited this place from my Aunt Mary and Uncle Tom who you can see in the picture behind me. As you already know, their little girl Alice disappeared 17 years ago. When we moved in, I started seeing the ghost of Alice. We also found a letter from my Aunt Mary written before she died." I showed them the letter and read part of it out loud to them. "So my aunt used to see her too. I followed the ghost of Alice to the bunker. Then I had trouble finding the opening.

"The answer to that came to me in a dream and that's how I found the bodies and Rachel Gibbs. I didn't know about anything else, heck I was even dating Jimmy. I knew something was up but I thought it was just him looking after his father.

"Making sure he was taking his medication and making sure he was eating properly and looking after himself. That's what he used to tell me anyway, due to his mental illness."

That's when the questions started. "Do you know where he is now?" I told them about the phone call I had heard while running to get home and how it saved my life.

"That was the last time I heard him," I said. They asked me about Silvia. I told them we had kept her on as a housekeeper. "We are still in shock about the whole incident. My sister and I had grown quite fond of them both," I said.

"What about Jimmy's father Reginald Slater, did you know him?" was the next one.

"I never met him to be honest." There were a couple more questions and then they were wrapping it up. I said, "Jimmy, if you are out there and you can hear me now. Please just hand yourself in, I love you and I don't want you to get hurt."

I looked at the lady beside me and she went into wrapping it up and removed the microphone. She thanked me and said I did well. I was glad to leave the front room and get back to the kitchen.

I thought about what I was going to say last night and talked to Maree about it. I didn't want people thinking I was insane but how else could I have explained what happened and how I found the bunker and the way to open it. *The audience took it really well*, I thought. I think people these days are a lot more open to this sort of thing. I was glad to have everyone leaving and not be camping out down the lane.

Jimmy was amazed to hear how Alice had led Amber to the bunker. He was wondering how she had managed to find it. That must have been why she was so nosey. He just hoped Alice wouldn't let on where he was now. He was finding it really hard to be stuck inside.

It had only been a small amount of time but already he was feeling hemmed in. He had always been outside busy doing something. He would have to find a way to keep busy, he thought.

I was enjoying a coffee. It was really hard to be open and honest about my gift. I was hoping the public wouldn't ridicule me and put me in the same basket they put my aunt into. I wished my mom and my aunt were here. It would be so much easier.

I looked forward to Maree coming home, I could really do with a hug about now. It was only 12:30. I made the guys some sandwiches and was happy to be busy and thinking about other people for a while.

Earl was telling me that all the bodies had been transported to a training facility in Gosford to be identified and returned to their families. I was glad that I could help so many people but at the same time, I felt like I was grieving the life I had.

I didn't say anything because I didn't want to bring the mood down. All three of the guys had just cracked the biggest case they would ever have to work on in their lives. So they were in quite a good mood.

I went and turned the television on and stoked the fire. I had jeans on but I just didn't feel warm. I went upstairs and grabbed a jacket and looked out the window. The news crews had finally left. I noticed the lawns were starting to grow longer.

We would have to get somebody to come and do Jimmy's job too, I was thinking. I looked over to the path in the woods. It was where I had first seen Jimmy but it was also where I was terrified, fearing for my life. It was a fear I would have to conquer. *I would have to go for a run maybe in the morning*, I thought. I turned away and looked at my bed, it was still messy. It made me miss Silvia and the way she looked after us.

Maree and I would have to have a chat about what we were going to do. I just knew I would have to keep myself busy or I would have too much time to think. It was good to know Aunt Mary was happy to see what we were going to do with the place.

One of the questions was about Alice still being here. I told them that Aunt Mary and Uncle Tom had come to get Alice. So she was not trapped anymore. I thought if I advertised this place, they may not come if they thought there was a ghost floating around.

Which reminded me, the guy that was welding the name on the gate was due to come tomorrow at nine am. I also remembered that the numbers for the rooms needed to be put on still. So just to be busy doing something, I would go and find an electric drill and put the numbers on the rooms. I went to the first bay of the garage and found one hanging on the wall.

I grabbed an extension cord as well that I found on a hook. I got the numbers out of the boot of my car and went back in via the veranda into the kitchen. Frank was still there and Eli and Earl had left. "Hey, I was wondering where you had got to. I am supposed to be looking after you and I didn't even know where you were," he said.

"All good," I gestured toward the stuff in my hand and said, "just went to get these numbers to put on all the doors upstairs. You can give me a hand if you want to."

"I'd love to," he said. I was willing to do it but if he was going to offer to help, I wasn't going to turn him down.

"Cool thanks," I said and he followed me upstairs.

We were still working on those when Maree arrived home. Lucky was the one that told me she was home. He was happy to go see her. Frank and I decided to stop and have a break. Maree had stopped at the bakery and got some cream buns on the way home.

I went to pour a bottle of wine and Maree went up to her room to unload her bags and kick her shoes off. It was Friday and she was glad to be home.

While Amber and Frank were upstairs, Jimmy snuck out of his hiding spot and went to the gym and got a set of 50-kilogram weights and a bar to lift them with. He didn't think Amber would notice them missing. When he put one on each end of the bar, he would be lifting 100 kilograms. He was happy to have something else to do while he watched what was going on in the house.

Frank had a coke and while we enjoyed the cream buns, Maree told us all about her day. She was really starting to get to know the kids and the principal had even let her take the class by herself today. It was the 2nd, 3rd and 4th grade class that she had to teach.

She was thrilled to bits and I was really happy for her. I put a chicken on to roast and peeled the vegetables. The news was still on the television in the background. They still hadn't found Jimmy and they were showing the interview that she did. I went over and turned the television up and watched it with Maree and Frank.

"I think he'll be long gone," said Frank when it finished.

I asked Maree if she wanted to go for a swim, she said she would love to so we both went upstairs to get changed. I put a dark blue one piece on that I hadn't worn before. I looked at myself in the full-length mirror and thought I looked better than I felt.

Maree was putting on a yellow two-piece bikini. Jimmy enjoyed watching them both at the same time, he was getting himself off in the process.

Amber and Maree met at the linen closet where they got themselves a towel and ran downstairs and out to the pool. Jimmy had a camera on the side of the pool maintenance building. We put our towels down in the usual spot and got in.

We noticed the pool was starting to look a little bit murky so we talked about advertising for somebody to do the lawns and maintenance as well as a cook and a cleaner. Instead of just one person doing all of Silvia's chores, we thought we may need a separate person for housekeeping and a chef.

"The people that do the kitchen inspections will be here tomorrow morning early about 8:30 as well as the wrought iron blacksmith guy that's going to do the name on the gate, he'll be here tomorrow too." I was starting to get a little excited thinking about all the stuff that was getting done.

I poured us another glass of wine and floated while I did a meditation. I was feeling so relaxed by the time I finished. We both hopped into the spa and chatted for a while and drank more wine. I had to go get another bottle. I wrapped myself in a towel and went to the fridge and cool room.

Jimmy was watching as my towel kept falling down and the cold had made my nipples stand out. He felt like he was being teased. I went down to the cellar and got a couple of bottles out of the fridge at the back of the room. I caught the lift back up and put one of the bottles in the fridge and took the other one out to the spa.

I poured us both a glass and hopped back in. I told Maree that I would do the advertising this weekend to get people in and ready for the opening. "We should have a big party and invite all the people in town," I said.

"That would be a fantastic idea," said Maree. "We just need to get some employees."

Frank was sitting at one of the tables in the shade reading the paper. "Hey Frank, did you ask your wife about the cooking job?" I asked.

"Yes, I forgot she told me to give you our number. I'll give it to you before I go," he said as he turned the page.

"Do you really think Jimmy would come back, Frank?" I asked.

"No not really," he said.

"How long do you guys have to hang around here for?" I asked.

"Well, the dogs couldn't nail down anything and we've followed up a couple of leads but we don't really have anything to go on. So in answer to your question, probably another day or two," Frank said.

Maree and I talked for a little while longer. Then I had to go check on dinner. The vegetables, potatoes and pumpkin needed turning and I put some peas and carrots on the stove to boil. Maree went upstairs to do a little marking and promised to be back at seven for dinner.

I turned the peas and carrots down low and went upstairs to have a shower and wash my hair. *I would definitely have to get onto hiring a guy for the pool*, I thought.

Jimmy was loving the chance to watch both the girls taking a shower twice in one day at the same time. He wanked himself again while he watched. It wasn't the same as the real thing though. He was starting to think he could come up with a plan that may work. He would have to give it some thought though.

Chapter 21

After dinner, I fed Lucky and took him for a walk. Then I rang Frank's wife, Roxanne, she agreed to come over and have an interview tomorrow. I wasn't sure what kind of hours she would be able to do with the two kids, so I decided to advertise for that position to. I was in the front room on the computer. Maree had retired early and I had a lot of work to do. I advertised on the job seekers website for two housemaids, two chefs and a grounds keeper. So hopefully, I'd see some response over the next couple of days or weeks.

I wasn't sure how long it would take. I had registered the business and paid all the taxes, levies and insurances. Hopefully, everything goes well tomorrow and we should be ready.

I took Lucky out for another walk before bed, he went straight to the lawn. Five minutes later, I had to struggle to get him to come inside. He had found a little field mouse and was chasing it all through the gardens at the side of the house, making a mess.

"Lucky," I said with a little anger in my voice, he listened then and followed me inside. I could hear Frank talking to Eli in the lounge, he had come to relieve Frank from his shift. I went around and locked the place up out of sheer habit. Said goodnight and went up to bed. It had been a busy day so sleep came quite easily.

Jimmy laid down to sleep as well, he was happy that he had made a plan. He was going to wait till the police stopped watching the place then he was going to go out and find himself a girl. He went to sleep with a smile on his face, thinking about his new toy.

Chapter 22

My alarm went off at 5:45 am. I got up and got dressed in denim shorts and a pink singlet top. I put my hair up and my runners on and went downstairs. Lucky followed me and I got my water bottle out of the fridge and took off with Lucky.

Out the front door and across the lawn and into the woods. I kept running all the way to the river. It wasn't as bad as I thought it would be. Maybe it would have been worse if it was nighttime. But during the day, it was nice and peaceful.

I sat down for a while at the river and reflected on everything. I was so glad I had the house to keep me busy and all the interviews as well. I ran all the way back home and went upstairs to have a shower. After I was dressed in a nice pink sun dress, I did my hair into a pony tail and went downstairs for breakfast.

Maree and Eli were already there, she had made some bacon and eggs with tomato and onion. She handed me a coffee and a plate full of food. "Thank you, I did all the adverts last night," I said.

"That's good," said Maree.

"Yeah, I have Frank's wife coming over at 11 for an interview. Can you stay and help? I'm a little worried she may not have enough time so I have advertised the position as well. That way I could do up a roster and it won't be too much for one person," I said.

"That's a good idea," she said. I had just finished eating and putting my plate into the dish washer when there was a knock at the door.

It was the inspector to look at the kitchen, pantry and cool room. Everything on his list was ticked, even the fire safety exit signs. Within 45 minutes, he was done and gone. When I went to see him out, I noticed the blacksmith out the front already working on the gate.

He had his son out there helping him, he even had his own welding helmet on. I took some refreshments out to them. I still had a couple of the cream buns

Maree had brought home and I gave them both a can of coke to wash it down. He was doing a good job; he had already done the STOKES and only had the VILLE to go. I left them to it and went inside.

I had all the stationery made up with Stokesville in the design. It arrived yesterday. I had the keys made up with the room numbers on and put a board up to hang them on and put a check-in desk in the foyer with a reception sign on and a bell to ding if nobody was there.

I also put an office chair there and a file cabinet. I had an eftpos machine linked up to a bank account, so people could pay with their card and put a little safe box in the top of the file cabinet for if they wanted to pay with cash.

I rang a lady off the internet to come and help me design a web page for the business and she was coming on Monday at nine o'clock to sort that out, so I had it all happening.

Roxanne Anderson arrived right on time at 11 o'clock. I was out the front with Lucky when she arrived. She waved as she came in the drive. I waved back and smiled. She was an islander lady, happy grin across her face; she pulled up in front of me in a white commodore and got out and gave me a huge hug and said, "Hi, I'm Roxy, you must be Amber. It's nice to meet you."

I hugged her back and said, "It's really nice to meet you too, Frank's been raving about you, says you're a good cook. Come on in anyway."

She followed Lucky and me in and we went straight to the kitchen where Maree was. She stood up and Roxy introduced herself and gave her a huge hug too. "Hi," Maree said, she got up to put the kettle on. I showed Roxy the kitchen, pantry and cool room and walked back out to the kitchen and asked her to have a seat at the dining room table.

Maree brought a tray of coffee and a plate of Iced VoVo biscuits to the table and took a seat. Maree was talking about Joey and Sabrina and what good kids they were as she put the tray down. Roxy was delighted that she said that. I asked her about her availability and if she would like full time or part time.

I knew she was new to the area so I didn't expect her to have many babysitters. But she said she would be happy to do five days a week if that was possible. She said she had a neighbor who had a teenage daughter that was happy to babysit.

So we agreed on Wednesday through to Sunday from 1:00 pm – 9:30 pm earlier if it's not busy. I asked if she could start tomorrow and said the hours could be flexible. Depending on us never having done something like this before. She was up for the challenge and we were happy to give her a go.

We said goodbye and waved as she left. The gates were looking amazing. They were just about finished. I took them out some ham and tomato sandwiches and made some for Maree and myself. We didn't have to have a policeman at the house any longer so we were going to enjoy a lazy afternoon in the pool. We knew by this time next week we may be busy, so we were going to enjoy the quiet.

We both went downstairs to get some alcohol; we were both in the mood to party. I grabbed a ten pack of southern comfort and coke cans and Maree grabbed a bottle of gin and some soda water to go with it. We both came back up the stairs and put them in the fridge.

They went to the second floor to get their togs on. Jimmy watched as always. There wasn't much more that he could do. He had already done a session with his weights and had a shower. He was thinking of Amber, hoping she would get really drunk so he could sneak upstairs and give it to her without her being aware.

He watched her trying to figure out which bathers she wanted to wear. Just walking around naked, he thought. He was getting turned on just thinking of the last time she'd had too much to drink and how much he would like to drink her juices again.

I put my original leopard print ones on and got a towel on the way downstairs. I grabbed a can on the way through and grabbed a cooler out of the bottom draw and met Maree at the pool. She was already in the spa sipping on her gin and soda water. We clinked our drinks as I got in and said, "Cheers." I had rung the pool shop in Murwoolinbah and they had sent someone out to do the maintenance on the pool. So it was nice and clean again.

We hadn't even thought of dinner but we were definitely in the mood to drink. I went and got the floating swan and unicorn and we mucked around on them for a while. Then when we were having a rest, we decided that we would have a barbeque.

So we wrapped ourselves in our towels and grabbed some sausages out of the cool room and chopped up some onions and sliced some potatoes thinly and went out and lit the barbeque while Maree took over the cooking. I went inside to make a salad.

I grabbed another can and poured Maree another glass of gin. I went out to the barbeque to see where she was at with the cooking. It looked good; for a couple of women, we were doing alright.

I got the music going and left the door open so we could hear it from there. Maree and I were bopping away, waiting for the snags to cook. I went and got another can and poured Maree another gin. Then dinner was ready. We ate at the table on the veranda and cleaned the barbeque plate off and put the dishes into the dish washer.

"Compliments to the chef," I said as I clinked our drinks again. I was getting a little drunk. I cranked the music up and we danced half the night. Around 10 o'clock, I went around and locked the place up. It had been a long day. I had let Lucky out for a walk and when he got back, I locked the front door. Maree and I said goodnight and went to our bedrooms.

I looked around for Lucky and he hadn't followed me up. I knew he was inside somewhere, so I didn't worry. I closed my bedroom door and headed for the bed. I couldn't be bothered getting my pajamas on so I just stripped off and got into bed. That was the last thing I remembered.

Jimmy had watched them drinking and dancing all night. When Amber brought the dog back in, Jimmy was ready with a snack. The dog could smell it in the front room and Amber was too drunk to notice. He had a drug in the snack that was going to put him to sleep for a few hours.

Jimmy waited a half hour after the girls went to bed then snuck out from behind the photo in the front room. The dog was already out to it on the floor. Jimmy stepped around it to have a look out the window. He longed to be outdoors.

He turned and went up the stairs in the foyer to the second floor. He went to the left. Maree's light was off according to the gap at the bottom of her door. He snuck past and across the hall and into Amber's room. She was laying on her bed stark naked with the covers only half on and her head was back with her mouth wide open, snoring like a freight train.

Jimmy was a little scared, he didn't want her waking up and screaming. So he had a bottle of chloroform and put some on a hanky and put it to her mouth and nose.

He folded the sheet out of the way completely. He had already locked the door just in case something went wrong and then he really took his time.

Exploring her whole body with his tongue, making her come in his mouth over and over.

Putting his fingers inside her and at times she would groan but then he would use the hanky again and then he fucked her long and slow. Then just as he was about to come, he pulled out and released himself into a towel. He laid beside her for a while till he got his breath back then he started all over again. Knocking her out when he thought she may be coming to.

It was almost daylight when he left her room and went back to his hiding spot in the panic room. He felt satisfied for the first time in a while. He just wished she could have been more alert and sucked his dick as well.

He slept till he heard the girls up and about. He watched Amber wake up and go into the shower, she was looking at a mark he must have left on her leg. At least she was so drunk she'll just think she did it herself, he thought.

I woke up and my mouth felt like the bottom of a cockatoo cage. I went straight to clean my teeth and turned the shower on. My head was pounding. I felt like I'd been hit by a Mack truck. I took some Panadol and put myself under the shower.

I know I had a lot to drink. I put a T-shirt on and some underpants and went back to bed. I wasn't ready to face the day yet. I went back to sleep and slept till 9:30. I woke up and still had a bit of a headache.

I put some shorts on and put my hair up and went downstairs. I noticed a mark on my leg. I remembered noticing it in the shower this morning. I knew I must have got it last night from something but it did look more like a fingerprint mark. I knew it couldn't be, so I let it go again.

I went downstairs and into the kitchen and put the kettle on. Maree came in looking better than I felt. I put the kettle on and got my cup ready. "Are you OK?" she asked, "You look terrible."

"Yeah, just too much to drink, I guess and a little too much dancing maybe. I'll be alright once I have a coffee and wake up a bit. I don't think I'll be doing much today though. We've got Roxy starting today at one pm," I said. Maree said she had nothing planned and would be happy to show her around.

"That's good. I'll have to check the computer and see if we had had any response to my advertisements for the jobs." I had a toasted sandwich with ham, cheese and tomato as brunch and took my second coffee into the front room.

I had two emails. I opened the first one, it was in response to the maintenance job, and it said 'Hi Amber. My name is Casey Dwyer and my wife's name is Tina. We would like to apply for the maintenance position. I have looked after an Equestrienne Center for about 14 years. My wife and I live in Tasmania and would love to move to a warmer climate.'

'I am very good with machinery and fixing things around the place and know a lot about cars to. I noticed you were also looking for a kitchen hand and a housemaid. My wife said she would be interested in helping you out with those things. Kind regards, Casey and Tina Dwyer.'

I printed it out and read the next email, it said 'Dear Amber, I am writing in response to the housekeeping job you have advertised. I live in the area, I don't have any experience but I have done some work in hospitality and am willing to learn, signed Sally Chambers.'

I printed that one out too and went to find Maree.

She was in her room. I knocked and she yelled out to come in, she was just getting her papers ready for school tomorrow. I showed her the emails. Maree read them both and said, "Wow that was quick, are you going to interview them?"

"I'll see if Sally wants to come on Tuesday because I'll be busy all-day Monday with the lady that's building the website. Which reminds me the guy that's taking the photos for the website is coming by this afternoon also. I found him online. He takes photos with a drone. It's what the lady told me to do. I can't think of her name at the moment. So what do you think?" I gestured toward the emails.

"The couple from Tasmania sounds perfect, I'll have to tee up a zoom meeting with them. What do you think?" I asked.

"OK, let me know how you go, I better get downstairs, Roxy will be here shortly," Maree said as we headed toward the door and downstairs. As soon as we entered the kitchen, there was a knock at the door.

I went to let Roxy in. "Hi, how are you? Come on in." I directed her toward the kitchen.

She said "hello," to us both and I gave her the tour. I showed her where to put her bag in the pantry and where we kept the cash for supplies. We talked over the menus and made some changes. Maree stayed with her while she cooked dinner and showed her where everything was and I went to make some calls.

I rang Sally Chambers first, she answered after the fourth ring, "hello?"

"Hi, my name is Amber Stokes, you were interested in the housekeeping job?" I asked.

"Yes, I don't have any experience but I would love to give it a go."

"OK, can you start on Tuesday?" I asked.

"Yes, I can do that, what time would you like me to start?"

"Nine am would be good. Do you know the address?" I asked.

"It's Sullivan's Lane, isn't it?" she said.

"Yes, that's right, I'll see you then." I got off the phone and felt good about what we were doing. I looked into wages and made a printout of the award wage list and was surprised how much it differed to what we were paying Silvia. We were totally ripping ourselves off.

I went out to the kitchen to see how Roxy was going on her first day. The smells that were coming from the kitchen were divine. She was stirring a pot on the stove and I didn't see Maree anywhere. "Hey, how's it going? Where's Maree?" I asked.

"She went out to get some wood for the fire," she said.

"That's good, what are you cooking?" I asked as I looked into the pot.

"It's a chunky steak pie and I'll put some vegetables with it."

"Sounds great," I said and took a seat at the kitchen bench. We talked about the case and how it was all going.

Roxy said, "As much as its police business, it becomes your business when you are married to a cop."

I totally understood. Frank had been pretty busy looking after me and working on the case lately. After talking to her for a while, it was plain to see how much in love with him she was. Her father had been a policeman and she knew what it was like when they were working a case. They had moved here because she didn't want that for her kids.

She wanted to get away from the crime. That's why they had bought the house out here. So she didn't have to worry. I had to apologize that she wasn't getting the peace she had expected when she moved here. She said it was not my fault that my boyfriend turned out to be a murderer. It brought tears to my eyes.

Roxy was so nice; she gave me a hug and told me that it was all over now and I wouldn't have to worry anymore. When I settled down, I thanked her and

I left her to do the pastry and went into the front room to answer the other email. I asked them to give me a video chat time.

They answered pretty well straight away. We agreed to do that at 7pm that night. I went back to the kitchen to see what everybody was up to. Maree was sitting at the bench chatting to Roxy. I went back to the reception desk and turned the computer on.

I had set one of the computers up there from out of the front room. I had bought an office program that I could use to do the bookings and keep track of all the outlays and expenses. It was going to help me with the rosters and wages to. I worked at setting it up till the photographer came at 4pm. He was over and done with within an hour. He handed me a USB with the pictures on and left.

Maree came to hang out with me. I showed her what I had managed to do with the computer and showed her how it all worked.

We went into the front room at 6:55 pm ready for the video call at 7pm. I keyed their number into the phone and pressed the video call button. Casey and Tina Dwyer came into view.

"Hi, I'm Amber and this is my sister Maree, as you know we are starting a new business and are looking for people to fill various roles. Your resume sounds good and we would be interested to give you guys a go. We are needing people pretty well straight away, so how soon can you guys get here? We would like to be up and running by the end of the week."

Tina was the one to answer, she said they had just sold their place in Tasmania and would be happy to be on the next plane out of there. She said they were staying with her mother till they found a place to settle down. "This job would be perfect for my husband because he has so much experience and I am happy to help in any way that I can. Whether that's housekeeping, reception or in the kitchen."

They both looked to be in their forties and seemed like the perfect candidates for the jobs. They were going to get back to me with their flight details so we could pick them up from the airport in Murwoolinbah. It didn't take long; they rang back half an hour later and said they would be on a flight tomorrow afternoon at 3pm.

Chapter 23

We went back into the kitchen and enjoyed our chunky steak pie and vegetables and were happily talking about the house and the people we had coming. We were going to leave Alice's room the way it was and the same with Aunt Mary's for now anyway.

I told Maree that I had an idea for activities to make up some pamphlets, one for Jet Ski hire and also hiring the kayaks and getting the guy back that took the pictures for the website and he could take the photos for the flyers. Maybe even hiring out the motorbikes too.

She agreed that would be a great idea and we talked about getting some coastal ones done for day trips. I was so excited it was all coming together.

I gave Gerry a call, he was the guy that did the photos and told him what I needed. He said he would be happy to help. He said he would go through some pictures he had already taken of the coast and said I could choose some from them. We set up a time on Tuesday afternoon to do the other shots at two pm.

I took Roxy down to the cellar after we all had dinner and showed her what we would need to stock up on. I also explained the $5000 limit credit card we had made up and how we did the orders. As in which companies we used for what and handed her keys to the house and said she could use Mary's old Mercedes if she needed to go to town or anything.

We also told her about getting the fresh produce from the markets on Saturdays. I asked her if she would rather start earlier for a while till we got up and running properly. She was happy to start at 7:30 and work till 4:30 till we had things sorted with more staff.

Roxy said she used to do all the orders for the pub so she was more than capable. I fed Lucky and took him for a walk after Roxy had cleaned the kitchen and left. He went straight to the lawn as usual. Maree and I had a hot chocolate and then went up to bed. It had been a long day but interesting. I was enjoying bringing it all together. I went to sleep pretty quickly and rose just as the sun was coming up. I took Lucky for a quick walk and gave him a feed.

I put some workout clothes on and ran downstairs to the gym. Maree surprised me, turning up when I was only 10 minutes into my workout. It was great we cranked up the music and did an aerobics DVD that we put on the screen out the front. It went for an hour then we did a 10-minute cool down and ran upstairs to shower and get ready for a new day.

Jimmy loved watching the girls undress and redress and watching them doing their workout. He did his weights while he watched and then had a tug while he watched them both shower.

Roxy was just coming in the door as we made our way through the kitchen and filled our water bottles up and put them back into the fridge. We said hello and left her to it. After my shower, I blow dried my hair and left it down. I put a pretty sky-blue sundress on and earrings to match and went downstairs to get a coffee. Roxy had already boiled the kettle so it didn't take long till she handed me my coffee.

She was cooking up a storm. When she handed me my plate, it was massive. I had not only bacon and egg but a lamb chop, a sausage, tomato, hash brown and some toast. "Wow that's a lot," I said.

She said, "You don't have to eat it all, just eat what you can."

Surprisingly enough, I ate the lot. Maree came along just as I was getting started. She too was shocked at how much food there was but enjoyed it just as much as I did.

Maree left for school and I talked to Roxy till there was a knock at the door. It was the web design lady right on time at nine am. She introduced herself as Helen Newbury. I shook her hand and got her to follow me into the reception to the computer. We both sat down and by midday, the website was finished.

It looked really good and had everything we needed, so as soon as I was ready to launch it, it would only take a second. The photos turned out really well and she also showed me how to add in the activity photos when I was ready. She made it all very simple and easy to use. I wrote her a check and went to see her out.

Roxy made me a ham and salad sandwich and she ate one too. I was telling her about the couple that I had to pick up from the airport at three. Which reminded me I needed to clean out Jimmy's house ready for them. I asked Roxy if she would give me a hand. She said she would be happy to.

I took some clean linen with me and some cleaning products. I started with cleaning the fridge and I made a mental note to put some necessities into it for them. Knowing they wouldn't want to be doing too much this afternoon. With Roxy's help, we managed to get most of it done. She said she would be happy to do the rest while I was gone.

I had put all of Jimmy's clothes into a garbage bag and threw them into the boot of the car. I was going to give them to a charity while I was in town. I managed to arrive just in time. Their plane had already landed and they were waiting for their luggage. I introduced myself and gave them a hand.

They seemed really nice. Casey was about six-foot, brown eyes and brown hair and looked reasonably fit. Tina was a bubbly personality, she had blonde hair and brown eyes and looked reasonably fit herself. She was telling me about the plane fight.

They had to change flights in Melbourne and how the smaller plane had met up with some turbulence. "I thought we were going down," she said. Her husband was telling her not to be so melodramatic.

"It wasn't that bad," he said.

We loaded the luggage into the car and Tina hopped into the front seat and Casey hopped into the back. I said, "I hope you don't mind if we grab a few things while I'm in town, do you?"

"Not at all, it will give us a chance to have a look around," Tina said and Casey agreed. They were both very excited. They had never been out of Tasmania before, so it was all new to them. They had both removed their jackets when we left the airport.

I put Jimmy's clothes into a charity bin and bought some groceries for the log cabin and drove home. They gasped when we came through the gates. "I didn't think it would be this big," said Tina.

"Wow, I'm loving the lawn and the gardens," said Casey. On the way home, I was telling them how we had inherited the place and they had a lot of questions about the news and about the recent events. I told them about Alice and Aunt Mary and Uncle Tom. Also about Silvia, Jimmy and his dad.

I drove them straight around the back to the cabin. We unloaded the bags and took them upstairs and into the cabin. Casey and Tina were over the moon with the place and I loaded the food into the fridge and told them if there was anything they needed to just ask.

I had asked Roxy to bring a bottle of champagne up and she had made up a beautiful fruit basket to go with it and two champagne glasses. I left them to get settled in and went back to the house.

Roxy was just getting ready to leave. I had told her not to worry about dinner after helping me with the cabin. I thought Maree and I could just get some takeaway from the general store. I just felt like one of their burgers. Maree came down and we had a bit of a chat.

She wanted to know all about our new employees and I got to show her the new website. She was very impressed with it all. I told her we were just going to get a burger for dinner and she was happy with that. She had had a busy day at school and Eli was coming to stay the night.

I told her I had a lady called Sally Chambers starting tomorrow. She was going to do the cleaning. "That's good, the dust is already starting to build," she said. At 5:30, I asked the Dwyer's if they wanted to get some takeaway for dinner over the intercom because that's what we were doing.

I also thought it would be good for them to meet Maree and Eli and I could show them around a little. Tina came on and said they would love to. "We will be down shortly," she said.

15 minutes later, I heard them coming on the veranda. I went to let them in. "Hi, come on in," I said as I opened the door. Eli arrived just before them so I did the introductions and then went to grab my purse. Maree went to get the Mustang and parked it out the front. I locked the front door and we all piled in. Maree drove slowly out of the drive and headed into town.

Jimmy took the chance to come out of his hiding spot and chose a couple of movies out of the DVD library. Stocked up on food and some Jack Daniels and coke. There was a lot going on in the house at the moment. He hadn't seen the place this busy since he was a kid.

Tina and Casey loved the little town. They said it was very similar to their town in Tasmania. The only difference was that theirs had a pub, otherwise it was the same size. We all got our orders and took them home to eat. We sat at the dining room table and we talked about the house and what kind of jobs we had for them to do.

After dinner, I took them on a tour of the house and promised to show Casey more outside tomorrow. I also told them that Jimmy's Ute was available for them to use any time they wanted to. I also told Tina that I had a lady called

Sally coming to start work at nine in the morning and they could start then as well if that was OK.

She agreed that would be great and they went back home via the veranda. I had given them a set of keys and told them if they needed anything just to give me a buzz on the intercom. I had relabeled the buttons.

Maree and Eli went up to their room and I went to the front room to check my emails. There was one from a guy asking about the maintenance job and another two from women asking about the housekeeping jobs. I didn't reply to any of them because I wanted to make sure the people, I had now would be OK or not first. At least, I knew I had people as back up if things didn't go well.

I turned the computer off and took Lucky out for a quick walk then went up to bed. It was good to be busy. I fell asleep quite quickly and didn't wake up till 7:15. I got out of bed and opened the door for Lucky to go downstairs and went to have a shower. I used the shower cap and put my hair up afterwards. I dressed in denim shorts and a T-shirt and ran downstairs.

Maree was just leaving and Roxy was just arriving. I acknowledged them both and went to put the kettle on. Roxy went to the pantry to put her bag away and came back out, tying her apron on as she did. She told me to have a seat and took over.

I wasn't going to argue. I took a seat at the kitchen bench and asked her how she was going. She was telling me about her little girl and how she was helping her with a school project this morning. They had to tell a story with a diorama so she was making up a farming scene with animals and the farmer and his wife and two kids helping to do the chores.

She handed me my coffee and I smelt the aroma, "yum," I said.

"So what is the plan for today?" Roxy asked.

"Well, I've got a lady named Sally starting at nine and Tina as well. I'll get them started on the cleaning, then I have to show Casey around. I've decided to have a grand opening party that I want you to cater for and if things work out with Sally and Tina, I'll get them to help you with service and whatever other help you need."

"I'm going to create a flyer and put it up in town and online. I want to promote local produce whether it's honey, eggs, vegetables or meat. We will have a big party and we could meet all the locals and really put ourselves out there," I said.

"Wow that sounds exciting. I will have to do a heap of finger food like canapés and sausage rolls and little sandwiches," Roxy said happily thinking about what she would make. She handed me a plate of scrambled eggs on toast with bacon on the side. I heard Tina knocking on the French doors.

It was 8:45 am. I went over and opened the door, she said she was a bit early but she hoped I didn't mind. I told her to sit and have a cup of coffee with us and she was happy to oblige. I asked her if everything was alright with the cabin and she said it was fantastic.

Jimmy was not happy that somebody had taken over his job and his house up the back. There was not a damn thing he could do about it though. He would just have to sit back and watch and take chances where he could.

Sally turned up five minutes early and I went to answer the door. "Hello, come in," I said. Sally was only young. She had left school at the end of grade twelve and did a little waitressing on the weekends. Now she wanted something more full time. I introduced her to the girls in the kitchen and showed her where to put her bag in the pantry.

Then I got Sally and Tina to come upstairs with me and showed them all the rooms and the cleaning closets. Then took them around downstairs and showed them the gym and the other games room and family room. I took them and showed them the pool and the changing rooms.

I finished with a tour of the front room and the bathrooms attached. I told Tina to take charge and to get started with cleaning from top to bottom making everything perfect and ready for the grand opening in two weeks' time. Then left them to it and went to see Casey.

I found him in the shed, he was checking out the machinery. "Hello, how's it going?" I asked.

"Yeah good," he said.

"I hope you know what you are doing when it comes to this stuff because I couldn't tell you anything about how it all works."

"Don't worry," he said, "I know how it all works, I'm quite impressed actually; this machinery is a lot newer than the old stuff I've had to deal with in the past."

"That's a relief because the grass needs doing already. Would you like to follow me and I'll show you around?" I asked.

"Sure." I showed him the pool house, he'd said he'd never had a pool before but he knew if he took a sample to the pool shop, they should be able to help. I told him there was a pool shop in Murwoolinbah. I always passed it on my way into town.

"The heating should be easy," he said, "just a motor." I took him to the garage and started with the first bay. He was like a kid in a candy shop with all the tools and the tidiness of everything. He made me laugh just watching him. I showed him all the others, of course it was the old T Model Ford that he liked the most.

I told him he could have a drive but he had to take me with him. We got to the last bay and I showed him all the things I wanted to take photos of and rent out. I asked him if he would help clean the bikes and get the jet skis ready. He said he would give everything the once over. I said Gerry would be here this afternoon at two pm.

I took him into the house and asked if he could light the fire everyday sometime between 4:30 and 5:30 in the afternoon. "If there is some reason why you can't, just let me know and I can do it." She showed him around everywhere including all the bathrooms. As we went if there was a problem, he started writing a list on a note pad he pulled out of his top pocket. I thought that was a good sign.

When we'd finished, I left him to it and went back to the house. The smell of cleaning products met my nose as I walked through the house. I found both the girls in the bathroom off the front room and I noticed the furniture in the front room was sparkling clean.

The dust bunnies had gone and the floors looked good too. There were two big mats and the rest was polished floorboards like the rest of the place downstairs.

I told them things were looking good and not to forget to have a lunch break. Roxy was busy in the kitchen. I got a diet coke out of the fridge and she offered to make me a sandwich for lunch. I said, "Corn beef and tomato would be nice."

She was asking me about what Maree and I would normally eat and was taking notes. I had seen her earlier with a clipboard in her hand. It made me smile. I thought it was good to see her taking her job so seriously.

After lunch, I went back to the front room to the computer to finish making up the flyers for the grand opening. I asked if the girls could go and do some laundry for me after lunch. They seemed to be getting along really well.

I answered the door when Gerry arrived at two and led him out to the garage where Casey already had the motor bikes, jet skis and the kayaks. I got the fishing rods out and arranged them for a photo and did the same with the archery gear I'd found.

After he had taken all the shots, he checked them out on a laptop he had bought. They looked really good. He put them on a USB and handed it to me. Then he came inside and showed me the coastal shots he had. They were fantastic. He put them onto the USB. I thanked him and walked him to the door. Maree was already home; she was talking to Casey out in the drive.

I went back to the front room and worked on the pamphlets now that I had the photos. I had finished the grand opening flyers. And printed half a dozen out and shared it online. I had made up a Facebook page with a picture of the gate as the cover photo.

It looked great, the profile picture was the house itself. I had so much content now with all these photos, I felt. I enjoyed making all the pamphlets and I printed them out on shiny paper. I had brought a pamphlet holder offline so I already had the measurements.

I hung it on the wall to the left so people would have plenty of space. I even put two chairs there against the wall. It was starting to look really professional. The pamphlets took a few days because I had to do a write up on each one that went with the picture.

I also had to research the coast a little to write about it and told Maree all about these things in case somebody had questions for either of us.

Maree had recently been to the coast, so she had a lot of knowledge for me to. It all helped and I got Tina and Sally up to date on everything from the reception desk and how to book people in and the costs associated with each room.

We were going to charge food and drinks to the room numbers so as to keep things easy. I also paid for Sally and Tina to do a bar course like I did myself. They went in the same car together and when they came home with their certificates, Maree and I got them to serve drinks to us so they could get used to how things worked.

I let them pour themselves a drink as well. They had a lot of fun learning different drinks and cocktails. I let Sally stay in one of the rooms that night so she didn't have to drink drive. We had a great night of dancing and just relaxing in general.

We had all worked so hard, Roxy and Casey came and had a few. Frank drove Roxy home about 11. I gave them all the next day off to recover.

Chapter 24

Jimmy watched us all drinking and having a good time. He was thrilled to bits when he found out the young one was going to stay over, he had been watching her while she cleaned. He thought the other two women were too old for him.

He waited till one o'clock in the morning before he came out of his hiding spot and headed to room eight, which was in the right wing of the house across the hall from Mary's room. Everybody was sound asleep. He stopped at the reception desk to grab the spare key to the room.

He had seen where Amber had put them in the second drawer. He snuck up the stairs and down the hallway. Room eight had the front room, so he let himself in and went through the front room and into the bedroom; he brought his chloroform hanky out of his pocket.

Sally was lying on her back and snoring quite loudly. Jimmy put the hanky over her mouth and nose and then he removed the blankets and took off her panties. He lifted her nightie off and over her head. He put the bedside lamp on so he could see what he had; she had quite a full bust and her pussy was shaved, he really liked the look of this one.

He put his dick in her open mouth and moved it around inside. He was getting off on watching. He removed his cock out of her mouth and started kissing and licking her face down to her nipples and licked and sucked each one then put his hand down between her legs.

He parted her legs and stuck his finger inside her and used his thumb to play with her clit and brought his mouth to her vagina and licked and sucked the juices as they flowed. Sally started to moan.

He got the hanky and put it back onto her mouth and nose and then continued with what he was doing. He eventually put himself inside her and making sure he didn't leave any marks or bruises this time, he fucked her for a little while then after using the chloroform again, he rolled her over and fucked her ass as well.

Just before he came, he pulled out and released himself into a towel. After he caught his breath, he started all over again. He must have come five times that night. Then redressed her and went back into his hiding spot. As he drifted off to sleep, he was beginning to think he might not have to get another girl if they were going to be coming to stay at this place anyway.

I crawled out of bed at 9:10 and had a shower and got dressed and put my hair up. I was reflecting on the night before and I was really happy with how everything was going and the staff were happy too. We were all looking forward to the grand opening and they were doing a marvelous job.

Sally had woken up with a massive headache and rang her mom to come and pick her up. She left me a note on the kitchen bench. I went to put the kettle on and Maree came in 20 minutes later. *We were both pretty hung over but not as bad as the last time*, I thought.

I spent the day doing a stock take in the cellar just so we could keep track of our spending. I asked Roxy to do the same and I gave her a couple of spreadsheets to work with. She said it would help with the ordering and the stock take. I took off and went for a drive into town and each shop let me put my flyer in their shop window.

I spoke to them about it and invited them. I said I wanted every person in town there if I could get it. The flyer said free drinks and canapés and the whole town was welcome to come and check out the new business. The whole town was really receptive and I drove home in a really good mood.

Eli came for dinner that night and told us the case on Jimmy had stalled and his mother, Silvia had got two years for aiding and abetting because of the phone call at that time to warn Jimmy. And also because the judge said there was no way that was going on without her knowledge.

"She could appeal and get a jury," he said. "But she'll be out in eight months with good behavior."

"True," I said. Apparently, Silvia refused to talk, so the phone call and her living arrangements were enough to prove her guilt, the judge said. So we would never truly know how much Silvia was involved.

Jimmy's Dad ended up getting 132 life sentences and a never to be released order. They didn't care about his disability; he could get his medication in jail. They said Jimmy would cop the same when they found him.

Maree and I went to Murwoolinbah to find a nice dress to wear for the special night. After trying half a dozen, we both settled on one. Maree's was green with flowers coming from the neck line to one side which really set off her eyes and I settled on an apricot dress, it had pearls where the straps were and a handkerchief bottom.

There was only one day left and the house was looking amazing. Roxy was already prepping for the big day. I had launched the website and already had the place booked out for the next three months. I stood in the foyer and looked, the pamphlets looked great and so did the rest of this place.

I went to find Maree; she was in her room studying. "Hey Maree, do you want to make the most of our last private pool time before the house is bustling with strangers?" I didn't have to twist her arm, she jumped at the chance to have a break from her studies.

It was so nice just to swim and float. Maree enjoyed it too. We had a good chat as well, she was talking about Eli and the job and how happy her life was now that things had settled down for Eli with work again. It was nice to listen to her and see how genuinely happy she was.

That night, we had a quiche with a salad and some cheesy garlic bread and both had an early night. Jimmy had gotten used to living in the panic room. He did his weights and abided his time till he could have another toy. He knew for sure he would be able to get something on opening night.

He was getting as excited as the rest of them just thinking about it. He had heard Amber taking bookings, so he knew he would have a lot to choose from. Not only then but in future. He fixed himself up while Amber and Maree had their showers like he always did and went to sleep.

Chapter 25

I woke up thinking today was going to be huge. I let Lucky out and I got up and dressed in a purple sundress and flats. Brushed my teeth and my hair and looked at myself in the mirror. I didn't look too bad. I had gotten a little sun yesterday, which gave me a bit of a glow.

I had one more look at the dress I was going to wear tonight. Maree was letting me borrow the pearl inside the heart earrings and necklace she got that first time she went to the markets. I had also bought a nice pair of shoes which had pearls on as well. I went downstairs and sat at the kitchen bench.

Maree and Eli were already there and Roxy was busy cooking. I said g'day and gave Lucky a pat and made him breakfast. By the time I had finished that, Roxy had put a coffee and a plate full of food on the bench in my usual spot. "Thank you," I said, "are you ready for the grand opening?"

Roxy smiled and said she was as ready as she would ever be. I ate my bacon and eggs with tomato on toast and drank my coffee.

After breakfast, I checked out the whole house room by room just to make sure everything was ready. I was pleased with all the hard work of the staff and still a bit nervous or a lot. I decided to do a tarot card for the day. I took them down off the dressing table and sat on my bed, which had already been made.

I shuffled the cards and one fell out; it was the three of cups which meant celebrations. I pulled another card to clarify and got the emperor which meant success but through your own hard work. I also did a card while I was thinking about Jimmy, I got the eight of swords which meant he felt trapped.

Then I did another card to clarify and was the seven of swords which meant getting away with something behind somebody's back. I thought about that card and came to the conclusion of Jimmy having to steal food and holing up in somebody's shed or something.

I packed the cards up and went back downstairs. Roxy had the whole bench covered in little pastry shells. She was putting a chicken and vegetable filling into them. They looked amazing and she had sausage rolls cooking in the oven and Tina was helping to put red jelly onto a slab of cheese cake.

Sally came in from the laundry. Everybody said hello and went back to their work. I had people starting to check in from one o'clock onwards. It was already almost midday. I went looking for Casey and found him out in the shed tinkering on a machine.

"Hi Casey, would you be able to help me out in the front room please?" I asked.

"Sure," he said. We went in the back door so he could wash his hands on the way through. I got him to help me roll up one of the huge mats and made room for the three-piece band I had coming. They were playing at the markets last weekend and I really liked them. They were thrilled to bits to be a part of the grand opening.

We made room for a dance floor as well and put about 50 chairs around that I got from the attic. Sally helped us with that. It was looking really good. Tina and Sally had also hung a sign up saying 'Grand Opening' and had it hanging on the front veranda.

There was a knock at the door. It was the first person to book into a room. I went to open it. It was Errol and Florence Harper. I had put them in room five which was two doors down from mine. I checked them in and told them about the bar in the games room, menus in the kitchen and gave them a little map of the house that I had made up showing where the pool and laundry was.

I had brought another two washing machines that were coin operated ones for the guests to use. I also had little signs made up for the door of the gym and the games room.

They were in their sixties and had come up from Melbourne. I gave them their keys and told them to enjoy themselves and make themselves at home. Maree entered the foyer and I introduced them to her and told them if they needed anything just to ask.

They had booked in for a week. Casey came in and told them where to park their car and they went up to their room to get settled in.

I went back into the kitchen and asked Sally to make sure the bar was stocked up and the lights were on and ready for customers. I had put a sign on the pool saying 'no running or glass in the pool' and the pool hours were from 7 am – 10 pm.

I had left the front door open and Casey was out directing the cars and where to park. I heard the bell chime on the front desk. I went to check the next person in, it was a nice young couple from Brighton in Brisbane. I gave them the same spiel and gave them their key.

When they left to go to their rooms, I went and made myself a corn beef and tomato sandwich. By four o'clock, everybody had arrived that were staying either the night or longer. As I walked through the lounge and out to the veranda and down to the bar in the games room, everywhere I looked people were happily chatting with a drink in hand and really enjoying themselves.

I went to the pool to see how things were going. There were people of all ages enjoying, talking and drinking. I had found a heap of plastic cups for the bar as well for people who wanted to drink in the pool.

I saw that Tina and Sally were handling things quite well and Roxy was loving being so close to the clientele while she cooked. She was laughing and chatting and cooking all at the same time. It was easy for her just to charge the food to their rooms and people were hungry, so she was going to be busy all day and night.

I took the chance to go and get changed. I showered and blow dried my hair and put it up on the sides. I dressed in the beautiful apricot and pearl dress, plus the earrings and necklace. I ran back downstairs, there were even more people that had started to turn up for the grand opening itself. I went into the kitchen and poured myself a wine.

Roxy was doing a fabulous job in the kitchen and I went back to the foyer to meet and greet. Casey was busy directing cars and people were coming from everywhere. I was surprised at how many locals came. The band was setting up in the front room and in the middle of a sound check, I went and said hello and made sure they had everything they needed.

I had a book in the reception area where people could not only say where they had come from but also if they had any local produce for sale. The front room was where we had champagne and fruit cocktail, and non-alcoholic punch if people didn't want to drink.

I went to the kitchen to see if Roxy had some platters ready, it was starting to get busy. Maree was there, so I got her to help and Eli came dressed in his normal clothes and offered to help to. It was looking like it was going to be a huge success. There ended up being cars parked all the way down the lane both sides full.

Maree went over to the band at one stage and asked for the microphone. She got everybody's attention and made a big speech. Thanking everybody for coming and giving me credit for being able to pull all of this together. Especially after everything I had been through recently.

She actually made a tear come to my eye. With all the things she said and everybody clapped while they all looked at me, I felt like we had been accepted into the town by all the locals. I took the microphone and thanked Maree for everything.

I also thanked my staff for all their hard work in pulling it all together and thanked the band. I also thanked the locals for their ongoing support and thanked everybody else for coming too. There must have been over a hundred people. I was really pleased with the turnout.

Jimmy watched everything on the television screens all night. He had his eye on the lady who was staying in room six, next door to the old couple, he thought. She was only 22, he had heard her say, and her name was Robyn.

He had a few Jack Daniels while he listened to the band and all the different conversations being had. He was also looking forward to playing with his new toy.

www.ingramcontent.com/pod-product-compliance
Lightning Source LLC
Chambersburg PA
CBHW061250120726
48001CB00001B/240